ATTACK AT KHODA BRIDGE

Gus Smith Book 1 – An International Thriller

FRANK MITCHELL

STORY MERCHANT BOOKS
LOS ANGELES
2015

STORY MERCHANT BOOKS

ATTACK AT KHODA BRIDGE

Story Merchant Books
400 S. Burnside Avenue #11B,
Los Angeles, CA 90036

http://www.storymerchantbooks.com

ISBN-13: 978-0-9963689-8-8

Author Website: http://PathfinderTales.com

To Gloria, my wife and inspiration.

ATTACK AT KHODA BRIDGE

1

RUINS OF THE FIRST KHODA BRIDGE, IRAN
NOVEMBER 3, 1979

G us drank a sip of vodka and red barberry juice from a worn Sigg bottle and put it back in the cargo pocket of his surplus fatigue pants. Glancing upstream, everybody was still busy relocating the survey equipment from the old stone benchmark on the Russian side of the Aras River to the new one on the Iranian side.

All morning, Gus had jumped back and forth on the north side of the river, pulling the engineer's tape. When hopping from rock to rock he used an extendable rod to counterbalance himself before setting a steel pin for the next angle, elevation and distance measurement from the theodolite. This afternoon the survey team was doing the same thing on the south side of the river.

As Gus scanned four hundred feet back up the Aras River, his Turkish assistant Berke Demir had just lay down the engineer's transit on its tripod beside the new monument and started wading back across for the rest of the equipment including his shoulder bag. Two months ago, they had finished geotechnical engineering after making dozens of borings and test pits throughout the soil and bedrock. Shallow water flowed across the exposed rock shelf at the proposed dam site. The only thing left was to finish the topographical survey downstream past the ancient ruins of the first and second Khoda Bridges.

Looking upstream again he saw Captain Zandt Mohsen, the Iranian Army engineer leveling the transit for the next group of survey measurements. Dmitry Antonov, their engineer from Moscow was writing in the field book getting ready to record the new line of topographic data as Berke called it out. Today's unshaven Russian bodyguard was looking upriver, out over the proposed lake. Gus thought he could take a few minutes to answer the call of nature.

Leaning the rod, pins and tape reel against one of the nine hundred year old oval arches of the bridge, Gus stepped through the opening and moved behind the large stone pier where he relieved himself against the squat buttress.

Moments later as he was finishing he heard a three-shot burst from an AK-47, a distinctive sound he would know anywhere. It was followed by several single shots and then another burst. Hurriedly buttoning up his pants, he moved to peek around the stone buttress and look in the direction of the gunfire.

Up at the road he saw a dusty white Japanese Datsun pickup hidden by an ancient cairn. It was a dozen yards behind the mustard colored *Ahoo*, their Iranian made Jeep Wagoneer. This morning Berke had parked their Jeep just behind the Russian's olive drab military 4-wheeler. Up at the transit, he could see several armed fighters pointing rifles at two of the engineers, Berke and Dmitry. Both were kneeling with their hands clasped behind their heads while the crumpled pile next to the rock must be the Russian's bodyguard. Zandt was sprawled just beyond the partially assembled tripod. Both of them were face down and had expanding dark splotches on their backs.

All four strangers were wearing olive drab uniform pieces and had longish dark hair, almost like Afros. Two had beards and the other two had Pancho Villa mustaches. They couldn't be soldiers of the regular Iranian Army like Zandt since they were wearing mismatched fatigues and carrying Soviet weapons rather than German battle rifles. They must be revolutionaries, bandits or Iranian Communists, definitely murderers since they shot both men in the back.

One of the soldiers turned and started winding his way down toward the bridge arches where Gus was hiding. The assailant coming toward him carried an AK assault rifle and wore army fatigues, a round woolen hat, and a loose fitting checkered scarf.

Glancing around Gus thought to himself, everything is just too open to try and run. He realized he couldn't leave cover without exposing himself to the gunmen. Next, he discarded the idea of circling around the base of the arch since he would make too much noise trying to sneak up behind the soldier.

Looking around he thought he could slip into the river, which was deeper under the bridge although it was the end of the dry season and the water level was low. His combat training took over as he remembered what one of his instructors at Fort Bragg had taught him a dozen years earlier. He should always hide and attack from the least expected direction.

Studying the gurgling water, he noticed a light growth of reeds along the bank and a few more clumps two-yards into the river where a boulder had trapped a pile of dirt and debris. The water in the eddy behind the rock must be four feet deep. However, it looked obvious.

When the terrorist looks around the pillar, I need to distract him with a red herring. I'll crumple a few sheets of white sanitary paper I always carry in my pocket. While he's looking down, I'll envelop him with my full size, take him down and kill him.

Looking straight up, he placed his decoy just beneath the outside edge of the arch. He realized it would be difficult to climb the huge stone abutment then out on to the spandrel. In addition, he would have to drop at least 18 feet without making a sound; but he thought he could do it.

Moving to the river, he pulled a flute reed out of the water, bit off the ends and blew the punk inside onto the riverbank. Throwing the plant downstream, he scuffed the dirt slightly before moving over to study the downstream side of the abutment.

The limestone wall was crumbling in enough places to give him finger and toeholds. He was wearing his scuffed ankle-high work boots whose sole was rigid enough to give him a slight purchase in each joint as he climbed the wall like a spider. Loosing only one hand or foot at a time, he always kept three in contact as he scrambled upwards.

He didn't have any weapons and his pocketknife was with the afternoon's apple and cheese snack in his field bag. Abruptly he remembered he did have a weapon. His crusty old Kiwi instructor at the British Jungle Warfare School in Malaysia had told him about this one.

As Gus reached the crumbling brick spandrel, he stared at the newer 700-year old second Khoda Bridge still operating about a klick further downstream connecting Soviet Azerbaijan and the new Republic of Iran. There weren't any signs of movement on the newer bridge.

As he perched on the ancient span just outside the crumbling balusters, he began reviewing every move he planned to make. He felt like an eagle waiting for a rabbit to run.

The early November rainy season had almost started. It was gloomy but still above freezing. He took shallow breaths to limit condensation and he remained absolutely still as he crouched in front of the remains of the coping.

He had tucked his arms into the drop position, protecting his head and face as he grasped the improvised device in his right hand.

From the shadows coming from under the bridge, he could see movement along the bank. The terrorist stepped from under the arch and turned to stare at the ruse.

Gus dropped straight onto his shoulders with both axe-like elbows, while he held his pointed feet together and smashed them into his calf and Achilles tendon in a perfect parachute-landing fall, dragging the man to the side.

The smaller man collapsed like a sack of potatoes. As they fell to the side, Gus grabbed the Islamic soldier's neck and upper chest with his left arm and drove the ballpoint pen in his right hand through his ear and into his brain.

His grandfather had given him the large Montblanc ballpoint when he graduated from college. Gus' SAS instructor from New Zealand had taught him the brass-reinforced barrel under the black resin turned the instrument into a weapon, as stiff and deadly as a knife.

The bandit jerked a few times as he lost all bodily control. Gus removed his weapons, jacket and hat before he went across to the river and rinsed the pen. The mujahidin's upper clothing didn't have any blood or piss on it.

On close inspection, he realized the man was wearing a red headband with yellow Arabic script reading *Sepāh e Pāsdārān* under his Persian pakol hat. He must be an Islamic Revolutionary Guard carrying a new AK47. It was the paratrooper version of the standard Soviet assault rifle with a folding wire stock.

Gus carefully inspected the weapon, removing the banana clip and checking to make sure the chamber was loaded. It was a stamped Chinese copy but it looked like everything was OK. The Islamist had three extra magazines in his bandolier.

Gus thought to himself, I have no idea where the bullets will hit. Did anyone sight the rifle correctly? It probably still has its armory settings. I'm going to have to get close, fire single shots, and keep moving toward them. If I just spray and pray, I may hit Berke or Dmitry.

Trying on the terrorist's jacket, it was much too small and he had to use the man's knife to split the back seam open. Luckily, Gus's pants almost matched the dead man's soiled trousers although he was wearing a tan safari shirt.

After draping the costume and donning the checkered scarf covering his neck and shirt, Gus pulled the hat low. He then unfolded the wire stock and clicked the safety lever down past auto to single-shot before starting upstream for the transit tripod.

He was carrying the assault rifle at the ready, not slung from his shoulder. He slowly made his way toward the three remaining enemy soldiers. Two of the Islamists were inspecting the bodyguard's sniper rifle, while the leader was questioning the Russian engineer.

When he was still almost a hundred feet away, the lead fundamentalist pulled a pistol and fired twice into the Russian engineer expelling a large cloud of smoke from the end of his revolver. Gus thrust forward into a hunch, crouching as he moved.

He raised the AK into the ready fire position. As he planted his left foot, he fired a single shot into the furthest Revolutionary Guard warrior, the one holding the rifle. He saw the impact cause dust to jump from his chest.

Quickly shuffling forward with a right and then a left foot, he acquired a hasty sight picture as he took a second shot into the next guard. The second man just looked down at his stomach in disbelief.

As he took two more short steps forward, he paused with his left foot fixed and shot another round into the first man. Another pace forward and another shot into the second man who was turning toward him in bewilderment as the first man collapsed.

The leader raised his Russian revolver in a classic dueling stance and fired a hurried shot at Gus expelling another cloud of black-powder smoke. Although now only 70-feet apart, he was still too far for the hurried pistol shot.

Gus was taking aim as he heard the buzz of the passing subsonic bullet. Berke dove forward, grabbed one of the rifles and fired directly at the center of mass of the duelist, followed by a second shot into his head. Gus rushed forward taking short steps instead of strides. He was ready to shoot each time his left foot hit the ground although it wasn't necessary.

He confirmed all three were dead by checking their throats for a pulse. Motioning to Berke, they started collecting weapons and *pasdaran* clothing. The two ordinary revolutionaries had been carrying Chinese copies of semi-automatic SKS rifles while their leader was carrying a Russian World War I revolver with ammunition that was just as old.

"Why did they shoot Zandt, the Russian minder and then our Russian engineer?" Gus asked.

"They shot the Russian guard first and then Zandt but it's strange since I'm sure they recognized Captain Mohsen, at least his uniform," Berke said. "The Iranian asked Dmitry for you by name, although he couldn't pronounce James Augustus Smith correctly. He was speaking Azeri. Our Russian replied in the same local dialect. I don't think he realized I'm fluent in Azeri as well as Persian and

Turkish. Dmitry said, 'I'm a KGB captain here on a mission watching this man Smith.' He then pointed to the ancient arch where you were located." Gus nodded and then motioned for Berke to continue.

"The terrorists sent a soldier to collect you and bring you in." Berke said. "Dmitry no longer looked or acted like our mild engineer. He was now acting like a KGB officer who must have thought these men were Iranian Communist Revolutionaries since they weren't speaking Persian and because of their Russian weapons. When the leader started to tell the men to tie everyone up so they could join the other hostages, Dmitry ignored him and threatened the leader in Azeri, still thinking he was a communist revolutionary. 'You Pooya Marxist had better follow orders. If I tell my Spetsnaz soldiers, they'll castrate all of you and kill everyone in your family.'" Berke looked over to make sure Gus understood what he was implying.

"Dmitry suddenly made a hasty move while he was still talking and the leader shot him. He must have been carrying a pistol hidden under his jacket." Berke walked over and pulled back the Russian's jacket exposing a leather holster. He took the pistol out and showed it to Gus, "Look, he was carrying a 9mm Makarov. It's the model with the short built-in suppressor. Pulling back the slide slightly he commented, 'It's loaded and cocked. It's also in an unusual speed holster,'"

Gus didn't respond as he realized his assistant Berke was revealing the fact he knew too much. Searching further Berke said, "The holster has a carrier for the second longer silencer and an extra magazine. They're both marked as made in New York City." Gus didn't say, but he had a lot of experience with this Russian Silent Pistol PB-*Pistolet Beschumnyj*.

Berke then went and checked the bodyguard. "You already know he was carrying one of their Dragunov sniper rifles and some extra magazines. He also has a knife in a sheath at the small of his back. It's a combat knife with the Cyrillic letter A and wings engraved on the blade." He set it beside the pistol and holster.

Gus glanced at the pistol and 8-inch knife before going over to check on Zandt. He called back over his shoulder, "He's unarmed but just as dead."

Berke asked Gus, "Where did these pasdaran come from? Why are the Revolutionary Guards attacking us now? Our contract was with the old Imperial Government of Iran and the Soviet Union. I don't know if it's still in force but hasn't our joint venture been trying to get a contract extension from the new theocracy?" Gus looked thoughtful as he answered Berke. "The revolution ended nine-months ago and the Islamists won. Maybe the rumors you told me about Russian movements along the border are true. Maybe they're threatening the Mullahs."

"I heard the rumors about Soviet movements from several different people." Berke confirmed. "However, I doubt if that's it. The terrorist leader was asking for you specifically. These men aren't locals. The pasdaran commander in Tabriz must have sent them, or they could be all the way from Tehran. The Russians may be watching you but they didn't plan this attack."

"Maybe it's their way of telling us our contract has been cancelled." Gus paused and thought before saying, "Today is Saturday, the 3rd of November and most of the Turkish workers including the rodman and chainman had the day off to visit the weekly market held by Shia Muslim villagers. I love these Saturdays since I usually fill in for the field crew while you, Zandt or Dmitry operates the transit. I wonder if the terrorist knew about the market and that I would be working in the field today. Is someone in our camp passing information about us?"

"What about your regular trips to Tehran?" Berke asked. "Has anybody been following you?"

"You know since I got here, I've been going into Tehran monthly to fly to Germany for my reserve training," Gus started to explain. "For the past half-year Bill and I have gone in a few days early to work in the classified spaces in the embassy or to repair some of their equipment. MJ has an open-ended purchase order for our costs and we're the only civilian construction workers with a high enough security clearance left in Iran. All the rest of the cleared American workers have evacuated."

"Just before Dmitry interrupted and the terrorist leader shot him, he was trying to say in Azeri that his men took everyone hostage," Berke said as they collected everything near the engineer's transit. "I think the terrorist was saying that our workers at the compound are already hostages." While Berke smoked one of his aromatic Turkish-Balkan cigarettes, Gus rummaged through his field bag and sneakily emptied the last of the vodka in his aluminum bottle. He ate his apple and slice of hard cheese while he drank water from a glass bottle.

"It's getting cooler," Gus said as he exchanged the split field jacket for his larger one. "I thought Dmitry, our counterpart engineer, just had a Russian minder with him every day." Gus commented. "I was bewildered when you just said he was in fact a KGB captain. I thought he was only a graduate civil engineer. He knew too much about math, surveying and dam design to be anything but an engineer."

Berke said, "I've been told that there is a twelve-man team of Russian Special Forces across the river even though only two of them alternated working on this side of the river as bodyguards for Dmitry Antonov. When they first arrived he told me that they were military draftees; but he was lying. They are in fact an active unit of the Russian KGB trained similar to their Army GRU Spetsnaz. I took telephoto pictures of each of them although I only got two shots of their leader, apparently called the 'Major.' He has a patch of grey on each side of his chin. Most of them are officers who have been learning local languages and the rest of them have beards or mustaches and long hair just like the pasdaran revolutionaries."

"From what you just said," Gus remarked. "These men aren't in the regular Soviet Army similar to American Green Berets; I think they're more like the paramilitary officers that used to work for the CIA's covert Special Operations Group." Gus didn't say it, but he was wondering just why Berke was collecting all this information.

2

Gus and Berke carefully inspected all the weapons. As he surreptitiously watched his Turkish assistant, Gus realized he knew too much about Russian weapons. For more than two years, he had accepted Berke at face value, now he was suspicious.

Gus searched through the bodyguard's pack and two loaded canvas bandoliers. Each held five of the 10-round steel magazines and several cardboard boxes of spare ammo for the long Russian sniper rifle.

There was also a bipod and a cased telescope in the backpack. Gus knew the Dragunov was issued to both snipers and to selected marksmen in a Soviet infantry platoon. However, each of his green-tipped bullets was a special sniper round, marked in Cyrillic on the boxes. Gus knew these bullets had a sliding lead knocker behind the internal steel core that would upset on impact causing tumbling and massive injuries, an assassin's bullet. As he was inspecting the sniper rifle Gus commented, "It's too long for what we need to do." After several minutes of discussion, he said to Berke, "If they've seized the other three Americans and all of your Turkish workers, they're probably holding the hostages in one or two groups, most likely on either side of the yard."

A moment later Berke asked, "Do you think we can attack the terrorist and recapture the compound without anybody getting killed? What do you propose?"

"We'll have to drive up to the gate in their Japanese pickup," Gus responded. "Give me the silenced pistol and extra clips. I'll also take one of the Chinese semi-auto SKS's and sling it over my back. You carry the paratrooper AK along with the bandolier and three magazines."

"I'll need to reload the missing bullets from the spare clips." Berke said. "We have lots of disposable 10-round stripper clips in the pile."

"I'll carry some spare ammo in my jacket pockets." Gus agreed. "After we hump everything of use up to the vehicles, I'll move the Ahoo off Road 12 and join you." He finished his comments by saying, "I'd better fire a round or two through the pistol with its suppressor attached to check the sight alignment."

Sliding the second six-inch suppressor over the interrupted threads and tightening it with a quarter turn, he shot at the end of his empty glass bottle from about thirty-feet. Although he was shooting a foot-long pistol, the bullet struck a little high. The second round shattered the glass. Gus knew the end-on the bottle was about three-inches wide and he had hit low and ricocheted into the glass.

He then changed magazines so the pistol was fully loaded, eight in the clip and one up the spout. After sliding the New York holster and knife scabbard onto his belt, Gus realized the longer pistol wouldn't fit in the custom holster. He stuck it with its extra suppressor in the flapped cargo pocket of his field jacket.

He then slung the SKS across his back. It was also too long, almost a foot more than the wire stocked AK47 although it was still eight inches shorter than the Dragunov sniper rifle. He'd have to carry it in the cab.

"We can approach the entrance gate in the terrorists' white Datsun," Gus told Berke. "It's almost a full moon but there should be enough cloud cover to keep them from seeing us clearly through the dirty windshield."

"I'll step out and shoot any gate guards with the suppressed pistol. You then go to the west and free the men they're probably holding in the dining hall while I go to the east and check the offices and the company house. I doubt if anyone will be out back in the shops or motor pool."

There was no sunset with the heavy clouds of the on-coming rainy season. By the time they got to the vehicles the feeble light was rapidly fading. He put the SKS beside him and sat down. Berke lit one of his Turkish-Balkan Tekel oval cigarettes to calm his nerves before he cranked the diesel engine.

"Do you have any aspirin?" Gus was starting to get a headache. Berke reached into his field bag and removed a tin of Bayer as Gus opened his last bottle of water. He put the tin into his jacket pocket.

Starting east on the ancient caravan trail they passed the first Khoda Bridge with its washed out approaches and just about kilometer further east they could see the fifteen-arches of the newer second Khoda Bridge in the gathering darkness. The dirt road they were on ran for several hundred miles along the Iranian side of the Aras River border with Russia.

The construction complex was the first thing MJ built after they picked the tentative location of the dam based on exposed bedrock, rock cliffs and reservoir size.

The fenced compound had workers dormitories on the western side, shops and a warehouse on the south with the large company house for the American construction personnel on the east, next door to the project office. MJ only had four American workers left in Iran. The rest had been reassigned.

The Russians had constructed a similar camp on their side of the river. "Don't turn on the headlights; both the revolutionaries and Russians across the river will be able to see us." Just a few hundred meters beyond the second bridge approach was the turnoff into the MJ compound. Berke gunned the engine to pull through the sandy ruts at the intersection leading into the fenced 4-hectar construction space and almost flew up to the striped swing arm. He came to a sliding stop in a cloud of dust. Gus stepped out the far door, raised his new pistol and extended it over the corner post of the windshield, bracing his shooting elbow on the chrome frame. Supported by his left hand, he held his arm and wrist rigid as he squinted down the sights at the armed guard.

He shot him in the center of his mouth. As the pistol recoiled and settled back into alignment, he fired a second double-tap just above his nose. Swinging his head around looking for a second target, Gus held his position as Berke got out of the car.

The two shots had been half as loud as regular pistol shots, not sharp but lower pitched, more like a board dropping on the floor. The rattle from the engine had helped to cover the noise. The 9mm Makarov round was less powerful than a Luger 9 mm Parabellum, about the same as a short Browning. When he fired it through the suppressor, it still made a good bit of noise; but it was just quiet enough not to carry across the river to the Russians or through the solid stuccoed walls and double windows.

He slung the SKS barrel down across his back before moving over to check that the man wasn't feigning death. Then he started moving slowly toward the office. Leaving the pickup truck rumbling, Berke crossed behind him and started for the two long dormitories separated by a kitchen and dining room. "Check the dining room first." Gus whispered back as Berke passed behind him.

The wind whipped up a swirl of dust and brought the smell of coal smoke, fried food and the odor from the latrines. The charcoal cooking stoves didn't give off much smoke but they flooded the area with aromas, while the coal heating stoves gave off an acrid black exhaust.

Walking around the guardhouse toward the office, Gus saw a guard carrying an AK slung over his shoulder only a dozen yards away. He must be coming to investigate the sound he had heard. He must think I'm one of the pasdaran revolutionary soldiers, Gus was thinking as he raised the pistol and fired into the center of the rover's face. He shuffled forward; firing each time his left foot hit the ground. His second and third shots were into the nose and eye socket of the slumping sentry.

He only had three left in the clip and one round in the chamber so he drew the long knife with his left hand as a backup as he stepped up on the office slab. Hearing a muffled sound, he slowly opened the door and saw an unarmed soldier in Bill Williams's office flipping through files of papers, his back to Gus. The papers from his matching engineering office were already spread on the floor.

Three quiet strides and he shoved the Spetsnaz fighting knife into his thoracic vertebrae, paralyzing him as he drove the blade through his spinal column, while simultaneously firing two shots into the base of his skull.

The acting clerk was dead, gasping out his last breath. There was another AK leaning against the far side of the desk. Gus checked; there were no other people in the offices.

He paused to move the singleton round from the used magazine into the one that was short two rounds. He had eight silent shots left. He put the empty mag into his jacket pocket. It tinkled against the aspirin tin so he moved the smaller container to his breast pocket.

There was a companion Japanese diesel 4x4 pickup with an empty machine-gun pintle mount parked between the office and the company house. Next to it was a dirty Jeep Shahbaz with the windshield folded forward.

Quietly sliding onto the veranda slab Gus dodged the heavy weightlifting bench, an Olympic weight set, and several homemade barbells built from pipes with different size cans of concrete on both ends. He quietly moved to the window beside the north door and peeked in. Gus saw a guard pointing his AK at two of the three Americans sitting at the dining table while an older man dressed in civilian clothes questioned Bill, tied to a chair. The old construction man had a bruise on his cheek and a dribble of blood coming out of his mouth.

If Gus entered this door, his friends would be directly in the line of fire. On the veranda beyond this entrance were a set of Adirondack style slat-chairs and drink tables which Bill had built using old wooden pallets. Gus tiptoed around them to the southern door leading directly into the kitchen.

He would not be shooting with his friends as a backstop but the distance would be an additional twenty feet. He didn't know if his hand would be steady enough to make the shots.

Kicking in the door, Gus advanced into the room holding the pistol with both hands in an isometric grip and started sliding toward the terrorists. Muscle memory from years of practice took over. He continually moved forward toward both targets. He fired two suppressed pistol rounds into the soldier's face and then another two into the Islamic boss' as he was trying to draw a Russian pistol and back away at the same time.

He followed up with a single shot into each man's eye socket. He bent over and checked both weapons before changing magazines to the extra one the leader was carrying. He put the singleton in his empty pocket.

Inspecting both dead men, Gus heard a burst of three AK shots from the dining room across the dirt-packed courtyard. They were followed only moments later by another three. Running out he saw a shadow dash from the side of the Turkish kitchen and start for the back motor pool fence. He realized the man was taking the shorter leg of an expanding triangle. Charging across the hypotenuse Gus ran to intercept him. After a hundred meter sprint, he dropped and slid like a base runner, kicking the feet from underneath the escaping man.

Berke ran up, followed by several Turkish workers. "I killed both terrorist at the mess hall but this one escaped out the back door. I'll take care of asking him questions," as he pulled the man to his feet holding both elbows.

His men grabbed him and started marching him back to the dining room. "Send some men out to bring in the vehicles," Gus said to Berke before he turned to follow. "Have them take a couple of sheets in the Toyota, cover the pasdaran, put the Russians into their UAZ and bring it back to the foot of their bridge. Treat the bodies with respect."

Starting back to the company house, he paused to look into the backs of the Iranian Jeep and the small pickup. There were two canvas cases in the back of the truck. One held an RPG-7 anti-tank rocket launcher and the other had six spare rocket propelled grenades.

Looking up he saw that both bodies had been moved out to the porch. Walking past the bodies, he inspected the broken lock on the kitchen door to the house as it struck him. Their contract had been canceled. They needed to get out of Iran, tonight.

Walking in he greeted his friends and then listened as Bill Williams said to everybody, "We have to leave Iran tonight. You know the final groups of construction workers on the other projects left during the summer and we're the last MJ workers still in Iran." Bill was a blunt old MJ International superintendent. "We need to take our Turkish workers with us and skedaddle across the border."

"Bill, let's go next door while I use the ham radio to contact some people." Gus told his construction manager. "You need to tell me what your emergency plans are. Since it's after dark maybe I can get a civilian operator on the west coast who can relay our call to MJ."

"I usually call Jan every night," Bill said. "Of course you know that Boise is ten and a half hours ahead of us so our contact window will disappear with the rising sun in Idaho."

Bill turned and said, "Vince, get the Mercedes bus and the fuel truck filled with diesel. Load the back of the big Chevy pickup with three extra drums of gasoline, check the oil, filters and get spare parts like hoses and belts for all of them."

"The Turks are bringing in our Jeep Wagoneer," Gus added. "It needs to be checked and filled." Turning to Bill Williams he asked, "Why don't we abandon all of our older trucks? Pick the best vehicles and arrange them into a convoy."

"It'll probably start raining tonight or tomorrow so get tarps for the pickup loads." Bill told Vince and then turned to Dennis. "Why don't you start collecting food, water and medicine for our trip? Repair the front door and clean up all signs of violence."

"I think we should leave as soon as possible and travel all night," Bill said to everyone. "We can lay over tomorrow during the day and cross the border tomorrow night. Afterwards it'll still take us a couple of days to get to Ankara and another couple to Istanbul. Pack the minimum of personal stuff since we won't be able to carry everything."

Gus followed Bill next door to the common room and switched on the radio to start warming up the tubes of the single-sideband shortwave transceiver. Bill went into his office and Gus joined him to help carry the terrorist body back out the front door.

Their antenna was a long wire dipole style running from the roof, crossing the top of a telephone pole out back and down to a ground stake. Since it was oriented slightly southeast to northwest, they could usually contact one of the civilian operators in the northwestern United States.

They used to talk every night to the now closed MJ offices in Tehran about 350 miles to the southeast and they could reach several other jobsites around Iran, unfortunately they were all now vacant. They could also usually get the reopened US Consulate in Tabriz since it was only 80 miles away.

While the tubes warmed, Gus went across to the Turkish dining room and started to tell Berke about cleaning up all signs of a fight. "Our prisoner is already talking, more like bragging," his Turkish assistant said. "He says his colonel has organized the northwestern districts and they are coordinating with the armed Revolutionary Guards in Teheran, commanded by his older brother. He bragged that tomorrow morning a few hundred student-agitators are going to storm the US Embassy. Behind them will be his brother with the most dependable Revolutionary Guards in the capital." Gus asked several specific questions.

"The pasdaran are going to take everyone hostage, break into the top floor vault, the disintegrator room, and snatch the CIA files and secret cables. That's why they needed you as a hostage; they think that you work for the CIA. They're not there to demonstrate, the students are supposed to handle that. The Revolutionary Guards are heading straight for the chancery building. He and his men are going to do the same thing at the US Consulate in Tabriz, just like they did last year."

3

Jogging back to the offices Gus tuned to one of the frequencies he knew the embassy monitored. He could hear nothing but a warbling tone intermixed with a static hiss on the radio. Someone was jamming the channel.

The same interference was on the frequency used by the newly reopened consular offices at Mashhad and Tabriz. Changing to a private channel used by Ed Warren, his acquaintance at the local Tabriz consulate, he immediately got his friend.

Gus had guessed that Ed was a CIA officer from the Directorate of Intelligence assigned to the diplomatic consulate under official cover. Gus liked Ed but he thought that he hadn't actually recruited or handled any agents during his four-year career; rather he passed on information he picked up at parties, from local newspapers and official sources.

There were only a couple of Americans consular volunteers still in Tabriz along with a few Iranian consulate workers. After Ed asked what was happening Gus told him, "A group of students plan to start a demonstration and then attack the embassy and your consulate tomorrow. They're backed by the Revolutionary Guard pasdaran who are going to seize hostages and break into the classified spaces." At first Ed had questions but when Gus revealed the details of the attack at Khoda Bridge he stopped talking and started making notes.

"I can't get through to Tehran so I suggest you call home and then evacuate to Turkey. I can meet you at the same place near the border where we first met, over."

Two years before, Gus, Ed and the officer he was replacing had met at the ruins of an abandoned caravanserai on the hillside over-looking the ancient caravan trail near the Iranian village of Jolfa, the train yards right on the border between Iran and the Soviet Union.

From the hillside, they could look out across miles of the Aras River just after it spilled out of the mountainous ravines and into the gentle valley it followed for two hundred-fifty miles down to the Caspian Sea.

Gus had been doing a quick survey of the upper river along the ancient Road 12, while Ed Warren was on his first visit to the border. Jolfa was the northern end of the Iranian railroad to the Russian border and more than 350 boxcars loaded with Soviet cargo crossed south while tank wagons with 250,000 barrels of oil went north between the two countries every day.

As he was still finishing work at the embassy in Prague but just before moving to Iran for his new civilian assignment, Gus had studied the Foreign Service Journal and the directory of the AFSA. He thought he had identified all the players in Iran working for the CIA. There were no officers' left from the CIA's Special Operations Group-SOG and he knew for a fact that none of the American Intelligence Directorate officers could speak Farsi, Azeri, Dari or Turkic, although most knew some awful French.

His next calls were to various ham operators on the west coast with Bill listening over his shoulder. After five tries, he finally got a good signal to a MARS station located atop Fairmont Heights in Eugene, Oregon overlooking the university. Giving him the private phone number of his uncle Richard Knowles, the CEO of MJ, he listened as the ham go-between called Boise through the AT&T operator, reversing the charges.

Although it was 6:30 pm at the dam site, it was 8:00 am at the corporate headquarters in Boise when Richard answered and told the operator to go ahead. After years of experience both men knew they had to say, over when they finished their thought and not to interrupt when the other was speaking.

The ham amateur at the station in Eugene had to key the microphone to transmit or release it to listen. Gus mentioned that Bill was listening-in and then asked, "Is everybody there OK, over."

Hearing an affirmative, he then told his uncle about the attack on the dam survey party. Gus briefly mentioned the subsequent battle for the compound and then the warning they had gotten about the upcoming takeover of the US Embassy in Tehran.

He did not say anything about dead men over the radio. Mentioning he had contacted the consulate in Tabriz, but he couldn't get the embassy in Tehran or the other consulate, he asked his uncle to let Washington know what was happening.

"Call the State Department, the Pentagon and my old employer and let them know what the Islamic radicals are planning for tomorrow. Please tell the people across the river that your man in Iran is using the code words *Prairie Fire Emergency* in reference to the facility in Tehran. You can also say I used the older phrase *Broken Arrow*. Tell them to raise the Threat Condition to Delta, meaning an overwhelming attack on an American compound. Give them those terms exactly." His uncle asked him to repeat the phrases as he wrote them down.

"We are implementing our emergency escape plan and should reach Turkey in two days." Gus transmitted. "I hope to collect the US personnel from Tabriz along the river. There's something unusual going on with our Russian counterparts. It turns out that Dmitry Antonov was a captain in the KGB and a full team of KGB Spetsnaz was on site to help the now dead officer, a special team." Uncle Richard asked what he wanted to do?

"I may take a few weeks off," Gus said. "I need to get to the bottom of why they had me under surveillance. We're going to have to leave most of our belongings and the equipment here at the compound, over."

"Bill Williams," Richard said to the listening construction manager. "Give Gus everything in the safe; he has special training and a lot more experience in things like this. Gus, spend what you need to get across the border and then call me. You'll probably need to temporarily deposit any money left over in a Swiss bank using your name." Gus didn't understand what money his uncle was talking about.

"We don't want it back here. It can't show up on MJ's books. The extra cash is there for special payments to tribal leaders and the Russians. The Shah's people included it in our deal. I'll sue Iran through the State Department for anything still due under our contract and anything you have to abandon. Call me if you need anything. The rest of the team can probably catch a flight out of Ankara or Istanbul. Over & Out."

"You know I've been with MJ since 1935 over forty-four years," Bill Williams said to Gus after he turned around. "What I've never told you is that your grandfather hired me as a young snot-nosed kid to work for him outside Las Vegas on the Boulder Dam project. By the summer of '39, I was leading one of the company surveying crews in the Cascades where your father and Dick Knowles worked for me." Gus said, "My father and Uncle Dick were in school. What were they doing working during the summer?"

Bill said that they were on their month-long summer furlough. "We all were on standby to fight forest fires in the Northwest since the company needed the extra money that the Forest Service paid to companies furnishing firefighters. Your father spent time with the team from Eagle Parachute, testing how to parachute people and equipment in on fires. The next summer he was one of the first volunteer smokejumpers in Winthrop although in the evenings we all met at a local roadhouse to drink beer and eat buffalo burgers. That's where I introduced him to your mother, an up and coming local singer."

Bill paused and looked at Gus to gauge his reaction. Gus had never heard this story before, but talking about his dead mother and father made him uncomfortable. His grandparents didn't talk much about them.

He said, "Maybe we can talk more later, I wasn't born yet and I don't remember anything about them. My grandmother told me my father died in the Philippines and mother died on a USO war-bond tour a couple of years later, but she never told me how they met."

Bill then motioned for Gus to follow as he went next door to his office and opened an antique looking armoire cabinet. He then unlocked the safe hidden inside the old cabinet.

From the top shelf, he took down oily rags wrapped around three Colt 1911 pistols and a Browning Hi-Power. There was a cardboard box holding a dozen empty magazines and two boxes of .45-ACP bullets and another of 9-mm Parabellum rounds. He finally removed three leather tanker holsters and a canvas belt holster. There was also a smaller portable shortwave radio.

"The evacuation plan is to head for Turkey in the company vehicles," Bill said. "We can use some of the special funds to bribe our way out of Iran if we need them. The first item is in two Zero Halliburton aluminum attaché cases."

Bill pulled out one case at a time and lifted them onto the desk. "Each is full of South African Krugerrands; 100-paper rolls of twelve 1.0-troy-ounce gold coins. I used folded silk prayer rugs to pad the contents, meaning each briefcase weighs almost 90-pounds. When I first got the gold, its 2,400 troy ounces was worth about $250,000. At today's price it's now worth a lot more."

Gus looked at the cases and picked one up. He realized he would have trouble carrying both cases more than a few hundred yards. The aluminum case and handle easily held the weight that would tear right through a regular leather briefcase. Bill wrote both of the three-single digit combination numbers on a piece of paper.

He then pulled out a locked army duffle bag using both shoulder straps and twisted the dial of its combination padlock. Before opening it, he added three new double-digit numbers to the list. "This bag has two larger silk rugs wrapped around stacks of US $100 bills," he noted. "The banknotes are worth $2.5-million, and weigh around 70-pounds with the two carpets."

Gus inspected the bag and noted, "It's only a third full."

"You should probably put some clothing on top of the contents," Bill replied. "I started out with the gold for emergencies and $5 million in cash for bribes. MJ's been bringing the monthly draw for the workers from Tehran and disbursing the rest from our office in Turkey. You can see there's still half left."

"Why silk carpets," Gus asked as he checked the pistols.

"They're a quarter the weight and volume of wool carpets. I bought two large and two small carpets to fold up and conceal the cash."

"We need to leave by 9:00 pm tonight," Gus said, as he and Bill went outside to check on everyone's progress. Berke came over and joined the group of four Americans with some new information.

"The leader of the mujahedeen soldiers is in fact a former SAVAK-secret police lieutenant colonel working out of Tabriz." Berke continued, "He's responsible for the five provinces in the Northwest District along the Turkish border. He and his brother in the capitol are famous for their ruthless brutality. Everyone knows that they torture and murder revolutionaries. Over the past few years both of them supposedly have found religion, and they now call themselves Mullahs. Some of my sources claim they turned against the Shah and fully supported the return and theocracy of Ayatollah Khomeini."

"What do you mean, some?" Gus asked. "Do others have a second opinion? Are they trained or are they just the typical secret police thugs?"

"One of my agents says that Muhammad Hassan, the colonel in Tehran is a true believer," Berke said. "He has given up all his connections with alcohol, drugs and tobacco. He also prays five times a day. His brother Ali Hassan is not so pure. My man swears that he maintains his connection with drug smugglers and is much more worldlier. For their first few years in SAVAK the Hassan brothers reported to the career CIA officers who ran the unit for the Shah," Berke reported. "I don't know if they had any special talents. Later, Muhammad went to the United States for additional training in Virginia. Ali followed in his footsteps just a year later."

Gus asked, "Is there any way to find out if the CIA polygraphers' uncovered any secrets? What do you think Ali Hassan will do next?"

"After the assault in Tabriz," Berke said. "Ali will be flying here to check on his most trusted team. He's got an Italian Agusta Bell version of the Huey. If he doesn't find us here he will sweep up the river toward the border. After the swing he'll have to go back to Tabriz to refuel. So, he'll probably send out patrols after us and try to intercept us before we can cross into Turkey."

Turning to Berke, Gus said, "I want you to select the best of the pasdaran Japanese pickups to lead the procession. Arm two of your construction workers and have them pretend to be Revolutionary Guards."

"Those two are the most likely to pass if they change their clothes." Gus said as he pointed to two of the three men standing on the veranda well to Berke's side. "The big one, I think he's called Achmed, can drive the Mercedes bus carrying the remaining Turkish workers. The fuel truck with its diesel, grease and spare parts should be behind them. The Wagoneer Ahoo with Bill driving can follow with Dennis or Vince riding shotgun. It can carry most of their personal gear along with food and medicine in the back."

"The Chevy K-30 pickup will bring up the rear with you driving." Gus told Berke as he nodded agreeing with what Gus said. "I'll ride shotgun beside you. I told Dennis to put a couple of bags of charcoal in the back for smokeless cooking. I've already told Vince to load three 55-gallon drums of gasoline centered on top of the rear axle." Gus first nodded to Vince and then snapped his fingers, "That reminds me, the Suburban from the consulate will need premium."

Bill added, "We'll need to bring a rotary hand pump. You can put the heavy bags against the Chevy cab and the rest the stuff like clothing and extra supplies covered by the tarp. Everything should weigh less than 600 pounds. Put some 5-gallon jerry cans with spouts against the tailgate for quick refueling."

Gus then mentioned the various weapons and ammunition they needed to spread out among the vehicles. "We'll need a couple of AK's in the lead pickup. Following the convoy, I want to carry the sniper rifle. Berke you bring the rocket propelled grenade launcher and the paratrooper AK."

"More than two-thirds of the Turkish workers in the bus won't be armed." Berke stated.

"If we get a chance we need to find some more weapons." Gus said. "Tomorrow morning, the housemaids will cross the bridge from Russia and discover the Russian's jeep and bodies at this end. They'll run back to tell their minders who will come across and steal every-thing not nailed down. By then I want to be a hundred miles away."

"I need to make sure we give proper Muslim treatment to the dead pasdaran revolutionaries," Berke said. "It should probably be away from the compound. Also we need to wrap the two Russians in some improvised shrouds before we leave them on the bridge."

Dennis turned to Gus and said, "I need to find the camouflage shade nets that we used during the groundbreaking two summers ago. I'll also need to bring the chain-link drags that we use to smooth out ruts in the road after it rains in the winter. They're somewhere in the storeroom. We'll need them tonight and tomorrow."

After telling the men to be back in thirty minutes Gus turned to Bill and asked, "Can you think of anything else?" As Bill left Gus looked over the compound thinking of anything more he needed to do.

He went to his room to pack, putting the half-full duffle and his field bag on the top bunk bed next to an empty rucksack he pulled from underneath the bed. In the top drawer of the dresser were his Dopp toiletry kit, loose items and camera bag. The next drawers held various clothes and finally the last drawer held his leather strapped Gladstone bag full of exercise clothes and a rectangular package. Stored in the bottom of the drawer, tucked under his sweats and hand-made German cross-country shoes were his Randall combat knife and back-up six-shot revolver with its Ches Gayheart pocket sheath along with a backup ankle holster and a leather reload pouch that held two 6-shot rubber strips. He had smuggled the Colt Cobra into Iran on one of the Air Force cargo planes.

Putting the weapons to the side and opening the rucksack, he packed a single set of winter clothes, underclothes and his trail shoes. He then filled the rucksack with field equipment and supplies. Gus checked to make sure his earplugs were attached to the strap. But he left his old fly rod and the basic kit to tie flies.

From his hanging rod, he took down a leather sports coat, a pair of Levi jeans and wool trousers, a couple of shirts and a sweater and then his prized possession, a dark khaki British Aquascutum trench coat. The same Kingsway model Humphrey Bogart wore in *Casablanca*.

He smoothly rolled everything and packed extra clothes in the Gladstone before putting it into the duffle bag on top the rugs and money. The two heavy briefcases were still in the office. From the top of his dresser, he took his sunglasses, passport, and wallet after checking inside the top drawer for various currencies and ID's.

He rearranged the Turkish lira, German marks and US bank notes in the gold-filigreed money clip, isolating the Iranian and Turkish currency in the gold paperclip. If he had to pay a bribe, he didn't want to show that he had additional money.

He finally turned his attention to the brown kraft paper package, which was stuck together with silver duct tape. As he unwound the package a series of triangular steel forgings were exposed. Each flat piece had a stamped slot in the center and three sharpened tips. Sliding two pieces together formed a four-point polyhedron. He started assembling a dozen modern versions of the ancient anti-cavalry caltrop. It always landed with one sharp point up, destroying a truck tire or horse hoof. He was going to conceal these on their back trail to discourage pursuit. If someone tried to follow, they would get flat tires.

He left more than a dozen field outfits along with another dozen suits and sports coats he wore when he went to Tehran. Luckily, his uniforms were in Germany with his reserve unit in Frankfurt. He had a sudden thought. Everybody knows I'm in the Army Reserve, even the Iranians and my co-workers. Does anyone know about my former covert job? I'll bet Berke does.

Removing his dirty OD fatigue pants and the tan safari shirt, Gus poured a pitcher of water into the basin, performed a quick field wash, and changed into a new outfit adding his plain black wool ball cap. He had removed the embroidered gold "A" years ago.

Loosening the heavy leather belt from a couple of loops, he arranged the Randall knife and spare magazines on his left hip and the holster for the Russian Makarov on his right. He packed the ankle holster and then put the snub-nosed revolver in his right jacket pocket along with the strip of spare ammo in the left. The Russian Spetsnaz fighting knife was too heavy and with an 8-inch blade, it was too long.

Spreading everything else among his pants and jacket pockets, he made sure he included his red Swiss Army pocketknife. He then slipped on his gold West Point ring with its old rounded onyx stone from his grandfather and father's rings.

After dressing, he loaded a canister of very fast film into his Nikon F2 camera and went outside to take photos of the dead men's faces before they buried them. Pausing in the common kitchen Gus started a large pot of coffee and rinsed out a quart Thermos before going out into the yard.

"Where is the prisoner?" Gus asked Berke when he got outside. "I don't know whether to let him go or take him to Turkey as proof of their plans."

"Zandt's Iranian batman was guarding him. He pulled a hidden knife and slit the prisoner's throat before stabbing himself." Berke lit another cigarette as he answered Gus.

4

As the convoy proceeded west on Iranian Road 12 the trailing pickup stopped at the top of the hill just beyond the future dam site. Climbing, the unpaved road switched back and forth like a snake. Gus got out and sent Berke forward as he took off his well-worn ankle boots and walked on the cold dirt in his socks.

Spreading out on a piece of cardboard, he used the pick from a Korean war entrenching tool to plant a half dozen of his modern version of the medieval four-pointed caltrops in the ruts any vehicle would have to take going up the hill.

Afterward putting his shoes back on, Gus stopped to relieve himself. Looking over the river valley, he smelled the coming rain and looked back for any signs of light. At the pickup, he poured himself a cup of black coffee and took two more aspirin with the first sip.

Everyone knew to keep his headlights off. To save light bulbs most Iranian drivers didn't use their headlights at night. Instead, they would use their sidelights and the cloud covered full moon to navigate. The drivers already knew the rear vehicle would occasionally fall behind to check for followers. Having taken this road several times, Gus knew they must quietly pass through a dozen small villages during the night on their hundred-mile journey to get to the old ruins outside Jolfa. The mid eastern farm houses were mostly mud-brick and their yards were filled with scrap equipment.

They needed to set up their camouflage nets before the sun rose. Gus hoped that tomorrow night Berke could get them through the border guards and customs. He must have some contacts with the officers in Turkish intelligence. Gus hoped that he knew some people at the border.

When he first arrived in Iran, MJ's Turkish partner sent them a new assistant engineer to work for Gus along with several dozen skilled workers. The bulk of the original workforce was local Iranian. At the beginning, Gus had wondered if Berke really worked for Turkish Military Intelligence-MIT. The Turks might have a qualified officer keeping an eye on any Russo-Iranian project. Was he watching both him and the Soviets for the *Company*? After working with him for a few months, Gus didn't worry as much since Berke was a trained engineer. He had never told Berke he suspected he might work for MIT.

Over the next few hours the two men drove silently, Berke smoking one cigarette after another. Gus finished the thermos of coffee and swallowed another two aspirin. Twice the truck held back while the two men listened for signs of anyone following, using the pause to relieve their bladders.

"At first the Russian team here was led by a different engineer, not Dmitry Antonov. The rest were workers from Azerbaijan SSR. A few months into the project a dozen men led by a bearded officer called the 'Major' and his brother, a fresh-faced much younger officer showed up. Dmitry came with them and took over all contacts on our side of the border." Berke confided during one of the pauses.

"Months later one of the local workers from Azerbaijan identified the team across the river as a KGB special operations unit Gruppa Spetsialnogo Naznacheniya *ALFA*. Rather than watching anybody specifically, he reported that they were one of four Russian teams overseeing the movement of opium tar along the Silk Road from Afghanistan to Turkey and then on to the Mafia in Sicily. He claimed he overheard them say that the American CIA was involved."

Gus interrupted, "Wait a minute, I remember reading somewhere that Spetsnaz Alpha was imaginary, supposedly formed to divert attention from the Russian illegals department."

"Why didn't you tell me your contact was telling you that they were KGB Spetsnaz?" Gus asked. "Did you report to anyone at Turkish or American intelligence about your contact on the Russian side of the border? That you were watching this group."

Berke answered, "I did have a contact at Turkish national intelligence who regularly asked me questions." He then continued, "As far as I know, the Americans thought the Alpha-Group were just a rumor and not a real unit, so I didn't say anything. I was afraid that you would discover that I was reporting to them." Berke said. "I graduated from the Turkish Army Engineers School in Istanbul with Masters Degree from Georgia Tech. I am a reserve captain in the Turkish Corps of Engineers who sometimes reports to active duty officers in MIT-Turkish national intelligence. MIT doesn't trust the CIA. Both the Americans and the Russians are trying to keep something secret from us. Why else would they assign so many secret agents to watch you? They must think you learned something about them while you were in the CIA and they want to keep it concealed."

Gus thought a minute and then opened up to Berke. "I assume you were briefed I was fired by the CIA in late 1977. The Halloween Massacre eliminated almost eight hundred CIA case officers assigned to the Directorate of Operations, including the few dozen who were working as *NOC*'s—covert officers with No-Official-Cover." Gus paused for a minute as he collected his thoughts. "The President and the Director also fired or reassigned hundreds of contract employees, most of who worked for the Special Activities Division of the directorate. During the house cleaning they eliminated almost all of the operations officers with specialized skills like languages, political action, propaganda, air or marine support while the rest of the men they let go were former Army, Navy or Marine special forces non-commissioned officer's working for Paramilitary Operations. The Clandestine Service was annihilated."

"I will agree many of the men fired were cowboys left over from the 50's and 60's; dead wood that needed to be trimmed." Gus paused for a minute while he thought about what he wanted to say. "The rest were dedicated officers and their mass-termination neutered international covert operations. The decision has hampered the collection of human intelligence ever since. The Directorate of Operations was left with less than a couple of hundred Ivy-league type staff officers, most with little field experience. None of them were qualified as NOC's to carry out covert operations where the US Government denies all knowledge. Unfortunately, the carnage didn't touch the Directorates of Intelligence, Support or Science and Technology, which also needed cleansing." Gus paused to take two more aspirin and drink half a bottle of water before asking Berke to stop so he could relieve himself.

"Why do you think the Russians are watching you?" Berke asked when Gus returned.

"I've been trying to figure it out since last night. After I graduated in Civil Engineering, I served four years in the Army and then went on to graduate school. Following that I spent eight years working for the CIA. I've certainly crossed the KGB before." Gus paused, waiting for Berke to ask him about his combat experience. There were no questions. Someone must have already briefed him.

"When we get out of Iran, I was thinking of taking a few weeks off to go see one of my friends in Germany. Maybe he knows something or can jog my memory. He usually has an ear to the ground and knows what's up. I can't think of any information the Russians may want."

"What more can you tell me about these former SAVAK officers?" Gus asked Berke after fifteen minutes of silence. "What do you think they'll do next?"

"Lieutenant Colonel Ali came by the camp a month ago while you were in Teheran. Have you ever met him?" Berke asked.

"Yes," Gus said. "In January, I had to escort our engineer trainee, Zahir Khan to meet him in Tabriz. Zahir was using a false name at the time and Ali was suspicious, although he didn't have any real power to do anything. He's one of the reasons Zahir took another job in Pakistan as soon as the Islamist took over."

When the convoy arrived at the ruins of the old caravanserai just across the Aras River from Armenia, Gus had them refuel each vehicle before moving it under the tent-like camouflage netting. An hour later as the sun was peeking over the mountains; the four-wheel drive station wagon from the US Consulate in Tabriz arrived. It was a Chevy K 20 Suburban, black and shiny beneath the dust. Of course, it had Arabic numbered "Corps Diplomatique CD" license plates on the chrome front and rear bumpers. The filthy mustard colored MJ vehicles had painted bumpers.

Ed Warren got out of the passenger seat and introduced his three American companions to the MJ personal who were standing near two small fires concealed behind a shoulder-high wall.

"We got out just in time, I had this Suburban parked behind my villa and all three Americans were inside with me. We came north on Highway 21 the road paralleling the railroad tracks but I don't think anyone saw us. We pulled off the road when one of the goods trains passed us heading south last night."

As he spoke, Ed realized everyone was looking at one of his consular employees. "I would like you to meet Dedee Anderson. Unlike the rest of us she speaks Farsi." She was an attractive young girl in her twenties with auburn colored hair. "Her father worked as a dairy expert here in Iran for twenty years before he retired."

The second man was wearing a safari jacket covering a holstered pistol. Noticing his interest Ed said to Gus, "Derek Cobb is an assistant RSO-Regional Security Officer who normally works out of Tehran."

"The third man is John, another young consular officer who speaks some Arabic. Although the consulate closed last year during the revolution, we reopened in a temporary office three months ago. Unfortunately, Washington will close us permanently with this most recent scare."

At the almost smokeless fire pits, one of the Turks was boiling a large kettle of tea over one charcoal fire and five dozen eggs on the other to go with yesterday's fresh bread, hard cheese and melting butter.

Gus told Berke to have one of his men refuel the new Suburban from one of the high-test drums. "Save the drum. We may need to refill on the drive across Eastern Turkey."

Gus was still in good shape, but since leaving the clandestine service, he had slowly cut down on his daily exercise routine. Now he usually warmed up with calisthenics and jogged five miles on even days or lifted weights and walked on odd days. Although on Fridays, the Muslim holy day he sometimes went for long hikes with Bill. Yesterday he weighed seven pounds more than he did when he graduated from college.

He thought he should lose a few pounds and start increasing his lean muscles so he only had tea and one hardboiled egg for breakfast. He had decided last night that he could no longer drink anything alcoholic, ever again. Last night he also committed himself to working out strenuously every single day until he got back into top condition.

After his boiled egg and bread, Gus drank his tea as he changed into his well-worn trail-runners and a brown cotton turtleneck. Bill was going with him but he was still wearing his work-boots. They left the old caravansary and walked south into the valley that was the heart of the Kaimaky Wildlife Refuge. The Shah had set up this refuge to protect the Persian Leopard just a few years ago.

Gus left Bill to hike while he jogged on up the valley heading for the foot of Kiyamaki Dagh, the highest mountain in the park. About an hour later he returned, although Gus had run five miles further than Bill had walked. He drank some water from his canteen before both men turned and started back.

"Have you quit drinking," Bill asked.

"Yes," Gus said. "I'm going to exercise every day until I can run a 26-mile marathon." Then he asked, "Was my drinking that noticeable?"

"When you first joined us you drank a six-pack of beer some evenings." Bill said. "It increased to hard whiskey and beer."

"When the Islamic revolution occurred and we couldn't get anything alcoholic, I know you started getting vodka smuggled across the river and mixing it with local juice. I'm glad you quit since I expected you to go blind any day drinking local moonshine."

Gus changed the subject and asked, "I didn't realize you knew my mother and father before they met, why don't you tell me what happened. My grandparents didn't like to talk about them."

"Your mother Mary was a wonderful singer and the most beautiful girl in the Skagit River Valley," Bill said as they walked back to camp. "She was good enough to become a Hollywood star. Then she met your father and decided to get married."

"That summer of '40 your father and Dick Knowles had just graduated from West Point and both were working until they reported for duty in September. The previous summer furlough they both worked on my surveying crew."

"Of course your grandfather, an engineer from the Class of '02 had been the chief engineer for MJ since he retired from the Corps in 1930." Gus nodded and asked Bill to continue.

"We were building the road across the Cascade Mountains from northern Idaho to Seattle. Dick worked for me, while your father joined the sixty professional parachutists from the Eagle Parachute Company to form the first smokejumper squadron in the US Forest Service. Your father wooed Mary all summer and they were married on Labor Day."

Gus asked, "Where did they get married?"

"Mary was an orphan so they got married at the Cathedral and held the reception in your grandparent's house. When their summer furlough ended Dick joined the Corps of Engineers and your father took Mary to Fort Benning where he trained as an infantryman and parachutist."

"By the next spring, Mary was pregnant and your father was assigned to the Philippines to form an airborne platoon of Philippine Scouts. In 1941 dependents weren't allowed to go to the Philippines.

So, Mary went to live with your grandmother and two aunts in Boise where you were born just before the attack on Pearl Harbor. During the Japanese invasion of the Philippines, your father was killed and later posthumously decorated. I remember when a classmate returned his class ring, dog tags and crucifix after the war. I think he was reinterred in the Punch Bowl." Gus nodded in agreement.

"The War Department asked your mother to go on tours, where she could sell bonds, sing and entertain the troops. She died in a plane crash in '44 and your grandmother and a nanny raised you. Your grandfather was off on dozens of projects during and after the war. Dick Knowles married your aunt after he got back in '45 and started with MJ."

Suddenly Gus froze and motioned for Bill to get down. About 2,500 feet up a Huey helicopter was thumping and whopping as it passed from right to left along the river. It continued on to the border crossing at Jolfa.

Circling there, it then turned southeast and headed back toward Tabriz, probably to refuel. Things weren't looking so good. Luckily they had covered their tracks with the drag when they turned off the main road and it was starting to rain. Gus hoped the weather would cover their tire tracks. They couldn't leave the hidden laager until dark.

With the warning of future trouble Gus set up perimeter lookouts and a forward sentry post using the men with military experience. The cook had already put up a canvas tarp under the camouflage netting to keep rain out of the two fire pits. He was roasting their formerly refrigerated lamb over the hot coals still burning in the pit. Tonight they would have lamb stew with root vegetables and rice, finishing the last of their fresh food. The 50-pound sacks of hickory charcoal gave off a lot of heat and almost no smoke. Tomorrow morning they would either be having breakfast in Turkey or eating prison food.

Later in the morning they were resting under a rain tarp beneath the camouflage net. Gus was cleaning his weapons. He had just changed his revolver from the pocket holster to his ankle rig, since it was more comfortable while driving. He practiced grabbing his left trouser leg with both hands, pulling it up sharply and then stepping forward while kneeling and drawing the ankle pistol

Gus took a couple more aspirins with a bottle of water and slept for several hours. Later that afternoon Gus set up the Grundig portable shortwave and stretched its shorter antenna wire over the wall. He raised the truck tarp higher so the English speakers could gather and listen out of the rain.

The BBC World Service would be broadcasting the news to Iran at 12:00 noon and again at 1:00 pm GMT, which was 3:30 and 4:30 local time. Everybody gathered and listened to the reports of the takeover of the US Embassy in Tehran. Almost a quarter of the broadcast was about events in the capital of the new Republic of Iran. There was no mention of the consulates or any expatriate Americans trapped inside the country.

The stew had been cooking for hours over almost smokeless charcoal but just before they re-started the second fire for tea, a group of three vehicles slowly drove along the river road. The first Chevy pick-up truck was mustard yellow followed by a smaller dirty white Toyota with a heavy machine gun mounted on a swivel pintle in the back and then a tan Wagoneer. The lead pickup must be one of the MJ vehicles they left at Khoda Bridge. It was slowly moving along Road 12 while two men leaned over the cab searching the road for tire prints. All of the windshields were muddy from the recent rain. The convoy was heading west for Jolfa.

Scooting to the forward wall, and cupping his hands to keep water off the lenses, Gus watched them through his Zeiss binoculars. It's a good thing they used the chain-link drag last night when they turned off the road. It looked like the convoy was full of pasdaran soldiers.

"No tea with dinner, everyone eat up the hot food and then smother the fire with dirt, so it doesn't make any smoke," he said to Berke.

As they pulled the sentries in for the last of the food, it was turning dark. Gus nodded to Derek Cobb and both of them walked down to the forward listening post to watch until everyone had eaten and the trucks were ready to leave.

5

The heavy rain had ended and a light misty drizzle was rolling up out of the Aras River valley. On their way out of the caravanserai Gus asked, "Which are you? All of the RSO's I've met are one of three types; a retired Marine with embassy guard experience, a sworn special agent trained by one of the federal bureaus or a CIA officer under cover."

Gus had left his AK and the long Dragunov in the truck and was carrying his Makarov PB silent pistol, his Randall Model 2 fighting stiletto and the back-up Colt revolver. Cobb screwed a suppressor tube onto a stainless Smith & Wesson 9mm, a "hush puppy" from Vietnam.

"Were you a SEAL in Nam?" Gus asked.

Derek realized Gus was asking about his unique pistol. "Yes, however I blew out the rubber wipers in my silencer a few years ago and I don't have any of the green-tipped subsonic ammunition. To answer your other question, I'm now a special agent working throughout the Near East, I'm not in the CIA." Gus glanced back at Derek as he continued. "I was a naval officer who entered the

Diplomatic Security Service and went through regular training before becoming a Special Agent. I now have the power of federal law enforcement, everywhere. I am empowered to make arrests, investigate violations of federal laws and I can officially carry weapons anywhere in the world. However your observations are fairly accurate, since my supervisor trained as a FBI Special Agent although the top boss transferred over from the CIA." He then pulled out a well-used Japanese made MACV-SOG knife. Gus didn't know whether to believe him or not.

As they neared the ledge of rock where their forward pickets had been, two indistinct forms materialized through the mist into revolutionary guards coming up the trail. They were followed by two more about six feet behind them. Gus gave the hand signal to spread out and moved toward the first man with his knife in his left hand and the long pistol in the other. Taking two quick forward steps, Gus feigned with his pistol and drove the knife into the man's throat and brain.

Derek was about to make a similar move when his man said in Farsi, "Someone's been smoking," and leaned forward to study the ground.

Cobb raised his pistol and shot him in the chest. The shot sounded extremely loud.

The "hush puppy" slide was locked into single fire so Derek moved to jack another round into the chamber as Gus fired his much quieter pistol into the first man's nose just after withdrawing the knife.

The two following men started to unsling their rifles as Gus moved forward rigidly holding the pistol in a two-handed Weaver stance, his knife held underneath. Using his whole body to aim, he shot twice into the man on the right and then swinging his pistol and body, he shot the man on the left two more times. The fourth terrorist had just fired a burst up the track to his left before Gus double-tapped him in the chest and head.

Moments later, the diesel pickup started its engine down at the crossroads and someone fired a long burst from the pintle-mounted machinegun in the bed. The truck then accelerated away from the action.

Gus checked the two farthest bodies and then turned back to check on Derek. He was down. The five round burst from the AK had put three bullets across his upper body.

As Gus checked, he realized he was dead. Picking up the weapons and his knife, he slung the body over his shoulder and headed back for the caravanserai. While the cavalcade wrapped and loaded Derek Cobb's body in the pick-up, Gus went back down and planted the last of his caltrops in the ruts of the trail leading down to Road 12. On the way back he collected the terrorist weapons.

They then drove around the town and headed off across the uninhabited mountainous high desert on dirt trails. Several convenient rain showers covered their tracks, especially when they crossed the railroad. Whenever they crossed a dirt intersection, they used the chain-link drag.

A couple of hours later they intersected Iranian Road 32, the old route from Istanbul to Teheran. It was a paved two-lane road running across the high desert for miles, passing through a few small villages on the way to the Turkish border crossing recommended by Berke. Once again they used the chain drag to wipe out their back trail as they pulled onto the asphalt.

Every half-hour they passed dozens of semi-trucks and trailers running in small convoys. "The border is just beyond the Iranian town of Bazargan," Berke told him. "Trucks usually back up on the bleak Turkish side for four or five kilometers. Once they cross into Iran, they usually travel in groups in case of breakdown since they don't have an escort or guide. Going west the first real town in Turkey is Karaköse, just before the famous Tahir Pass on the old Silk Road; it's almost 135 kilometers inland from the border." Gus asked a few questions to pass the time.

"To bribe the customs inspectors I'll need some cash." Berke asked an hour later. "I have a few thousand Turkish Lira and about 15,000 Iranian Rial's, maybe three hundred dollars. I'll need to spread the money out among the men on duty in the early morning darkness. Do you have enough cash to give me a couple of hundred US dollars to bribe the inspectors?"

Berke continued driving while Gus pulled out his two wads of cash. He used the chance to get rid of his few hundred in Iranian currency. He had enough $5's, $10's and $20's to divide it evenly into five packets, half Iranian and half American.

"At our next stop, while everyone stretches I'll collect all the passports and yellow exit permits to take into the customs office for submittal and stamping while the rest of you wait for me to get back. We can't wait in line to cross the border since red haired Dedee will never make it through regular passport control; neither will the body in the back." Gus nodded agreement and then asked what they were going to do?

"Once I've paid, we'll drive through into Turkey as a convoy with no stopping. Make sure our girl covers her hair with a shawl. When we pass the first Turkish town it'll still be early, but I believe four of my men will get off there and go home. The rest live further into Anatolia."

At about four in the morning, the two men in the Datsun pickup arrived just outside Bazargan at a Turkish owned trucking compound with a solid wall around the entire enclosure. After a momentary discussion with the guard, he admitted the entire convoy.

Berke and his two men collected all the passports and immigration papers and then got into the Japanese pickup. Berke scooted his man into the middle and they left in a cloud of dust. By the time they got back, it was after five. Sunrise would be at 6:20 am according to Gus' almanac.

When they returned Berke walked down the line of vehicles passing out stamped documents to each person while one of his men got on the bus to pass out the Turkish papers.

When he got to the MJ pickup he said, "Lieutenant Colonel Ali Hassan has already called the border post and is offering a large reward for our capture. He used your name specifically as one of the wanted men. He also had the names and pictures of all four consular employees and the other three MJ Americans. He's aware we killed another four of his Revolutionary Guards just outside Jolfa, in addition to the dozen more at Khoda Bridge."

It was nearing 6:00 am when they left the covert compound, driving straight for the border control post. Gus was snapping pictures with his camera. The convoy didn't pause as the bribed guard waved all six vehicles through.

As they crossed the border into Turkey, everyone seemed to exhale and breathe in the clean air. Taking dozens of pictures of the trucks waiting to cross into Iran, Gus noticed almost half of them were carrying military equipment.

After finishing the high-speed roll, he changed to a slower film for daytime pictures. After a few miles, they drove forward and honked for the convoy to stop so they could take pictures of everyone with the mountain in the background. They were in the first high valley of Anatolia, eastern Turkey. To the north, Gus could see the rising sun strike the 17,000-foot high snow-covered peak of Mount Ararat. It looked like the first storm of the season had deposited snow in the high mountains. They needed to stop and rest, change drivers and make pots of hot coffee and tea before pushing off for the next town, which was still hours away. They used the rest stop to test fire the weapons and check his sights after installing the telescope on the Dragunov. Gus was starting to settle down, no more shakes as long as he braced himself.

"Did the American Special Forces train you as a sniper?" Berke asked during a pause. Gus didn't respond as he continued to reveal too much. "You must be aware that you can't hit much with an RPG beyond about four hundred meters. You know the range of the Russian Dragunov sniper rifle is almost a thousand meters. Didn't you capture one of the first examples in Vietnam?"

"You know I'm a major in the Army Reserve," Gus snapped almost as if he was counter-attacking. "I've never mentioned I was a sniper. How do you know for sure? Are you an officer in Turkish Military Intelligence?" Berke didn't say anything.

They arrived in downtown Agri around noon and the convoy divided with Berke taking the Americans to the newest and only clean hotel in town while the rest found space at a truck stop dormitory on the bypass route. They had been on the road for eighteen hours.

Each room in the hotel had a private toilet, tub and shower and half overlooked the lake running through the middle of town. It was the middle of the night in Boise, so Gus waited to call his grandmother and uncle after they had breakfast. In the meantime, he went out for a jog around the city. Returning he took a hot bath and looked in the mirror at his stubble. Usually he got a haircut once a month and shaved almost daily. It had been seven weeks and his Walrus mustache and sideburns were getting long. He decided to leave his German travel razor and the French badger-hair brush in the Dopp kit and start growing a beard.

Later after his calls to America and the evening supper down-stairs in the café, he washed his dirty clothes in the sink, everything except the field jacket. After wringing his things out, he arranged them over the steam radiator.

That night was the first in months he slept all the way through to sunrise. He didn't jerk out of a deep sleep in alarm, real or imagined.

The next morning, he changed into the wool surplus trousers, an olive safari shirt, his commando sweater, black ball cap and the brownish-khaki trench coat with its thick cashmere lining and similar lined gloves and neck scarf in the deep map pockets. It was weather-proof, a copy of their double-breasted model including the original d-ring accessories, belt, and epaulets. It was made with finely woven sea-island cotton called Ventile cloth that swelled when damp to eliminate the passage of rain or snow, although vapor could still pass through the garment.

It would be cold in the mountains however several travelers had mentioned that the pass should be open. For the past two days, the first storm of the winter had kept it closed while road crews plowed the snow. After breakfast, everyone was going to assemble at the truck stop on the main highway west.

The black diplomatic Suburban had trouble starting and then it constantly stalled. Vince stopped the mustard MJ Wagoneer, changed cars and drove the newer consular four-wheeler. By the time they got to the truck stop, he had identified that the load of gas from the bottom of the spare drum last night must be contaminated with paraffin wax.

They needed a new fuel filter. "We're carrying several spare filters in the box of parts," said Vince. "But, I'll need some time to put it on the lift, drain the tank and replace the filter." Ed told John, his male consular employee to ride in the MJ vehicle and he would catch up before the next stop in Erzurum.

While Gus and Berke waited for the work to be finished, his assistant said, "I dropped Agent Cobb's body off at the hospital and checked in with my headquarters. Then I took a few of the Turkish workers to the local Army depot where I had them issue some Turkish made G-3 battle rifles and loaded magazines.

Every vehicle now has a fully automatic AK47 and a few sighted-in semi-automatic 7.62 NATO rifles.

I also picked up some American army radios, batteries and accessories for each vehicle," Berke told Gus. "I made sure everyone is on the same frequency for communications."

Gus checked with Vince to see if there were any problems. "Go ahead and catch up with the others. We'll be another 15 minutes and then I have to fill the 40-gallon tank with fresh ethyl gasoline. These big-block 400 cubic-inch engines and automatic transmissions use a lot more fuel than our smaller manual straight-sixes. She only gets about 10 miles per gallon, less in the mountains."

As Berke pulled out on the old Silk Road, he called the lead Datsun on the radio and checked that everything was OK. "We'll be going up the old Tahir pass in a few minutes," Gus mentally translated the Turkic response. "However, the bus will slow us down because of the steep grade and continuous switchbacks."

"The top of the pass is above 9,000 feet," Berke said to Gus. "In winter the graveled road can be in terrible shape, covered with snow and numerous potholes. The approach road on this side is steep and has more than three-dozen 180-degree switchback curves. They rebuilt the roadway a few years ago to allow trucks to use it in winter, as long as the drivers don't slide off one of the sharp turns. This is now the main all-weather road into Iran; the one further south takes an extra day since it has to go around Lake Van in Turkey and then Lake Urmia in Iran."

Just 45-minutes later, they were only a couple of miles behind the convoy when a broken call came over the radio. Berke tried to raise somebody, but only heard static.

Suddenly they could hear the steady pounding of shots from semi-automatic battle rifles and regular AK47's interspersed with the unique rap of a new small caliber automatic firing numerous bursts of four or five rounds.

"It sounds like the new Russian copy of the American M-16." Berke said.

Slightly further away was the sound of a Soviet medium machine gun firing six round bursts, different and much deeper than either the old or the new AK's.

Abruptly there was the sound of an explosion, either an RPG or a hand grenade. "Don't drive into the ambush," ordered Gus. "Look for a side trail up one of the parallel ridges overlooking the pass."

Simultaneously they spotted a graveled road on the left rising a hundred feet above the new road. Berke said, "When they rebuilt the new serpentine switchbacks, they abandoned part of the old route."

Gus and Berke leapt out of their pickup and jogged up to the overlook, carrying all their weapons. They spread out and got on their bellies, crawling forward to look at the scene below.

White snow covered the pass although dark rocks protruded in many places. Low-crawling up behind several rocks overlooking the pass, the battle landscape spread out in a perfect scene with the warriors sprinkled across the backdrop like little insects.

Gus and Berke settled into two firing positions about thirty feet apart and he started studying the far slope with his Zeiss binoculars. Pausing long enough, Gus inserted his earplugs.

6

Finished with his binocular sweep Gus aimed the long-range Dragunov telescope at the enemy, glassing them for a counter-sniper armed with a similar weapon.

All of the enemy soldiers were wearing mottled white snow smocks, but he could occasionally see a brownish pattern peeking out from the reverse side of their uniform. The ambushers were definitely wearing Russian Special Forces uniforms.

He finally spotted his sniper opponent slightly higher and behind the forward positions. Mindful he was firing downhill, Gus carefully adjusted the optical sight, locked his weapon to his shoulder, cheek and forearm and intertwined it with the leather sling. He then fired his first round, squeezing the trigger.

As the scope recovered from the recoil, he saw he had hit the sniper in his shoulder. Close but no medal, it was a good thing he had checked the sights yesterday along the desert road or he might not have hit anything.

Berke simultaneously fired his first rocket-propelled grenade into the vicinity of a much closer forward fighting position.

Lying next to the Russian sniper was his spotter, now trying to untangle the Dragunov from the wounded shooter. Gus aimed and shot him in the throat, with the bullet ranging down the length of his prone body. He put a second round into each man for assurance.

For Berke the range was about 600 meters to the leading positions and with the wind, it was difficult to hit within a dozen feet of his targets. After reloading the launcher tube, his second rocket hit nearer the closest position blowing up near one of the occupants who had just stood to move.

Gus looked around and realized the medium machine gun had redirected its aim and changed targets firing a six-round burst at them on the hillside. The loader was pointing at the ridge where Berke had exposed himself by kneeling while he frantically rushed to reload his third rocket-propelled grenade.

The gunner had missed by a dozen feet, but he was squirming around readjusting his aim so Gus shot the machine gunner, followed by a second shot into his still moving body.

His loader rolled the man onto his back as Gus shot the assistant twice and then fired a third round into the principal machine gunner and changed magazines.

He saw a Russian rise up with an RPG and fire it at maximum range toward the pass. Gus shot him twice before the explosion erupted fifty-feet short of their position.

In the meantime, Berke finished reloading his third and fourth rockets firing both at the second closest pair of Russians firing AK-74's at the bus.

Both longer-range weapons were out of action. Left were the much lighter automatic weapons firing their smaller and lighter bullets. In fact the Russian .22-caliber round wasn't any better at long range than an American M-16. Gus had read it was not as good as the old AK-47 bullet, which was almost the same as the old lever action Winchester 30-30. Each soldier could just carry more bullets.

After ten rounds, Gus changed magazines for a fresh ten. He continued to kill or wound their ambushers, one shot at a time. His barrel was getting hot, so he paused, packed snow on the barrel-receiver and carefully glassed every single position, shooting a round or two at suspicious movement before changing magazines again.

Berke had fired the last of his rocket grenades and switched to the Turkish Army G-3 rifle firing NATO rounds.

No enemy soldiers on the hillside were still moving, but there were people crawling near the bus and the mustard colored Wagoneer. There was no movement from the white Datsun or the fuel truck.

Wriggling backward Gus finally stood and called out to Berke, "Let's go and check out what's happening."

When they pulled up behind the bus, Berke got out and started checking the wounded while Gus went to check out the Wagoneer.

Dennis and the consular employee were dead, one sitting in the front passenger seat and the other in the rear seat of the MJ Iranian Ahoo.

Bill Williams, who had been driving was wounded in the arm. "I was on the side of the switchback away from the ambush," said Bill. "I think the bullet that hit me passed through Dennis first. We were only going about five-miles per hour so I rolled out and hid behind this rock."

Gus rooted through his field bag and pulled out a surplus battle dressing. Removing the plastic wrapping, he stretched out the OD bandage and wrapped it around Bill's arm as he observed, "The bone isn't broken."

Gus started up the slope to check out the enemy. He recognized a number of the troops as Russians from the team across the Khoda Bridge on the Alma River. He would have to take photos of the dead men to compare with his files.

He was sure he had telephoto pictures of all twelve men across the river although only two regularly came across the 2nd Khoda Bridge with Dmitry. A third man used to bring him vodka. There was a trail of footprints coming up from a saddle in the hillside more than a kilometer away. Looking around Gus saw several drops of blood leading away from the battle.

Raising his binoculars, he searched through the rocks and snowdrifts until he saw movement. He fired and hit his target as the Russian moved from behind a boulder. There were seven bodies scattered among five improvised fighting positions and he could see the sharpened entrenching tools they had hastily used to improve their hides. Their snow smocks had an inner lining with a camouflage pattern of brown, OD and dark gray; it almost matched the Vietnam Tiger Stripe pattern.

As he left to check out the eighth body, two of the unwounded passengers came up to recover any usable weapons. "Pick-up all the weapons and equipment and take it down to the road." Gus told Achmed, the senior worker who had driven the bus.

The dead eighth man was the youngest Russian officer. He had been one of the first who arrived at the Khoda Bridge to backup Dmitry Antonov, their Russian engineer. Gus thought as he cautiously moved down to check a suspicious looking clump of bushes the eighth man was trying to reach. Where are the other three missing Spetsnaz?

As he moved into the sloping field, he discovered a cache of eight oxygen mask and rectangular splotchy blue and grey parachutes with harnesses.

They looked like HAHO, high altitude-high opening paragliding models. Gus was surprised since the US Army was just starting to use similar equipment.

They must have glided into the pass last night. He waved for the Turkish worker to collect the hidden equipment.

On his way back to the road he thought, the only way these Russians could get enough information to jump blind was from the call Berke made to MIT headquarters yesterday afternoon. Or, someone could have betrayed him to the Russians. Since he trusted Berke, it must have been one of his Turkish bosses. There's no way regular intercepted telephone communications could have made it to the Spetsnaz in time.

Both men in the lead Datsun were dead. The driver of the fuel truck was dead along with five of the bus passengers while seven were wounded.

Only nine passengers of the twenty-six driving into the pass were free from wounds. Berke had already changed frequencies and contacted the military back in Agri.

"Doctors and ambulances are on their way." He told Gus when he got back. "I used the extra medical supplies in the pickup to stabilize most of the wounded, however I need Ringer's Lactate IV bags. Everybody needs to go back to Agri to be checked out and to answer questions. As far as I can tell, the consulate Suburban and your pickup are the only vehicles still running." Gus mentioned that he needed to continue on to Ankara.

"At least, I'll need your pickup to carry the seriously wounded back to town. If you want to proceed, you'll have to go in the official Suburban with Vince, Ed and his female employee."

When the black official Chevrolet arrived three military ambulance-trucks followed it. Gus took Ed aside and explained what had happened. "We need to continue on in your vehicle while the wounded go back to Agri," Gus told Ed. "I'm sure that once in Ankara, we can send a charter plane back to get the workers while Vince and Dedee fly on to the states."

Gus didn't say anything to Ed but the MJ money was burning a hole in his pocket. He needed to get it off his hands. He thought mentally, I'm half-a-step behind everything happening. I didn't suspect the Russians or expect them to ambush us. Colonel Ali almost caught us at the border. He was half a day ahead of where I thought he would be. The next time I won't be so lucky.

"I contacted my man at Langley last night and they told me to go anywhere you go and give you anything you need." Ed told him. "We can take the Suburban. The embassy in Ankara is expecting us."

Gus was suddenly thinking; surprise, surprise, two different government agencies knew about my travel plans for today. Someone at either one of them could have told the Russians where we were going, not just Berke's MIT.

He agreed saying, "You should report the ambush and death of your consular officer, just don't announce our future plans or route."

Gus then started transferring everything into the black Suburban. Opening the glove box he spotted a Browning Hi-Power with two extra 13-round magazines. He thought, I guess Ed Warren will want to ride shotgun. If we take this wagon with diplomatic plates no one will be inspecting our belongings or checking us for weapons. We'll be able to drive across Turkey and Greece, take the ferry to Italy and drive north to Switzerland without anyone checking. I know MJ has a bank in Switzerland. I'll call Uncle Dick and set up a deposit for the gold and the cash.

He cleaned and reloaded the weapons and magazines while Vince topped up the fuel tank in the pickup. The drum of hi-test for the Suburban was empty, struck by a bullet. He put the new weapons from the eight Spetsnaz into two piles.

Every one of the eight men had a primary military assault weapon, a smaller backup, and a winged A combat knife. The larger stack had the sniper rifle, the medium machinegun and the RPG along with five AK-74's.

Their backup weapons included a mix of pistols with a few Makarov silenced pistols. One of the men had a new replacement suppressor in his rucksack while two of them carried wire stocked Czech Skorpion mini-machine pistols.

Gus exchanged his used Makarov suppressor and kept the fast New York holster on the right side of his belt. He buckled the new tan Skorpion shoulder holster under his trench coat and then dropped the Czech machine pistol into the pouch loaded with a 10-round magazine, snapping the retainer.

He then snapped two magazine scabbards to his left belt. While nobody was looking, he put several of the guns and magazines into the duffle.

Pulling Berke to the side he said, "Both you and Ed Warren reported our movements to someone higher in your organizations. I trust you, but that doesn't mean I trust your MIT." Continuing in a low voice he said. "I have my own issues with Ed Warren, although he's going on to Germany with me. Either the Russians were listening in on phone conversations to your agency or Warren's call to the CIA alerted them."

"In any case someone is betraying us to the Russians." He went on to explain about the impossibility of blind HAHO jumping into the pass. "I've heard MIT listens in on every pay phone call in Turkey, particularly those along the major truck routes. If I radio you the location and time, could you get a recording of what was said, and maybe what phone number was called."

Berke replied, "I'll call a friend. He can get the recordings to me after I get to Ankara. However there will probably be a delay of a day or two for any new calls."

Gus looked over and said, "Let's set up a series of short-wave frequencies and procedures for sending a burst of Morse keyed transmissions in code."

"I have a few dozen double-pages of a US Army Whiz-Wheel neon yellow code pages and several plastic grilles," Berke replied. "We can use those."

7

Gus Smith was driving the shiny black Chevrolet Suburban as they left the Tahir Pass and made it through the intervening mountains of eastern Turkey. Ed Warren was riding beside Gus in the passenger seat while Vince Boxleitner and Dedee Anderson rode in the rear. As they crossed the final hills and drove down the high valley into the town of Erzurum it was their first chance to stop and top-up with gasoline. Gus was still upset by the ambush in the mountain pass. He knew there was a Turkish Air Force base to the north of town called the *Rock* by NATO so there should be international fuel stations.

Ed's official State Department vehicle was a heavy monster with armor plate around the body and laminated ballistic windows. It got terrible mileage although it had a 40-gallon tank. Since Ed was uncomfortable on the twisty dilapidated road across the mountains, he had asked Gus or Vince to take turns driving.

Rather than take the new bypass, they drove into town where they found an Esso service station. The tank required high-test gas. While Gus filled the armored car, Ed went to a phone booth on the corner and made several calls. Vince and Dedee walked down the street to try and buy some Cokes and dried snacks. Funny how even in the worst of times people still think about things like Coke, Gus thought as he cleaned the windows, then checked the oil and coolant. By the time everyone got back he had added 33 gallons of premium gasoline.

"I called the operations center in Washington." Ed said. "Even though it's 6:00 am there, my earlier report about the seizure of the embassy and consulate has stirred up a hornet's nest. Everyone reported in early for duty. The Deputy Director of the entire CIA immediately put me on the speaker and started to ask some serious questions." Gus now knew for sure that Ed was a CIA officer; he hadn't called State Department Operations. He was probably in the Directorate of Intelligence rather than Gus' old Directorate of Operations. Over the last two days he'd handled himself fine, garnering a measure of respect from Gus who had years more field experience.

"For the first time, I told him about your actions during the Revolutionary Guard attacks on your compound. Then I described our escape from Tabriz, and the shootout at the caravanserai. I could tell by the DD's tone that everyone there was extremely upset with what was happening in Iran." Gus asked him to explain realizing that Ed's tone was growing angry and doubtful as he recounted the reaction from Langley. He was more interested in Ed's responses than he was in the CIA's.

"I reported there were two dead Russian KGB officers, an Iranian Army captain, his orderly, sixteen dead Islamist revolutionaries and a Diplomatic Security agent." Ed told him, ignoring Vince and Dedee. "The news hit them like a bomb, Gus. Especially when I mentioned that their civilian engineer was responsible. You could hear the sudden chatter of listeners in the background. When I continued with information about the unusual Russian response from Spetsgruppa Alpha of the KGB, they didn't believe me." Ed stopped.

Gus said nothing, learning early in his career that silence is often the best offense.

"The DD interrupted me to say, 'Group Alpha is a myth.' He suddenly became alarmed when I told him the Russian attack in Turkey had killed a US Consular officer, an American contractor, and thirteen Turkish workers, two of them probably agents for MIT. Then I said, 'We recovered proof of the mythical Spetsgruppa Alfa including the bodies of eight dead Russians wearing unique camouflage and carrying engraved knives.' The Deputy Director was flabbergasted. He couldn't say a word." Ed was telling his story while he gestured with both hands, reminding Gus of his nanny. Rachel was an Iranian Jew expelled by the Muslims and later sponsored by his family. Gus's father, mother and grandfather were away at war while his grandmother took a job teaching foreign languages so she became his surrogate mother.

"How do you know?" Gus asked.

"How do I know what?"

"That he was flabbergasted."

"What?" Ed said, slapping his hand against the Suburban.

"If he didn't say a word, how do you know he was flabbergasted?"

Gus' question was a direct attempt to make Ed concentrate. He ignored it and continued with his story.

"After a minute, the Chief of Operations came on and told us to stop at the embassy in Ankara. I told him about Vince and Dedee and he said they'd take care of them at the embassy. He wanted to put you on the payroll as a technical consultant where they could issue you a new black diplomatic passport. I told him you weren't interested in working for the CIA. He ordered me to go on to Germany with you."

"You're right about me not working for the Company." Gus replied and then thought to himself. How did you know? Bill Williams is the only person who knows I plan on going to Germany. Who's talking about my plans?

"He gave me a couple of phone numbers," Ed continued. "For support if we need it." Gus wondered if Ed was telling him the whole truth and nothing but the truth. Could his uncle in Idaho have spilled his plans to someone in Langley at CIA headquarters?

They piled into what everyone was calling the tank. It was cool outside but since the windows including the rear couldn't be opened it became humid inside as they drove over 500 miles to the embassy in Ankara. It was too cool for the front and rear AC units and too warm inside for the heater. They stopped for tea, sandwiches and to fill up with premium every few hundred miles and change turns at the wheel. As the roads got better the passengers tried to sleep even though their average speed was creeping up to seventy.

It was just past 8 o'clock at night when they got to the Chancery Building at the front of the US Embassy compound. Ed turned off Ataturk Boulevard and then into the main entrance stopping at CAC-1, the guardhouse manned by uniformed local security guards. An older Regional Security Officer was waiting for them at the main Compound Access Control. He passed the official vehicle.

They parked in the main lot and walked to the entrance at the inside corner of two wings. In the lobby, the RSO led them up to Marine Post One, although it didn't look very well protected. Surprisingly, there was no bulletproof glass although it looked like the reception booth was made from cement blocks parged with plaster. Gus thought, the cells must be reinforced and filled with concrete. It would be criminal not to protect this vital area.

The corporal was wearing Delta camouflage pattern fatigues and had an M-14 and a shotgun in a floor-rack just beside the counter. He asked them to hand him their papers and put any weapons in the basket.

Vince and Dedee handed over their passports after saying, "No guns," in unison. Ed had a small Walther PPK pistol in a shoulder holster, just like the one James Bond wore in the movies. He must have left the Browning in the car along with the rifles.

The Marine was staring at Gus when he first took off the plain black ball cap followed by the long khaki trench coat. He realized that to the Marine he must look tired with his bloodshot eyes and razor stubble. He then removed the shoulder harness, various Soviet weapons, and the Randall Number 2 knife from under the commando sweater. Lifting his left foot, he unbuckled the ankle holster as he exposed his worn Wolverine lace-ups

The starched guard was too young to have served in Vietnam but he knew he was looking at a Soviet submachine gun and a silenced pistol carried by only a few covert agents. Motioning to the Marine Gus said, "There's a folding knife and extra magazines in the trench coat pockets. I don't think everything will fit into your basket."

"I called my sergeant at Marine House. He'll be here any minute with another Marine to stand guard in the lobby. He's going to escort you anywhere you need to go in the building."

The sergeant and another Marine arrived both wearing starched cammies. You could see that the sergeant respected the RSO by the deference he exhibited. When he saw the weapons on the coffee table, the gunny sergeant raised his eyebrows. Looking first at Gus and then the other three, he said to the guard, "Don't enter this visit in the official logbook. Give me their passports."

Of course, Ed Warren had diplomatic papers with several entry and exit stamps for Iran and several stamps for Europe. Vince and

Dedee had similar documents. The senior sergeant then inspected Gus' well-worn standard green covered document. "James Augustus Smith," the Marine said, holding up the passport and glancing from Gus to the picture and then back again before continuing.

"My friends call me Gus," he responded with a scratch in his voice. He could really use a nice cold beer about now. Pensively he realized that he could never use this crutch again.

Pausing about halfway through, the gunny turned back and started counting. The passport office in Washington had stitched-in pages A through X between pages 12 and 13, and then several years later they repeated it again. Originally, the book ended at page 24, but Washington had added 48 more pages in the middle of the original. Of course, each page had room for more than four entries and exits.

The sergeant thumbed through the pages and realized Gus had visited Vietnam, numerous Asian countries and every country in Europe and the Mideast except maybe Greenland and Andorra. He had half-page visas to many of the countries controlled by the Soviet Union along with stamped entries and exits from several of their internal republics.

"My passport expires next June," Gus told the sergeant.

After telling the extra Marine to escort Vince and Dedee to the guest quarters, the sergeant turned and asked Gus. "What size shirt and coat do you wear?" He dialed four digits and then called in the sizes that Gus gave him.

They entered the chancery and took the elevator to the top floor. From there they walked up a set of concrete and steel stairs to a vault-like doorthe entrance into a separate suite of windowless rooms.

While the sergeant waited outside the vault door, the security officer escorted Ed and Gus in to meet two men. "I'm the head of the station here," the older man said. "My consular associate will take your picture and issue you a new diplomatic passport. The Regional Security Officer will be sitting in on the questioning; I believe you already met John Campbell." The RSO asked Ed to start with describing what happened at the consulate in Tabriz.

Gus and the consular officer stepped into the next room; where he took his sweater, safari shirt and olive tee shirt off and changed into white shirt, striped tie and a dark blazer. The second man then took several pictures. Gus disrobed within seconds of the last flash and the consular officer left to process the new documents taking the temporary clothing with him. Gus hadn't even unbuckled his heavy leather belt until he went to put his dirty clothes back on. He waited in the empty room next-door as Ed finished his report. No sound penetrated from one room to the next, even though Gus listened at every crack and crevice. It took more than half-an-hour even though he thought that Ed shouldn't take long trying to explain he had nothing to do with the death of Derek Cobb and he had not been present at the ambush in Tahir Pass.

The door opened and Gus entered as the older man turned and said, "My name is Charles Metcalf and I run the Asia-Minor portion of the Near-East South-Asia Section for the CIA. I am also the station chief for Turkey, the largest Company operation on the southern perimeter of Russia." Gus nodded.

"As the Chief of the NESA Section, I am responsible for everything along the southern border of the Soviet Union along with the Arabian Peninsula. My counterpart in Morocco covers all of Northern Africa, and a different office handles Israel."

"The senior RSO here oversees Diplomatic Security for all US facilities in Turkey and handles administration for other stations along the southern rim of the Soviet Union. Derek Cobb worked for him and was his friend." Metcalf told Ed to wait for them downstairs and then waited for the vault door to close.

"Tell me everything that's happened," he asked Gus as soon as Ed left. "Start when you first arrived in Iran."

Gus began by stating it was the second time he had lived in Iran. His first was to rebuild the executive floor of the Sheraton in Teheran in 1972. He then casually mentioned he had been a covert SOG officer for the Deputy Director of Operations during those years. "My cover was an engineer for MJ International who had the construction contract." Gus seemed to put a formal emphasis on this statement, almost like he was testifying in court.

"We'll get into that next," said the station chief. "First start by telling me what you did on the day after Halloween of 1977." Gus stared thoughtfully at the CIA official.

"I then want to know what you did afterwards; when you finished up in Czechoslovakia and then took a couple of weeks to move to Iran. I already know you turned in your official equipment. I want to know every step you made from Prague." Gus had a puzzled look on his face and started to answer when Metcalf continued.

"What did you do with the Soviet firearms and covert stuff you had collected across Europe? I mean the listening devices, two-way radios, telephone taps, miniature cameras, and false identities. By the way, I first served with the OSS in China before transferring to the Directorate of Intelligence after the war. The RSO was a special agent for the FBI before he joined Diplomatic Security."

"A half-dozen of us were fired by a cable that arrived overnight and we were immediately cut off from any more contact with Company employees." Gus started to explain. "The new politically connected station chief made no effort to process any authorized expenses, outstanding vacation time or severance, but the old General Services Officer needed to finish my project. He knew it would take us a few more months of construction at the embassy." Gus explained how a single plane arrived later in the week to pick up the other five men and their household belongings. Metcalf was starting to make numerous notes in a wire bound steno book.

"The construction director for Foreign Building Operations sent a letter to the National Industrial Security Program requesting that they maintain my Top Secret clearance being held by MJ International." Gus explained and hinted that there was some political pressure from MJ corporate. "When I left Prague I kept working for MJ and they transferred me to the Iranian dam project. You do know I'm also an officer in the Army Reserve with the same clearance and I meet for monthly and summer training with a unit in Germany. The result was I kept both of my Top-Secret clearances, Army and Industrial."

"We know," said Metcalf. "Our polygraph expert is going to be in tomorrow morning. He's going to flutter you based on your answers tonight. You know that you need to regularly pass a polygraph using control questions as a requirement for keeping your SCI clearances."

For the next three hours, Gus answered question after question about his entire life history. He mentioned that for the past year, "MJ has been issued small purchase orders to perform classified work at the embassy in Tehran. It takes forever to get a Seabee in from Germany and the embassy staff is way down from a thousand to less than a hundred."

"Since I'm the only civilian construction engineer with a top-secret clearance, I do anything they need when I'm there. I was already making the trip into Teheran once a month to fly to Germany for reserve duty." Gus explained how the Military Airlift Command had a worldwide route structure to and from the Far East. The northern route stops in Tehran and then Germany every day. He was able to hitch a ride to and from reserve duty.

"Starting last year they've had me and my construction superintendent coming in several days early to fix small items." Gus paused and answered several questions. "After the GSO transferred out, I've been working throughout the facility. Although the embassy compound is almost four-dozen acres, the local maintenance men can't work within the classified areas or the vault on the top floor of the block-long Chancery Building. In fact since they weren't Cleared Americans they couldn't work in most of the sensitive areas. Bill Williams has a Secret clearance and mine is Top Secret-SCI so the two of us can work almost anywhere." Gus paused and asked for a glass of water. When Metcalf asked if he wanted a beer. "I don't drink anything but water when I'm answering questions."

"We've fixed broken toilets, electrical systems, welded and remounted equipment," Gus said after he took a long drink. "I've even painted a Top Secret conference room. Bill and I can build or machine anything and the Chargé gave us free reign in the almost-empty facility. The barrel shaped disintegrator in the vault was a special case, it broke down almost every month and they had to wait for me to get there and fix it."

Metcalf asked, "How does Tehran handle payments?"

"MJ has been charging them costs and a standard markup for every hour we worked." Gus continued to explain. "For my first trip back to the capital I took the train from Tabriz to Tehran, but never again. It was jam packed with pilgrims headed south to Qom and took 12-hours. Because of traffic I learned at least half-a-dozen detours around potential blockages leading into the eastern side of the city. With the extra income over the past half-year we've had a small plane pick us up for flights between Khoda Bridge and Tehran."

When he got to the details of what happened at the dam project Gus was rather surprised when Metcalf didn't have a lot of questions.

He accepted the sequence of events, the escape and the later shootout where Derek Cobb was killed. Gus thought to himself, where did he get these details? Nobody told Ed Warren anything about Khoda Bridge, yet he mentioned telling Langley about the shootout. Was the CIA listening when my friend Berke reported this information to MIT Turkish intelligence? When he didn't have any questions about the Russian ambush in Tahir Pass, Gus looked at him and asked, "I'm curious that you're accepting everything I say without any questions."

"Do you remember any of the names used by the Russians?" Metcalf asked, ignoring his question.

Gus looked at him in surprise before he answered, "I've written the names for four of the dead men that I remember on the list that goes with the film I took. The leader of the unit always stayed across the river but I heard them call him major several times, probably his rank. I also heard them refer to a Boris, Georgi, Vlad and a Peter." Gus though, something's up. Metcalf knows way too much.

"I know about your actions as a CIA sniper during the NVA Easter offensive in 1972 where you held up the entire 33rd NVA regiment from joining the siege on An Loc." Metcalf continued. "It's apparently a repeat of what you did for the Special Forces in 1967 just before the January Tet Offensive. I was told you shot more than several dozen officers, sergeants and many more soldiers before running out of match ammunition." Charles Metcalf commented. "The CIA gave you an award for valor, didn't they?"

Gus remained calm saying; "I had to leave Vietnam because of the reward the NVA put on my head. After the Company fired me, they sent the award to my grandmother." Changing the subject he said, "The Russians must be monitoring phone calls in Turkey. They either have a double agent in Turkish intelligence or one of your CIA officers is a turncoat. Their Spetsnaz were waiting for us in the pass and only the two agencies knew we were coming."

Metcalf picked up the phone, depressed the conference switch and called downstairs to Ed Warren. He asked him to relate whom he had called in Washington and what they said before the Russian ambush. Ed must have replied that he didn't say anything unusual. "He only let his supervisor know what had happened," Metcalf said. As he hung up his final comment about the Russians listening to their conversations was, "I'll check on it."

Changing subjects Metcalf stated, "My man is going to wash and then exchange the Arabic numbered Iranian plates on your Suburban for a set of United Nations diplomatic plates good anywhere in Europe. I want you to sleep for a few hours, and then shower and change before we test you and then you get out of here. I'll make sure breakfast is ready when you wake up."

"I've gone ahead and made official reservations on the winter ferry between Greece and Italy. I agree the only way you can carry weapons into Europe is through the diplomatic bag, free from customs and border control. It's too bad every gun you're carrying is a Soviet version."

"When I was behind the *Iron Curtain* I carried Russian weapons," Gus responded. "But I was lucky, I didn't have to shoot anybody until the last week. I also have Cobb's 9mm hush puppy however it's way too loud."

"Derek complained his suppressor needed new rubber wipers," RSO Campbell finally entered the conversation. "He said the old ones were worn out, and he was out of subsonic ammunition. Why don't you leave his pistol here with me?"

"My first tour with the Army in Vietnam I carried a sniper rifle, a shotgun and an old OSS .22 pistol." Gus started to explain as Metcalf interrupted, "Was it the one with the built-in silencer?" Gus said yes as he continued. "Later, back in Vietnam with the CIA I carried a Browning Lightweight Hi-Power in 9-mm with two extra magazines and my backup Colt Cobra. Always nearby, I also had a Winchester riot shotgun that I carried broken down and a sniper rifle. In Europe I carried a custom lightweight .45 pistol and a backup 9mm made by a gunsmith in New York City. He also made me a silenced Ruger .22 similar to the old OSS pistol and a new sound suppressor for my Colt."

"I'll bet you got a 9mm ASP from Paris Theodore at Seventrees Ltd. in the garment district," Metcalf said as he nodded to Campbell. "The gunsmith was a former CIA operative who also built holsters, silencers and other pistols for SOG covert agents. Who made your .45?"

"After I came back from Vietnam the second time," Gus said. "I asked a Connecticut gunsmith named Larry Seecamp to build me a lightweight Colt Commander with his new double-action trigger mechanism. He also adjusted and tested five 7-round magazines." Metcalf and Campbell both nodded as Gus paused.

Since Metcalf was finished, he sent the RSO down and had a private talk with Gus. "I'm aware you're carrying financial material for MJ. I called Richard Knowles in Boise and he gave his full approval." Gus thought, how does he know about uncle Dick and our problem with getting bribe money secretly into Switzerland?

"There will be an external seal for your bag so nobody will open it," Metcalf continued. "I'm also giving you a standard diplomatic pouch with a few extras lead seals inside. He had nothing but high praise for you and I found out a lot more about your background." Gus was thinking that many of the senior officers in the CIA were accomplished liars.

"I'm going to use you as my stalking horse to root out any possibility of a double agent within the service," Metcalf continued. "I understand that you don't want to work for the CIA so John Campbell is appointing you a Special Agent for Diplomatic Security and issuing you with an ID and badge. He's waiting downstairs to swear you in." Gus was surprised. The federal government was actually going to help.

"We don't know whom we can trust at Langley, but I have full confidence in Office of Security at the State Department, John Campbell's department. It's even more dedicated to releasing the hostages in Tehran and discovering if anyone is leaking American secrets to the KGB. You can call or radio back here but don't call anyone at CIA Headquarters until I set up a special channel." Metcalf quickly said. "When you get to the states don't tell anybody what you know about the internal workings of the embassy in Tehran."

"What about all my friends with the Special Forces?" Gus asked. "I've been training with them for the past eleven years. They all know about my knowledge of the embassy in Tehran and they'll be asking questions."

"Pick out a few snapshots of the embassy and give the package to them," answered Metcalf. "Don't give them any specific information until we find out who has a need to know."

"Can I send you a burst of Morse over the single-sideband?" Gus didn't tell him what he and Berke were doing with Turkish pay phones to get information about Ed Warren, but he went ahead and told him a little of what he was thinking. "I don't trust Warren and think he has been collecting information on the side." As Gus said this, he looked over at Metcalf and saw a strange look, almost like amazement or shock. The expression disappeared in a second.

"We'll see. If he's talking to anybody outside channels, he may not know whom he's working for. He may think he's making regular reports to his supervisor."

Downstairs in the Security Office, Campbell swore him in. Afterward the RSO said, "Here's a phone number in DC for Keith Allison, the Deputy Director of Diplomatic Security and Chief of Special Agents in the State Department."

I met him in Vietnam," Gus responded. "He was a Washington Warrior that the CIA brought in to get some field experience."

"Please call him as soon as you land in the US," Campbell said. "Keith will set up a debriefing for you with the appropriate authorities. In the meantime study Title 18 of the US criminal code." He handed him a three-ring binder."

Gus was escorted over to the hotel like guest room where he stripped and got under the top sheet. Although he had asked for a daylight wakeup call he tossed and turned having trouble getting to sleep. Among other things he was worried about the lie detector exam tomorrow.

8

G us jerked out of a deep sleep in a pitch-black room. He was thirsty and had the start of a headache. Starring at his watch, the 15-year old luminous dots were barely visible since green crud was starting to cover them. Realizing that it was still night and the feeble light outside was peeking around the blackout curtains; he made his way to the bathroom and turned on the light. It was a few minutes past one o'clock in the morning. Taking the last aspirin out of the Bayer tin, he took it with a glass of water. He realized that he had tossed and turned for the last hour mentally reviewing events from the past three days. He still didn't recall anything from his past that would cause the KGB to target him. He tried to remember as he went back to sleep.

Gus slept for five more hours before waking. He put on exercise clothes and went out for a jog around the diplomatic neighborhood. He then showered, and put on fresh clothes before eating breakfast with Ed. He didn't have a headache.

Gus' facial hair was beginning to match his luxurious mustache, although his head and sideburns were too long, like a movie star.

The Marine sergeant had cleaned and pressed his dirty clothes. He had also replaced the worn laces of his old-fashioned Wolverine miners' half boots. Now, instead of worn into a natural suede, they were spit-polished brown. It was too warm for his long khaki trench coat without removing the cashmere lining.

Gus went to the main reception area where the examiner was waiting. He led him to an interview room off an adjacent hallway. The room had a mirror on the back wall, probably two-way so Gus wondered who was watching. He spent an hour hooked up to the machine where he answered short questions. More than halfway into the questions they became different, things he didn't expect but had no problem answering. He knew that there would be one or two trick questions coming up.

When he became a NOC in Moscow his preparation included training in how to answer lie detector questions without showing signs of deception. When asked the first "out-of-the-blue" question, "Have you ever met with a Soviet agent and not reported it to your case officer?" Gus clinched his sphincter muscle, as he answered "No," without breaking the rhythm of his responses. A few minutes later the tester asked, "Have you ever had contact with a homosexual KGB officer?" and Gus once again followed his special training. The next unusual question was, "Have you ever been recruited by a Soviet agent?" Gus knew that these three questions related to his "off-the-books" work with *Mongolian*. He had not reported his contacts since he was doing it as a favor for his SAS friend working for British MI-6. The final question was, "While you were working for the CIA did you ever kill a Soviet KGB officer or asset." Thinking quickly Gus answered, "Yes." The examiner immediately stopped the machine and asked him some questions. Gus explained that he had killed a famous Russian sniper in Vietnam and several different European looking intelligence officers during various clandestine operations throughout Southeast Asia. "In fact I had to kill more than one Russian with my silenced pistol."

The tester gave him a clean bill of responses, no deception. However, Gus knew that someone had inserted these trick questions with a different motive. He needed to get to Germany so he could discuss this with his friend Andy.

The embassy was taking care of transportation for Vince and Dedee so Gus and Ed proceeded in the official Suburban. Four hours later, on the outskirts of Istanbul, Ed stopped at a roadside café for coffee. He excused himself to go to the restroom and then call his girlfriend.

Gus took his glass cup in a copper holder outside where he extended the nine-foot whip and used the sideband shortwave to call Berke. He reported the latest call and then listened while he learned Ed had made one call to northern Virginia from the hotel in Agri followed by a second to the District of Columbia.

"The next day he made three calls from the service station at Erzurum," Berke reported. "One was to a blocked number in the Virginia suburbs of Washington while another was to a company called Safeguard Consultants International in downtown Washington and the final call was to the US Embassy switchboard in Ankara. We don't have recordings of any of the calls, but I put the numbers on the watch list for future recordings." Gus thought, Ed told Metcalf he made only one call to the CIA Operations Desk, not three.

After driving across the Istanbul-Bosphorus Bridge from Asia to Europe, they continued for the next ten hours, stopping only to change drivers and get gas.

There were a few more hours before the winter ferry left for Italy. They filled up and had the Suburban washed, even though the gasoline was more expensive in Greece. In Italy, they would be busy as soon as they arrived.

They then went to a waterfront restaurant and had fresh seafood. Gus had a spicy Mediterranean fish stew with two huge prawns on top, eyeballs and all. It came with a salad, and hot Greek bread with olive oil. He ate the salad, skipped the bread and drank a bottle of the local still water from the island of Cephalonia.

The ferry left Greece for Italy a few hours before midnight. Gus and Ed were sharing a double bunk cabin while the car was locked on the car-deck.

For the past day Gus thought that Ed Warren was trying to recruit him to join with his group of intelligence officers. He didn't come right out and say they worked for the CIA, hinting at some other agency working for the federal government.

He had been keeping an eye on Ed since leaving Ankara except for the twenty-minute phone call he made at a filling station outside Istanbul. They had stopped in Greece to get gas, but the station didn't have a pay phone. At dinner, Gus kept an eye on him.

While Ed went down the hall to the marine toilet, Gus went up to the top deck of the RORO ferry, stretched out his short dipole antenna from a rail to a stanchion and contacted Berke who was now in Ankara.

"Whoever was talking on the phone at Safeguard Consultants gave him a new number in Geneva, Switzerland. He then called and a woman answered with the Safeguard name. She connected him with the boss who had new plans for them in Italy."

Berke reported and then continued by playing the tape made by MIT. "Bring this Gus Smith to meet with me for breakfast at the Café de France near the docks in Brindisi. Your "New" team has lost half of its people and you need to regroup. I understand that the special Soviet Alfa unit you've been monitoring has lost nine of its twelve men. Do you think that Gus Smith actually has some special information about their codes over the past decade."

After listening to the recording Gus said to Berke, "That may be the reason Ed is trying so hard to recruit me. Have you ever heard of a 'New or Gnu', spelling the two different words. What is it? Is it a Serengeti Wildebeest?"

"I think they're talking about a special unit working for the State Department dedicated to tracking transnational narcotics and crime." Berke told Gus. "It includes all the different agencies trying to track international crime, money laundering and drugs, it's called the Narcotics Intelligence Unit."

Back in the top bunk for the next half-hour, Gus stared at the painted ceiling as he tried to figure out what was happening. He finally decided to scout the café location before he went in, although he would send Ed straight in to grab a table. Rising early well before the ferry reached harbor, Gus went to the small workout room on the upper deck and did strength exercises for about thirty minutes in the early morning darkness. Once again, he was headache free although he was still drinking a lot of water. Their first stop after leaving the embassy in Ankara was at a chemist to get a couple of new tins of aspirin.

As he walked back to their small room, he could smell the sea. Wisps of fog were spreading out and covering the approaching harbor. A half hour later, Gus waited to drive the Suburban off the well deck of the ferry. He was using the headlights and windshield wipers to see through the fog. Unexpectedly, Ed mentioned his superior had the same name as he did. "So he's called Edward," responded Gus.

"No my name's not Edward, it is Edwin. You may recognize the name of the man we're meeting, since before he retired he was a major player for the last four administrations in the Treasury Department. He later moved to Switzerland as a consultant for the US Government."

He went on to explain his organization. "My older sister died from a drug overdose when I was still at Princeton majoring in International Relations and French," Ed told him. "I joined the Drug Enforcement Agency and went through Special Agent training in Georgia. Two years later I was selected to transfer to the CIA and go through their training. I work for the NIU-Narcotics Intelligence Unit, a joint international section. It includes agents from the CIA Directorate of Intelligence, DSS, NSA, the DEA and Treasury Department. Dedee Anderson works for the State Department Bureau of Intelligence. Derek Cobb was a special agent for Diplomatic Security and John was a radio expert with the National Security Agency. We're meeting my mentor who worked for the Treasury and the Bureau of Narcotics before the DEA. In Iran we were setting up a series of radio repeater transponders and connecting them to our INMARSAT satellite. At the same time we were tracking transmissions from the Mafia and certain government sponsored criminal organizations including drug smugglers." Gus was suddenly very interested. He listened in amazement.

"NSA intercepted a phone call on the morning of the 4th from Georgi to his brother and father in Moscow. He was temporarily in command of the KGB Spetsnaz team on the Alma River." Ed continued. "The brother is a Major Boris in command of the unit. Their father is a Lieutenant General in the KGB. We suspect that he's the same officer who first involved the KGB in drug trafficking from the Golden Triangle to American troops in Vietnam." Gus quickly asked several questions about KBG involvement in Laos and Burma

"Boris told his younger brother to send the team across the river and collect everything," Ed continued. "He then asked about you, Gus, confirming that Dmitry Antonov had first reported your presence in Iran, but his brother was the one who identified you as the only survivor of an ambush outside Salzburg. He then mentioned that the coded documents must have burnt up during the ambush." Gus was listening intently trying to remember anything.

"Georgi asked his father what he should do about the escaping Americans." Ed continued. "The general said he would send an Antonov from the Baku Kala Air Force Base to the gravel strip just north of the river. He ordered his son to parachute the remaining men somewhere in front of the fleeing refugees and kill you. He was sending Boris to Ankara, Turkey to clandestinely meet with his American turncoat in case you got through. He was also going to send a couple of men to New York to meet with Arkady and brief him into the picture. If something went wrong he could ask the Mafia to help."

The dozen cars were first in line for customs and immigration, while scores of trucks followed. The grey uniformed Border Police Officer inspected both passports and asked if they were carrying official material. Gus said, "We're diplomatic couriers, carrying sealed diplomatic pouches and both of us are armed."

The Guardia di Finanza stamped the entrance and date, November 8, 1979 and then waved them through. The sun was nearly an invisible yellow spot, rising as they drove into the old port. They took the Via del Mare, zigzagging past several docking basins and starting around the harbor on the old maritime business road.

9

E d explained that the Café de France was near the end of Garibaldi Street, a main route running east from the business district and ending at the new seawall. On the far side of the old harbor road, Via del Mare was a newer park where there had once been numerous docks and warehouses. He directed Gus down several back streets so they could check the area, ending on a one-way narrow alley crossing Garibaldi just a block up from the café and Via del Mare.

Ed told Gus, "I'll go in and get a table while you circle behind the café and find a place to park. The man we're meeting may already be there." Gus parked on the secondary street behind the restaurant. Deciding to circle the block, Gus started walking along the back street down to the park.

Although it was 6:30 am, there was almost no one out on the foggy streets. He guessed the early shift was already at work and the later workers wouldn't be out for another hour.

Crossing the two-lane Via del Mare, Gus saw a younger man sitting on a concrete park bench at the other end of the park facing Garibaldi.

Just then, he saw a second man wave from the bank catty-corner across the street. The bystander ran across into the park and started jogging down the sidewalk. He was putting something in his ears.

The bench sitter opened a briefcase on his lap and started fiddling with the contents. Something was wrong so Gus ducked down, out of sight.

There was a huge explosion from around the corner. The blast broke windows across the street. Almost nothing came his way since Garibaldi Street channeled it down toward the harbor.

However, the blast affected both suspicious men in the park. The explosion drove the man running down the sidewalk on a knee. Both men must be terrorist bombers.

Gus drew his Skorpion machine pistol and attached the sound suppressor as he ran across the park, twisting it a quarter-turn to lock the interrupted threads into place. Pausing at the vertical statue with a dog and horse wrapped around the base he flipped the wire stock to the rear and raised the compact machine pistol.

Both bombers saw him starting to lean forward in a gunfighters crouch as they turned to flee. Gus grasped the submachine gun with both hands pulling it into his shoulder pocket. From their expression, Gus realized both men were dismayed when they recognized him.

They were trying to draw weapons when he opened up with a five round burst at the first man, advanced a pace and fired a second burst at the other. Changing to a 20-round magazine, he fired another burst and advanced another pace where he fired a fourth burst and then forward again for a fifth and then a sixth.

Thirty rounds expended, he changed magazines before moving forward to check his accuracy. Both men had numerous bleeding holes in their chests. A lot of the .32-ACP rounds had hit each man in the upper torso with some penetrating all the way through and out their backs. The rest must have ricocheted around inside their rib-cavities.

Kneeling down, Gus used his kerchief to open the briefcase where he recognized a radio-control unit for a model airplane. The spotter must have thought he saw Gus join Ed in the café. Maybe it was an innocent bystander killed along with Ed Warren and the restaurant staff.

There was nothing more in the briefcase but both men had cash, Italian driver's licenses and a few credit cards in their front pockets. Their registered addresses were in Sicily. As Gus started shooting they had drawn Beretta Brigadier 9mm pistols. They just weren't quick enough to fire a shot.

Going up Garibaldi Street to Café de France Gus pushed through the wreckage of the front patio. The striped overhead canvas was torn into fragments and remnants of chairs and tables were thrown against the perimeter, even across the street. Ed and a second older man were crumpled against stone pilasters that used to support glass doors on either side. As Gus knelt he realized that Ed was blind and his face and neck were covered with blood. Putting his handkerchief against the worst neck wound, he applied pressure. Calling out in English Ed said, "My ankle, make sure that mother gets my badge."

Gus reached down and discovered a back-up pistol and a leather case. Opening it he realized that it was the gold badge and credentials of a special agent for the Drug Enforcement Administration. Ed's voice was weak. "Derek and I were trying to track opium shipments along the Silk Road from Afghanistan to Sicily. The Russians get it to the Mafia who convert it to heroin and then send it on to New York." He was getting slower, finally a whisper. "My boss is …" Ed expelled his final breath and passed on. Gus realized that Ed had forgotten that he gave him the same information just an hour ago, before the explosion.

The dual and triple-horns of the emergency vehicles were getting louder as Gus rummaged through their pockets collecting both sets of ID papers and badges. He left the passports and other information. He then retraced his shortcut to the black Suburban. He headed west and then north out of town along the coast to Bari where he joined the Autostrada Adriatica to Bologna. He should have stayed; Ed was a good guy after all.

Although the toll road was two-lane for most of the distance, there was a state run service station every fifty or so kilometers. Since the speed limit was 120 kph, Gus made very good time reaching Bologna in six hours where he stopped to buy groceries for his lunch.

He drove into the hills just outside town. Gus turned off on a road to a Catholic Shrine, engaged the 4-wheel drive and drove to a hilltop. Measuring the hundreds of feet off his roll of copper wire to form a full-wave dipole antenna, he climbed a pine tree as high as he could dropping four wires to the ground after he fixed a transformer-balun to the two wires running down to the radio.

He had to use the car bumper to stretch each section of wire to eliminate its catenary curve. Gus was planning on talking to Ankara even though it was still daylight here and in Turkey. He would try to reach Boise later this evening when reception should be better.

After assembling the radio and antenna, he wrote out a message about the bombing death of Ed Warren and his American acquaintance. He included a description of the two dead men from Sicily. He then took the time to study the documents he had collected. The older man had an ID and business card identifying him as a consultant to the DEA. In his badge case was gold shield of a Retired

Director of the old US Treasury, Federal Bureau of Narcotics. Gus decided to send his name but skip any DEA references.

Gus then used the one-time pad from Metcalf to write out the transposed characters into each new Morse code. He keyed his groups of coded numbers into the burst-data transmitter. Using the neon yellow Whiz-Wheel code he rekeyed the same message for Berke.

He used SSB-voice to contact the special office located on top of the embassy. Bringing them up to date on the death of Ed Warren, he then sent them a burst transmission with all the details he had learned. There was a pause of half-an-hour while they decoded the recorded burst and Metcalf had a chance to review the information.

"Someone blew up Ed and we don't know who did it." Metcalf said after he had received the decoded transmission. "The takeover of the other facility happened four days ago and the pressure for information is doubling every day. I'll run your suspicions through the Company, but it may take weeks."

"You should avoid talking to Washington until you are stateside and can call on a safe phone. Check back with us every other day since we might have a new phone number and the name of a contact I can trust at headquarters."

After signing off, he changed the channels slightly and contacted Berke in Ankara by voice. There were no new calls from Ed Warren intercepted. Gus told him about the new information he had collected and then sent everything is a burst of code to his Turkish friend after warning him to start recording. A few minutes later Burke reconnected by voice using the SSB radio.

"In fact, I know the intelligence officer at the army facility you're headed for." Berke told him. I'll send him a coded message with any information we develop.

Gus drove through the Italian Piedmont into the foothills of the Alps. It was November and the lowest point in the tourist season so he didn't make reservations for a hotel. He crossed into Switzerland and arrived in Lugano in the early afternoon.

Leaving the A2, he drove along the lake to the five-star Hotel Eden. They had plenty of first class rooms so he let them copy his diplomatic passport and had the bell captain take the single bag to the room while he arranged for the official containers and duffels' concealing his cash and extra firearms be moved to the hotel safe.

Going out to his Suburban, Gus toured around the town to check for escape routes. There was a sporting goods store on a main corner, well back from the lake so he parked and went inside. Among the ammunition in the gun section were several boxes of Swedish Norma pistol cartridges, .32-ACP.

He was short by 30-rounds after the affair in Brindisi. Looking at a bullet, Gus realized they were duplicates of the Super Vel hollow point round. Understandable since he knew Norma made the components for the designer of the high-speed anti-personal cartridges.

Asking about purchase requirements, the shop owner started to talk about Swiss citizens. Gus interrupted and asked about diplomatic passport holders. "It's legal for diplomats to purchase non-military handgun ammunition." Gus immediately asked for the 50-round box.

He could leave a couple of magazines loaded with full-metal jacketed bullets in case he needed to fire into automobile doors or windshields. He asked the shopkeeper about the lakeside mountain he had passed on the way into town and learned it was a nature preserve. They allowed hiking and climbing throughout the park, however there were a number of houses on the ridge top road running south from Paradiso.

He could drive along the lakefront beyond the Grand Eden Hotel and find numerous places to hike up the rocks to Monte San Salvatore.

Gus drove back along Lake Lugano until he found a spot where he could drape his pre-cut dipole antenna, tension it with the car bumper, and then talk to Boise. He contacted a ham operator on the west coast who transferred the call to his uncle who was having coffee. After bringing him up to date about the DS agent in Iran and the MJ personnel killed at the pass in Turkey, he mentioned the explosion and deaths in Italy.

"Throughout my years with the CIA everyone suspected that the KGB was instrumental in the drug trade in the '60s from Burma and Laos into Vietnam. Later I heard that they were involved with opium shipments from Afghanistan to Europe. Several people even mentioned that the American Mafia was directly involved with the Russians and that they were now moving into cocaine from the Soviet revolutionaries in South America."

Uncle Dick said for him to take as long as he needed. "You can safely use our bank in Zurich, UBS-the Union Bank of Switzerland. I've already called them and set up a personal account for you and a large safety deposit locker for the gold owned jointly by you and me." Gus asked about using the MJ accounts.

"Everything must be in our names; you can't use the company name." Richard said. "In fact, I told our banker to issue you a new worldwide charge card and tie it to the personal account. I hope we've fixed it so no one can use your spending to track you. The bank concierge at the entrance gate on Paradenplatz will let your car into the inner courtyard and assign someone to help with the containers." He asked if Gus had any questions.

"As soon as you are ready, whether in New York or DC, I'll send a corporate jet to pick you up and fly you out to Boise. I'll be in

Washington late next week where I plan to have a stern talk with our Senators and Representatives. I need to make sure you are insulated from the activity that seems to be occurring with the various executive agencies. Out."

On the way back to the hotel, Gus stopped at a men's haberdasher and went in to look for a set of business clothes; he had abandoned everything dressy in Iran. He purchased a pair of black tasseled loafers, a matching belt, tan-colored wool slacks, an English made white button-down dress shirt and double-breasted navy blue wool blazer with a multi-color silk tie along with several other items including a new briefcase. His surplus feldgrau wool pants were dirty and wrinkled. In addition, they weren't in style having narrower legs for boots, rather than relaxed cuffs. So when he went back to the hotel he sent them, the shirts and his trench coat out for dry cleaning and pressing before ordering a steak and vegetable plate from room service.

10

Rising before daylight, Gus went out for a 5-mile run along the lake getting back in thirty-five minutes, a 7-minute per mile average. Gus realized he was feeling good for a change.

Getting back, he stretched and then dove into the freezing lake from the swimming platform. Using an overhand stroke, he swam a hundred meters down to an empty mooring buoy and used a backstroke to swim back.

Weighing in, he was down 2.3 kilos, although his old scale at the dam was probably not very accurate. He cleaned up dressed in his new business clothing and went down to breakfast overlooking the lake. The sun was just rising. His eating habits were changing. For breakfast, he only had coffee and muesli cereal with fruit and skim milk. Later, he loaded the car and was on the road to Zurich before 7:00 am.

He still wore the back-up revolver on his left ankle and had moved the Makarov with its short integral suppressor to the small of his back. His new London made harness leather belt tightly fit through the trouser loops but it had no trouble supporting his weapons.

Gus didn't button the double-breasted blazer. Instead he placed a loaded magazine in each pocket so when he swept the coat to one side to draw his pistol, his coat tails would flow with the weight and not interrupt his actions. He put the machine pistol, extra magazines and knife in the new briefcase.

Two hours later he made his way into downtown Zurich, headed for Paradeplatz Square in the middle of Bahnhofstrasse, the Wall Street of Switzerland. As he pulled into the square, Gus saw the arched entrance into an inner courtyard, beyond the sidewalk.

Driving in, the concierge came over and asked in German for his passport. Gus replied in the perfect "Hochdeutsche" dialect his grandmother had taught him. Saying, "I have an appointment." When the former Swiss military man, carrying a concealed pistol was satisfied, he directed him to an elevator in perfect English, "The porter will help you with your bags." Apparently, the High German didn't fool him.

Arriving at the next floor, Gus was surprised the room was plain oak and stone with a polished wooden floor. In addition to the reception desk, there were two long tables down the center of the room, with high windows on one side and ten steel vault doors along the wall. Waiting for him was a well-dressed but slightly overweight Swiss banker.

"My name is Dr. Rudolf Halter and I am President of the Union Bank of Switzerland. Your uncle has instructed me to set up a new checking account with a gold American Express Card automatically paid by the account. He told me to tell you to charge the cost of all of your replacement clothes for the ones you left in Iran." Gus mentioned the money he spent yesterday in Lugano.

"Give me the receipt and we can reimburse you from the deposit." Dr. Halter said. "He wants us to send him copies of all correspondence and the monthly bills, so he can forward them to you. He's already transferred money into the new account. We'll need copies of any passport you want to use and your signature." Gus handed over the documents for a clerk to copy.

"He also said you would deposit cash money into a new Intrag AG mutual fund account and you would need one or more secure vault drawers for gold, and other items. He's the co-signer of the Intrag account and for vault access. If you want to store weapons, make sure the chambers are unloaded." Gus realized the concierge downstairs had reported that he was armed.

"I've got two briefcases with 2,400 gold Krugerrands and they need to go into a safety deposit locker because of their weight," Gus replied. "I also have twenty-five thousand $100 dollar bills, $2.5 million." He paused to let the numbers sink in.

"First put the Krugerrands into safety deposit," Gus instructed. "Then my uncle and I want you to buy an additional $1.5 million in gold bars and put them into a second and maybe a third safety box if we need the space. The remaining million dollars should be invested in a mutual stock fund. We would prefer American stocks. I want to take all four Persian carpets with me as Christmas presents. You can put them in the empty briefcases."

"We'll need time to count and inspect the bills," Dr. Halter said. "We have to inspect your money for counterfeit hundreds since I understand the bills come from Persia. We'll then bring the gold bars over from our refinery, Argor. It'll take at least an hour to count the currency and then bring the gold here. Each of the UBS marked bars weighs one-kilo, slightly more than 32 troy ounces. At today's price, you're talking about almost 4,300 troy ounces. That's almost 133 kilos, or about 294 of your pounds." Gus nodded his head as Dr. Halter explained everything.

Dr. Halter continued, "Intrag Asset Management handles a number of different investment vehicles. We call one of them the America-Canada Trust Fund. AMCA only buys North American stocks and bonds."

"In the meantime, I can't help but notice that you wear your wristwatch facing the inside of your wrist. It's an extremely worn Rolex Submariner with a scratched dial and some corrosion around the crown. It looks like it leaks. It's also five minutes slower than our master clock up there over the desk. Are you trying to protect the face?"

"I've always worn my watches that way. I bought it fourteen years ago at a military exchange in Saigon," Gus answered as he compared it against the master clock. "It replaced my old Hamilton that wasn't really jungle-proof. I also got a red Victorinox Swiss Army knife and a Leicaflex camera with an extra 135mm telephoto lens. The camera and lens were stolen but I still carry the red knife. I believe the watch cost less than $250, but now I have to reset the time every week against the BBC noon signal."

"There's a jewelry store just down the street where you can give them your watch. The factory will renew it and recertify it as a chronograph. You'll need to buy a new watch since it will take them a couple of months to fix your timepiece. The concierge will give you directions. I'll see you back here in an hour." The gatekeeper directed him one block up Bahnhofstrasse to Beyer Chronometrie at Number 31.

The storeowner came to the door and said, "Dr. Halter called and said you wanted to look at watches while your Rolex is at the factory. Let me see your old watch."

He studied it through a loupe. "The stainless case and bracelet have numerous scratches and it leaks. It had a black tropical dial that is turning brownish and it needs new luminous spots. Do you want them to change the color of the dial? You can have Black or Blue. If they renew the luminous hands and dots it will look like new when they finish. Of course this model doesn't have a date." Gus said black would be fine.

Heer Beyer took him to look at the various advertising brochures for a replacement watch. "Should it match the gold ring you're wearing?" Gus responded, "Stainless will be fine. Do you have any that don't flash?"

He waited while Gus looked at the different brochures. Gus thought a minute and said, "I want a non-flashy Rolex with luminous dots and a 24-hour bezel with the extra hand showing a second time zone. It's named the GMT in the brochure."

The owner led him to a case with two-dozen different watches. Gus liked the first watch he pulled out. "It's a solid platinum GMT model," the shopkeeper warned. "We also have several gold or stainless GMT models with different colored dials and bezels. If you want something really plain you can get our least expensive Datejust model, or one of our many cheaper brands." Gus studied them and then said, "They're all too flashy, everybody will notice if I wear a shiny watch. But I still want a GMT model."

The shopkeeper asked Gus to wait a minute as he went into the back room. "I want to show you a special-order made for an over-weight *Schwabian* planning a big game hunt in South Africa. The German died before he could pick it up." He handed a box over to Gus.

"It's stainless with a white dial. The case and President Bracelet are matt-frosted metal. It has an anti-reflective sapphire crystal with a Cyclops magnifier over the date. The bezel is matt stainless and the twelve even numbered hours are incised black. We call the hour hand a Mercedes style while the 24-hour hand is an orange outlined triangle. Rather than radium they now use tritium luminous *Pearls*."

"I'm assuming you want the same properties on your renovated watch. I can have them matt-frost the stainless and install an anti-reflective crystal."

"Have them go ahead with the matt; I love the dull finish. How does this one work?" Gus asked.

"The main dial is already set for European time and the orange hand is set for London GMT one hour ahead. You should change the main dial to your local time and leave the 24-hour orange one on GMT time. You could then rotate the bezel so it matches a third time zone."

"Leave the orange triangle on GMT London time; I can change the regular dial for whatever zone I'm in. I doubt if I'll ever need a third zone." Gus told the owner.

"I've got an unrelated question. Do you have one of those hydrosonic cleaners?"

The storekeeper answered with a positive yes. Gus asked him to disassemble his Montblanc ballpoint and give it a thorough cleaning. While it was cleaning in the blue liquid, the owner asked if he would like to look at matching fountain pens or mechanical pencils.

Gus told him, "No thanks. Just the watch and ballpoint." Heading back to the bank, almost everything was ready so he handed over the Colts and Browning to put in the top of each safety deposit drawer.

After signing the paperwork and packing both aluminum briefcases, Gus put the Gladstone and rucksack into the surplus duffle. Gus went downstairs, put everything in the Suburban and headed east for Innsbruck, Austria.

One of his friends owned a bookstore there on the main street. He was holding an Army surplus duffle bag with Gus' American pistols, spare magazines, holsters and harnesses, along with his riot shotgun.

Two years ago, he had filled the rest of the space in the duffle with other specialized equipment. Gus called ahead and told his friend he was on his way. It took him a little over two hours to drive the 180 miles, arriving in time for a late lunch.

He followed his friend to an uncrowded restaurant where he asked, "Why's the town so empty? Hasn't the season started yet?"

"It's early November and the groomed high slopes don't open until the weekend. The rest of the backcountry ski trails don't have enough snow so they won't open for another week or two."

Gus explained he was collecting several of his old reliable friends to go with his new Russian equipment. He thanked him for his help and then gave him more money to keep his bag for a few more years.

When he left, he was now carrying the custom Colt aluminum framed pistol in .45-ACP, the 9mm ASP backup pistol, and the .22-caliber Ruger. He also collected his 20-inch barreled featherweight Winchester pump-action shotgun that he carried broken-down in a leg-o-mutton case. Among the various accessories were suppressors, several holsters, magazines, and extra ammo in pouches and other various accoutrements including lock picks, custom molded earplugs and a complete set of listening devices.

After lunch, Gus headed east for a few miles before turning north toward Germany, crossing the mountains through two lake valleys he then drove along the Isar River to Bad Tölz, the headquarters of the 1st Battalion of the 10th Special Forces Group.

His forward operational B-Team was attached to the 11th Special Forces Reserve, the sister group to the 10th. They were stationed in Frankfurt since the location there was more convenient for personnel flying in from all over and deploying for the weekend or two weeks of active duty. They supported Army Reserve "A" teams training throughout Europe, Africa and the Mideast. Of the dozen Green Berets in his unit, half were on active duty while the remainder were working in Europe but serving in the reserve. Fort Meade was the headquarters for the 11th Group with its three battalions and "A" teams located up and down the east coast from Miami to Boston. Its area of operations was to back up the 10th Group in Europe, Africa and the Mideast.

Every third Friday of the month, he flew into Germany for regular reserve duty, and every summer he spent two weeks with his unit. The Pentagon promoted Gus to company commander of the reserve support element two years ago. For three years, he also attended the 3-year long correspondence and monthly non-residence Command and General Staff school courses in Germany, graduating last summer. Each summer for the residence training he always flew to the United States on Air Force transports.

He was going to Bavaria to see his good friend, the retired and paralyzed sergeant major, Andy Johnson. He lived in a private house just south of the old SS officer training school, which the American Special Forces 10th Group now occupied.

The main reason Andy stayed in Germany was his daughter, a medical student at LMU in nearby Munich. It was one of the best medical schools in Europe.

After graduating from Harvard, she wanted to go to medical school near her German mother who was sick. Sergeant Major Andy Johnson was planning on retiring in two more years. Of course, her mother passed and Andy became wheelchair bound because of his accident.

Gus had never met the daughter, but he thought she should have graduated this last summer. He couldn't remember her first name.

11

G us was already on the east side of the Isar so he took a shortcut to Mühle and then on north to Andy's house. It was a rented farmhouse and outbuilding, south across the fields from the golf course.

When he knocked, a truly stunning girl answered the door. She was an inch under six-feet tall, maybe five inches shorter than he was. She looked better than the Lorelei statue in the Bronx, the blond siren of the Rhine.

"You must be Papa's friend Gus. I'm Mary his daughter. He's in the back workroom. Why don't you follow me?" He felt like an idiot since his mother's name had been Mary. Why hadn't he remembered her name?

She was wearing a loose sweater and skin-tight blue jeans. They weren't Levi's or Wranglers so they must be "hip-huggers", Gus thought. As she turned to escort him into the house, he noticed the low cut of the waist, showing her taunt abdomen and the tops of twin dimples just above her buttocks.

Gus greeted his old friend and slapped his back although he was a little unsure how to act with someone in a wheelchair.

"We served together in Vietnam," he told Mary. "Starting in 1968 we met again whenever I was here for annual summer training with the 11th. Since the accident in '77, I haven't seen Andy although we've often talked on the phone. He's mentioned you a number of times but I don't think we ever met." His explanation started to falter and die out.

"Mary graduated as a Doctor of Medicine from Ludwig-Maximilians-Universität in Munich last year," Andy explained as Mary blushed. "She passed both her American and German medical license exams before she finished her clinical internship in Public Health and Tropical Medicine this May."

"Over the summer and this fall she's been studying for an additional post-graduate Master's degree in Epidemiology, you know epidemics and infectious diseases. Her dissertation will be submitted next week and she must verbally defend it two weeks later. By Christmas we're going to move back to the US and she's going to join the Army." Andy paused and looked to Mary and then Gus for any comments. Both were too shy to say anything.

"I plan to settle into a Fayetteville apartment outside Ft. Bragg while she goes to Ft. Benning for orientation and airborne school." Andy continued. "Then she's off for another three months in the basic officer course for doctors at Ft. Sam Houston before coming back to Womack Army Hospital at Bragg for her two-year residency in Family Medicine."

Gus finally spoke as he congratulated Mary and asked her some questions about what she expected as a woman in the new Army.

She answered in a sweet voice, "Of course you know the WACS disbanded almost two years ago and women now join the regular army. All direct commission officers, including women go through two weeks orientation and weapons' training at Benning and Papa has set it up for me to continue on to jump school before I go to the basic officers' course at Fort Sam Houston." Gus realized that she was firmly putting him on notice.

Mary looked directly at Gus as she asked, "Would you two like me to get you a beer?"

"No thank you. Black coffee would be fine." Gus responded.

"I'll fix a pot while you two catch up on old times."

"What's happening in Iran?" Andy changed the subject after Mary left. "Tonight, I plan on having a few friends over and they've all been asking questions."

Gus responded, "Our friends have ordered me not to say much."

"You may not want to discuss the details but I want to know what's been happening to you. Just after midnight on November 4th, our intelligence S-2 got a flash top-secret cable from the Pentagon declaring a *Double Take* alert in Europe. The warning order included our two standby teams and the entire covert Detachment A in Berlin. DefCon 5 was increasing to 4. We were put on a one-hour notice for deployment to support an unidentified US Embassy. Of course you know that the embassy in Tehran was seized a few hours later. A few days later we got another report from Turkey and I just heard about a bombing and shootout in Brindisi yesterday morning." Andy paused and waited for Gus to respond. "Just an hour ago the intelligence shop brought me a sealed top secret message for your eyes only."

As Gus opened the brown envelope marked Top Secret, he saw there was a long Teletype inside. It was full of information about dozens of contractors and a few case officers from the old Directorate of Operations. Berke had delivered everything in the MIT files.

It looked like every one of them had been cut either before or during the massive Halloween Massacre in '77. After reviewing the package, Gus realized he would have to study this information and ask questions about some of these men from his contacts within the secret world of special operations, starting with his old friend Andy.

Turning and looking back he said, "Tonight, I need to question all of the old-time Green Beret sergeants and warrant officers, include anybody who's retired. This top-secret document includes a list of rogue Special Forces personnel and a few CIA trained Special Activities Division officers. There is some detailed information about them and a number of front-companies and banks that a sister agency suspects might be smuggling drugs. I would like to get more; especially anything about drug smuggling in southeast Asia or more recently between Afghanistan and the east coast."

Andy said, "I'll invite a few more of my old friends." He called out to the kitchen, "Mary you had better drive by the commissary and get more rolls, sausages and beans." Waiting for her to leave Andy realized Gus had more to tell him.

"Now that I'm out of Iran it looks like I'm being targeted by two different groups. The biggest and oldest is the KGB and their Spetsnaz Section A or Spetsgruppa-Alfa."

Andy looked at Gus almost in disbelief. He said, "They're just a rumor not real. No Americans have every operated against Section A."

"I helped kill eight of them in a Turkish high mountain pass four days ago," responded Gus as he tossed the long combat knife with the engraved winged *A* on the table. "In fact, this whole mess started less than a week ago when a hostage team from the new Iranian Revolutionary Guard killed my watchers. For two years I've worked with a Russian engineering counterpart and of course the soviets insisted he have a bodyguard when he was working on our side of the river. On Saturday I found out he was a KGB captain and his bodyguard was from Section A. He was there to watch me. Just before the Iranian terrorist killed him, my friend overheard them tell him that they were there to take me captive." Gus paused to let the information soak into Andy's thoughts.

"Of course the next day they seized the embassy," Gus continued. "I don't know what to think. I had a problem with Islamic fundamentalists, but I'm out of the Middle East. At first I believed the Russian mission might be tied to what happened almost three years ago. Did I know something about their agents who may have penetrated the American intelligence community, secret codes, spy stuff?" Andy asked a few sharp questions before Gus continued.

"Now I've found out that the Soviet group may be drug smugglers and it may involve former American special operations agents. Do the dealers still work for the CIA smuggling drugs or do they now work for the Russians, smuggling drugs. Apparently most of them are mercenaries selling weapons, drugs and laundering cash for either one or both sides. I've heard that one is even selling young boys and girls to the Arabs." Gus then told Andy what he discovered about Ed Warren and his boss.

"The two groups may be working together. In fact I am beginning to believe that the American traitors passing information to the Russians are just drug dealers who are being blackmailed."

That evening, Gus stayed outside and cooked bratwurst on the wood-burning fire-pit. It was freezing out there, although there was no snow yet in this part of southern Bavaria. All of the active duty Green Berets stayed with him, drinking beer.

A few of the Green Berets were wearing their fatigues but most were dressed in jeans and jackets. The older retired men stayed inside with Andy and Mary who was in the kitchen fixing sauerkraut, beans, rolls and German style potatoes. After Andy talked to a few friends about what had happened, they started asking numerous questions about Iran and the gun battle with the Russians in the pass.

After dinner, everyone met in the living room and discussed the list of rogue actors Gus had gotten from Ed and from Turkish security in Ankara, particularly the ones who were known drug dealers. Gus used Mary's blackboard to write out the name and past assignments as he passed around notecards for each man to write information on each man. The heated discussion took more than two hours with some surprising disagreements.

Later after their discussions, a Chief Warrant Officer-CW4 waved Gus and Andy into the workroom, closed the door and said, "I'm Dean Mitchell a former sergeant major and the second in command of intelligence for the 10th. I know all the men here."

"Although most of them would never betray the United States, I'll bet you at least one of them knows someone in your group of suspects and will tell them about your suspicions. Why don't you talk to the colonel?"

Gus responded, "What colonel?"

"You do know that retired Colonel Bankhead is here in Germany on a boar hunting trip. I know tomorrow is his last day of hunting. Since he's one of the fathers of the Green Berets, he's planning on stopping here on Sunday and spending the night." He mentioned a suite at the BOQ.

"The next day, our Pilatus courier plane will fly him over to Frankfurt where he's catching Pan Am to New York. He lives in California not far from Richard Nixon's old Western White House in San Clemente." CWO Mitchell continued, "He's also an advisor to Governor Ronald Reagan who will probably run against Jimmy Carter next year. I'm planning a formal officer's dine-in for Sunday night. Do you have a tuxedo to wear, how about your decorations?"

"I don't have any decorations with me," Gus said. "I have a set of Class A's, some fatigues and civilian clothes in Frankfurt with my reserve unit. It would take hours to get them and I would still have Greens, not Dress Blues."

"The PX will have some miniature devices, shoes, socks and dress shirts," Mitchell said as he pulled out a notepad and pencil. "Give me your sizes, I'll send someone out to rent you a penguin outfit. However, you'll have to buy the shirt, bowtie and shoes. Of course, you'll have to break-in the shoes for a few hours and then spit shine them for the formal dinner."

"Can you get me an appointment to talk to Colonel Bankhead for a few hours Sunday afternoon?" Gus asked.

"Sure, he gets here about noon and has lunch with the troops. You can meet him after he inspects our museum; it's full of his stuff. By the way, do you have any souvenirs to donate?"

"Since I can't easily get them back into the US, I was planning on giving you a few Soviet weapons I've collected in the last week." He told the chief warrant officer.

Gus was keeping his American guns he picked up in Innsbruck, along with a few other devices. He could donate the rest of the communist guns to the Special Forces.

After everyone left, Mary asked, "I guess you'll take Papa in your black Suburban tomorrow. You'll need to push him around if you go into the woods."

"Andy needs to use his stipend from the VA to purchase a handicapped van with a hydraulic lift and hand controls. When do you think he'll get to Fayetteville? I could arrange for one to be waiting for him." Mary agreed and they talked for a few more minutes.

"Before sunrise, I'm going for a long jog and then run through the SF obstacle course. Would you like to go with me?" He felt like a fool; rushing through multiple thoughts without giving her a chance to answer anything, she could only nod her head in agreement before she left to cleanup.

"You never told me about the ambush three years ago?" Andy said after everyone had left. For a long minute, Gus didn't say anything.

"I've never told anyone about it," Gus said in a quiet voice. "The Russian KGB has been watching me for the last few years and it's because of something out of the ordinary in my past. I was thinking that you would go to the site in Austria with me tomorrow, so I can talk you through the action. I'm still missing something. It's at the back of my mind, but I just can't remember."

Rising before six, Gus went into the kitchen and drank a glass of water. Mary was making noise in her room so he went out and walked around the perimeter, stretching and looking for any signs of activity.

It was a few degrees below freezing and hoarfrost covered the grass and tree twigs. Once again, he was wearing his old cross-country trail-runners, black sweatpants and a matching black jersey. He would warm up as he ran. Later he could strip down to his old army gym shorts and the OD tee shirt he was wearing underneath the sweats.

Mary came out wearing skintight running pants, Addis shoes and a loose Harvard sweatshirt.

She directed him up the road to the start of the running trail as she explained, "The team here designed a 10-kilometer cross-country running course. At the start, and then every kilometer there's a pause for stretching and doing exercises like push-ups, sit-ups, or pull-ups. Every other kilometer you have to do one of the five-standard PCPT items; the 40-yard low crawl, the horizontal ladder rungs, the run-dodge & jump, the 150-yard man carry and finally a timed one-mile run to the finish.

You can carry me over your shoulder for the man carry," Mary said. "Even though I only weight about 52 kilos, I'll run back with the 30-kilo set of sewn sandbags put there for singletons. At the end is the Special Forces obstacle course. At each stop, I'll just stretch and jog in place while you finish the assigned task."

"If you're going to jump school and then Ft. Sam Houston," Gus said. "You should do several of the exercises to start getting into shape. At a minimum you have to do seven dead hanging pull-ups to complete airborne."

"Women have a different requirement for timed bent arm hanging rather than pull-ups," Mary replied. "But you're right the other trainees will respect me more if I take the men's test."

The trail ran up and down hill, across double foot logs and dodged around trees. By the time they got to the low crawl, Mary offered to race him. Gus did it right, always keeping his chest in contact with the ground, just like an alligator. Mary stuck her ass up in the air and finished first.

He was sweating so he took off his jersey and pants, tying them around his middle. She took off her sweatshirt and tied it around her narrow waist. Under her crimson shirt, she was wearing a tight tee shirt cropped off at her rib cage. It didn't look like she was wearing a bra since her nipples extended as she realized he was looking.

As they ran to the next station, Gus followed and noticed she wasn't wearing any underpants under her tights. There she was able to do six correct pull-ups.

When they got to the man carry Gus just grabbed her off leg, swung her over his shoulder and took off to the turn. Treating her like a sack of potatoes.

She ran back with the sandbag slung across her shoulder. She didn't complain as they ran on. When they got to the obstacle course, she just ran the trail beside the individual obstructions. This course could be extremely dangerous for someone who wasn't trained or ready.

Gus realized she was taking it easy. He was panting and she was hardly breathing. He told her, "I'm trying to get back into shape."

12

I t was snowing in the foothills of the Alps. As Gus and Andy drove east parallel to the rising mountains, Andy asked, "What do you plan on doing with this bulletproof Suburban? Who's keeping a record of the diplomatic plates?"

"It's armored for handguns and light assault rifles and not on anybody's books. As far as State knows it was captured in Iran by the Revolutionary Guard. In fact its European Diplomatic plates aren't registered in anybody's records. Maybe the 10th SF could keep it under cover and use it for special activities."

"What are you going to do about the US Embassy in Iran?" Andy asked a few minutes later. "I had a telephone call last night my old friend Dick Mead in North Carolina, you remember him from Da Nang, don't you?" Gus remembered Dick as one of the toughest Green Berets in the Army. "He retired as a Major a few years ago didn't he?" Gus asked.

"He's a consultant now and said that he's working on a plan for Colonel Charlie Beck and the new group he's running at Fort Bragg.

They've been operational since fall, but they haven't gone on any missions yet."

"I've been advised to not discuss Iran with anyone until further notice. Today's the 10th of November." Gus commented, "The hostages were seized almost a week ago. The government needs to start working on some plans to get them released. Maybe I should work with the guys in North Carolina. What do you think I should do? I was considering asking Colonel Bankhead what to do tomorrow."

"You need to lay it all out for the colonel and carefully ask him about your options." Andy advised him. "He's retired and out of the action, but he knows what's happening politically. Talk to him; forget about any warning the CIA gave you. He's not a secret agent."

"Also you need to be more observant." Andy commented. "For example what are the colors of the three cars behind us? Don't look in the mirror." Gus couldn't answer.

"Then where was the last policeman we passed?" Again he hadn't noticed. Gus realized that three years ago he would have seen everything.

They passed Salzburg and it was almost 11:00 am when the A1 Autobahn passed between a lake and steep mountain and turned north starting up a long rising valley. About 8-kilometers further Gus turned off the East-West Autobahn and drove fifty-meters up a gravel road.

Getting out he pushed Andy's wheelchair up a bumpy path. The roadway was to their left and about 5-meters lower.

"You have a Top Secret clearance and know more than anybody else. Let me go over everything, step by step," Gus said to Andy. "As you know the main reason I became involved was the weekly routine that I had established in Prague during the preceding year. In 1976 the CIA promoted me to Core Collector within the Operations

Department because of the three low-level border guards I was running as a case officer. I also had a mid-level agent we called Martin in the StB-Czechoslovakian State Security that almost no one knew I was grooming to give me information." Gus set the brake and knelt down so he and Andy were face-to-face. "Every Friday evening just before they closed the border crossing, I would arrive in my mustard yellow MJ crew-cab pickup. Often I brought along an American or an Austrian construction worker. I'd pass out a few bribes and drive into Austria. On Sunday I would come back with construction supplies addressed to the US Ambassador, and give the guards on duty western goods like chocolate, blue jeans or records." Gus turned to Andy and explained how the Russian KGB and Czech StB were running weapons through the same checkpoint from the Brno gun works to the Palestine Liberation Faction terrorist training camps.

"For fifty-hours a week I was an MJ engineer, while the rest of the time I was a covert operations officer who had always served as a NOC. Occasionally I also acted as a paramilitary officer. My reports went straight back to Langley and not to the Prague Embassy."

"I thought you were in the Green Beret reserves." Andy asked.

"Of course I went to monthly reserve meetings and took two weeks off every summer for training, although for the year I was under deep cover in Moscow I skipped the monthly meetings."

"I first met the Soviet defector Mongolian in Tehran before he started passing information to the west. He was a senior officer working for the KGB rezidentura who was tasked to recruit British or American agents. Just transferred in from Vietnam I had a great cover as an MJ engineer rebuilding the top floors of a hotel. On my fourth night in country I ran into my old friend, I'll call him Sergeant George. Under the buddy system, he had been my partner through-out the entire half-year SAS training course. We had drinks together and although circumspect, each of us realized the other was under-cover. What we didn't realize was that a Soviet officer was studying us in the only pub serving beer in Tehran; it was in the basement of the hotel I was renovating. George was not a case officer in British MI6; he was an undercover shooter from the Special Air Service protecting the exalted SIS officers." Gus paused and made sure that Andy was comfortable.

"Over the next year Mongolian tried to recruit both of us," Gus continued. "Finally George turned him and gave him over to his superiors. The British assigned him their next available code name. Mongolian was promoted and transferred back to Moscow in 1975, and the British lost all contact."

Gus continued, "In the meantime, when they announced Russia would host the 1980 Olympics, international businesses and hotel chains started a huge building boom in Moscow. By 1975 construc-tion contracts were starting to be issued without local Russian partners. I went to Russia pretending to be a Swiss engineer working for a French engineering, architectural and construction company with a contract to build a huge new hotel. My French bosses had no idea I was an illegal agent, working undercover and that I wasn't from Switzerland. Although as a junior engineer from a neutral country I had some freedom of movement. We took over an old building on the edge of the site and converted it into small dorm-type rooms for the expatriate workers. Of course I also had additional night and weekend chores. I was dark in Russia, completely out in the cold with no local contacts. My case officer flew into Russia once a month and my only contact was through dead drops. I'm not really supposed to talk about what I was doing for the Company." Andy didn't ask any more questions.

"In Moscow the CIA had a problem," Gus continued. "A new female case officer pretending to be a low-level secretary with diplomatic immunity was going to be the single contact point for a Russian double agent working for their Foreign Ministry. The KGB was tracking all of the male case officers working at the U.S. Embassy. Usually when one case officer went out for a pickup the rest would go out to distract the enemy watchers. She had to find someway to remain sterile when she picked up information. Someone clean had to loosely shadow her and check for KBG followers when she went out. I was the only covert NOC in Moscow. I watched over her and would usually leave her a signal when she was clean. I also set up new dead-drops for her and her agent. I never contacted any of the other American case officers."

Andy asked, "Did you have contact with any Americans?" Gus' answer was, "Not any working in Moscow."

"Once again my instructions came over the shortwave and the British serviced my supply caches," Gus responded. "Of course within the first month I got a message from my old SAS friend George asking me to re-establish contact with their loose agent. He wanted me to help him get back in contact with Mongolian since the KGB was watching the British embassy too closely.

"Finally away from Moscow," Gus continued. "In 1977 I was back using my own identity as a project manager for MJ at the US Embassy in Prague, but once again without any diplomatic immunity." Gus then explained about how he changed identities back to his real name as he moved to the US Embassy in Prague and took charge of an MJ contract to renovate one of the buildings. "I did run into my friend George but we never actually talked until I got a message at my apartment to meet him clandestinely and head for the border."

"That winter," Gus continued. "The British had discovered my routine in Prague. George also knew you and trusted you to get them to the airfield at Bad Tölz. When you were injured in the parachute accident, George told me about your predicament and I decided to cover the entire trip from Prague to Bad Tölz. Mongolian did recognize me there, giving me a warm greeting. Other than George, I had never met any of the British officers." Looking over Gus could see Andy was intrigued and wanted to hear more.

"There were two MI6 case officers and the defector in the first car," recited Gus. "I was in the second car with my friend George, both of us heavily armed. We left the MJ truck a couple of miles into Austria where we rendezvoused with the fast sedans. That night was cold but still with patches of snow remaining on the north slopes. The plan was to drive across northern Austria and on into Germany to Baker Field, the PSP airstrip just north of here. There was a short-takeoff Pilatus Porter waiting there to fly them to RAF Gütersloh where they would go on to a safe house in England."

Gus paused and said to Andy, "I've never told anyone this story and if it ever got out, I think I would be in a lot of trouble." Andy agreed to keep it confidential.

"The British were handling the exfiltration of Mongolian as an emergency." Gus continued. "George later mentioned they were trying to keep everything from the CIA, which is why they were using us. I asked him 'Why?' and he then told me there was a traitor at headquarters in Virginia." Andy motioned for Gus to continue.

"So, unless you told someone, nobody at the Company knew my name. I was just a gunman in the second car." Gus looked to make sure that Andy understood. "Under my trench coat, I was wearing my .45-ACP pistol, with the suppressor attached and six full magazines. In addition, I was carrying my Model 12 Winchester riot shotgun loaded with man-killing rounds, one in the chamber and six in the tube magazine along with two twelve-round pouches in each deep pocket."

"You remember it from Vietnam, if I held the trigger down, it could slam fire all the rounds in a couple of seconds by fast pumping the forearm." Gus looked at Andy as he remembered Vietnam. "Three hours after we left the border, we were approaching this spot right here. The other highway lane was closed and traffic was two-way in this section headed to Salzburg when we were ambushed. The lead car's radiator exploded in a blinding flash and our car skidded, leaving the passenger door turned away from the sudden ambush. I rolled out and got behind the steel wheel and engine block." Gus pointed out the spot just a hundred feet up the road.

"A Soviet medium machine gun was perforating the drivers side of our car with bullets which flew on out my side. The lead car exploded with a second direct hit by another rocket-propelled grenade. Its hood peeled back and the carburetor caught fire. I leaned around the front bumper and slamfired six-shotgun rounds into the machine gun position. The gunfire slowed so I must have hit the occupants. Running around the back of the car I leaped up the bank, slinging the shotgun around my back and drawing my pistol as I ran." Gus pushed Andy's wheelchair downhill to the natural depression and log where they had set-up the machine gun. The enemy was set up in an L-shaped ambush with the hinge at that culvert under the road." Gus pointed back uphill to the improvised fighting positions and then the culvert.

"The team in the drainage ditch there at the road was firing their rocket grenades directly into the front of the first car. I came down the long leg of the ambush firing a silenced round into the head of each bloody carcass beside the machine-gun as I ran by, down this path to the next fighting position. It was the apex, the hinge position. Just to the left side of your wheelchair." Gus rapidly pushed Andy slightly upslope to the next fighting position.

"One of the ambushers was stepping out onto the path," Gus continued. "He was carrying an AK-47 and must have been confused by the strange noises and dazzled by the sudden flames. He tried to raise his assault rifle as I shot him just beneath his nose and followed with a second bullet into his eye socket. Stepping around the body, his partner was looking through the scope of a Russian sniper rifle. He didn't know there was any opposition until I blew three holes into the side of his head." Gus then looked down at his hand as if it were a pistol.

"One round left in the pistol, I slammed a fresh magazine into it, putting the empty magazine in my rear pocket. Running to the front edge of the hinge position, I looked out at the culvert, near the road. I fired six silenced .45-ACP rounds into the two men, one holding two grenades and the other with a fresh rocket in the launcher." Gus had been acting just like he was reliving the action, making hand gestures, ducking and moving like he was in combat.

"I reloaded the pistol and shotgun," he continued. "I then began quietly moving down the trail to the turnoff where we just parked the Suburban. I had no idea if there were more enemy soldiers. There was a van and a Mercedes sedan parked there. No one was with the cars, so I went back and checked each body."

He said to Andy, "I was using Super Vel bullets, hollow-point projectiles; you know the ones that aren't approved by the Geneva Convention. Every headshot seemed to almost explode as the bullet punched through the skull, expanded in the brain and then blew out the far side. I had loaded alternating military buckshot rounds and green flechette shells in the shotgun and each charge clustered into a three or four inch pattern. Both machine gunners were hit in the face by several of my 12-gauge shots. The three men in the lead SIS car looked like crispy critters while George was hit dozens of times by machine-gun bullets and our rear car was starting to burn. I don't think anyone was expecting me to be there. I recognized at least one KGB officer who I had followed in Moscow before reconnecting with Mongolian. Four of the young men were wearing dark red Che

Guevara sweatshirts, almost like uniforms." Gus explained how he had gone back to the Russian's Mercedes and drove back toward Vienna before anyone drove up to the scene.

"I stopped for a coffee in the early morning hours at the first open rural roadside cafe." Gus continued. "In the parking lot I used the dome light to inspect everything I had collected. There was very little identification on the bodies, but the car trunk yielded separate plastic bags with alternate identities. Three were regular West German driving licenses; two of them with police ID's. There were another four East German licenses and Humboldt University ID's with library cards, probably for the Red Army Faction, Baader-Meinhof gang."

Andy said, "Pay attention. You just said there were seven ID's, but only six dead bodies. Where's the seventh man? Surely someone was guarding the Russian vehicles. When you took the Mercedes did you disable the van?"

"I don't remember, I've never thought about it." Gus responded and then thought a moment. "Maybe that's why the Russians have been following me," he continued. "I hid the extra weapons in an old hollow tree near Vienna. On Sunday I crossed back into Czechoslovakia and drove to the job in Prague, getting there by evening." Andy asked what was said in Prague.

"By the next morning, a few people in the chancery building were talking about the events in Austria on Friday, but no one suspected me of any involvement. Unfortunately, I have no idea what the Russians think. I don't remember picking up any information in Austria. However over the next six months the Red Army Faction seemed to go crazy attacking numerous civilian and police targets throughout Germany. They even tried to hijack that Lufthansa plane in the middle of October." They got back in the SUV and started downhill for Salzburg.

119

"Did any of this help?" Andy said.

Gus answered. "No, there's something I'm still missing although you're right the seventh man must have told Moscow that it was me." Gus then said he might have been followed back to Prague.

"Can I ask Mary to help?" Andy asked and Gus said sure.

Arriving in Salzburg they stopped for a late lunch. Andy ordered beer and raised an eyebrow when Gus ordered water. "What's up with the water?"

"After I was fired by the CIA on Halloween day in '77 I sort of went downhill and started drinking too much. I can't handle it so I went cold turkey last week."

Later they continued on back to Bad Tölz. When they arrived, Mary came out and said to Gus, "There're three items on the front porch, one's probably your tuxedo along with a package and a box." Opening the package, he pulled out a shirt, bowtie and vest.

Opening the shoebox Gus looked at a pristine pair of leather dress shoes, Bates low-quarters. The soles were unmarked leather with rubber heels. The unblemished black uppers weren't particularly shiny.

"I have an ammo can with polishing equipment," Andy commented. "There's even mink oil for your running shoes. I guess you know what to do from your time at the Point."

"I'll need to sand the soles and soak them in water. Then I should wear them into town and back out, maybe five kilometers. I probably need to buy a couple of pairs of cotton socks to wear inside the wet shoes."

"I'll also need some fine linen handkerchiefs. Tomorrow morning, I'll run the 10-K course in them. Then, I can use the time tomorrow to re-polish all of my shoes."

"I'll go into town with you for the socks," Mary said. "We can stop for an espresso at a coffee shop I know." She continued on saying to Gus, "I already know Papa always broke in boots by soaking them and walking them dry before he polished them."

13

On the way into town Mary asked, "Why did you start working for the CIA? Last night I discovered all of Papa's friends know you from the Green Berets and they highly respect you. In fact I overheard two retired warrants say you were the best warrior that ever served in the army. Why did you leave active duty and transfer to the reserves."

"It's kind of complicated, I've avoided thinking about why," Gus told her. "However I can say I was disenchanted with the actions of senior army officers in Vietnam. My spotter and best friend persuaded me to leave active duty, get a master's and go to work for an agency dedicated to winning the war. However, it turns out the most of the Ivy League managers at the CIA were left wing liberals. I can't really talk about my time working undercover but it seems like I jumped out of the frying pan and into the fire."

As they walked along the path beside the railroad, a darkened van flew past them on the far side of the tracks. Gus looked over and then commented to Mary, "Those two men looked suspicious, there was a curtain between the front seat and the rear. I also spotted several small observation windows hidden by the letters of the paint scheme. It's supposed to be a Deutsche Telekom van, however they weren't wearing the correct uniforms."

"I didn't notice," Mary replied. "Why did you notice them?"

"Your father scolded me yesterday for not paying attention. I'm trying to get back into a combat mindset, noticing everything and taking mental note of any discrepancies."

"Why do you carry two pistols, one with a silencer?" Mary asked. "Papa told me about your Gladstone and I've noticed your ankle and waist holsters, although with your overall size and "V" shaped torso the holster and scabbards around your waist aren't very noticeable as long as you wear a jacket."

"It's a sound suppressor not a silencer. Since I left the Company, I usually don't carry a gun at all." Gus responded. "I left all my combat guns with a friend in Austria and just picked them up yesterday."

"When I worked for the government, I usually went unarmed when running around during the day. However, I always kept a pistol hidden near work or near my apartment. I only carried the small backup pistol when I was working undercover at night or on the weekend. But, when I was expecting trouble I carried two handguns and a lot of extra ammunition. I was always prepared."

"I enjoy my job building things." Gus said as he looked at Mary. "For the past two years I've been living with the thought there may be a traitor at Langley, but I couldn't say a word to anyone. It's good to talk to someone."

"Do you think the turncoat at the CIA is still there? Could he be the one giving instructions to the men running drugs?" Mary asked. Gus didn't reply, he was just thinking.

It was almost dark by the time they made their way back to the house. The temperature had dropped below freezing. The DT van was parked in the distance with its motor running.

Gus reported his suspicions to Andy and asked how he could get in contact with Mitchell, the chief warrant officer from last night. "We need to set up a rotating watch of armed Green Berets; near the van, not near the house. If they make a move toward the house, we need to seize them."

Andy pointed out his quarters on a map. Gus changed into warm, earth-toned clothes and his work boots, fastened his pistols and ducked across the road into the high weeds, always keeping the house between him and the van.

Once across, he slowly rose and moved toward the cantonment using the trees for cover. He was carrying the shotgun tucked under his arm like a hunter wearing his plain black ball cap.

The next morning, just before 4:00 am, the two watchers got out of their DT van and pulled shortened carbine versions of the new AKS 74U's out of the back. Both men paused to screw long sound suppressors on the short barrels and slip-on brassiere like bandoliers with extra magazines before inserting a rust colored magazine and charging a bullet into the chamber.

As they turned to start for the house, four trained Special Forces warriors rose like wraiths from the back and both sides of the partially concealed van. Tackling each man low and high they smothered both men to the ground, hand cuffing them and shackling leg irons on each assassin. They then searched every pocket and folds in their clothing as two more men went through the van.

The Green Berets bundled them into the back of a military truck that arrived after a radio call. Another pair of men hopped out of a second truck and hooked up the counterfeit DT van to the back of their military tow truck. Both trucks started off to the south.

Gus was watching what was happening from just outside the house still carrying the shotgun. Mitchell and his men had no idea he was their final backstop.

He knew they were taking the men to an old house in the middle of their maneuver acreage. The American agents would question them for the next week. But in all likelihood, the men would turn out to have diplomatic immunity. They were definitely there to assassinate Gus and the Johnsons since they loaded both small-bore assault rifles and attached the sound suppressors in place of the flash hider assembly; both actions illegal in Germany.

Later the next morning after a short nap, Gus removed his still damp shoes from a plastic garbage bag and put them on along with his running clothes. He went downstairs for a glass of water and saw Mary waiting for him.

She was wearing different colored combination of running tights and top, however they were just as revealing. He really liked her. He was also starting to trust her. She was the best looking girl he had ever spent much time with.

"Let's check around the perimeter before we start our run."

"The telecom van is missing." Mary said. "I woke up several times last night worrying about them watching us." Gus didn't say a word.

As the two went behind the old barn, a camouflaged soldier with face makeup stood up and told them, "Everything's clear. Early this morning, we picked up the two in the DT van as they were checking their guns before assaulting the house." With that reassurance, they went for their morning exercise. Gus didn't mention he had been watching everything happening at 4 am.

As they cooled down and walked back to the house, Mary asked about the ambush nearly three years ago. "Papa told me everything the two of you discussed yesterday. He also explained to me why you think there's a Soviet spy at the CIA. Think about driving the Russian's Mercedes back after everything was over." Mary said. "When you got back to your pickup what did you have in each of your pockets? Did you put anything in the company truck?"

As Gus tried to remember what was in each pocket, he realized he had a Zippo lighter in his right pocket along with his Swiss army knife. He remembered worrying that one might scratch the other since he didn't usually carry anything in the same pocket with his knife.

"Mongolian, the defector gave it to me when we met in Prague just before we left," he told Mary.

"When the Russians transferred him back to Moscow he went dark." Mary asked, "Why did he do that. Was it unusual?

"No," Gus responded. "When an officer looses faith in the communist system of government and turns into an agent for the west, he can get paranoid if he is transferred back to Moscow. He probably worried that someone had discovered what he'd been doing. The British Secret Intelligence Service lost all contact and they couldn't get anyone free from their embassy to re-connect. The KGB was following everyone. My old friend George from the SAS had been transferred from Iran to Russia as a driver. He had discovered I was there undercover and had much greater freedom of movement. He covertly brush passed me contact information one evening." Gus then briefly explained what he did in Russia.

"I watched and then snuck into Mongolian's apartment a few days' later while he was at work and searched everything," he explained to Mary. "The KGB had installed microphones in every room, but no video cameras. That evening I was waiting in the street outside his apartment. We went out into one of the parks and talked for hours while we shared a bottle of vodka. Mongolian mentioned that one of his reasons for turning coat was how his bosses treated prisoners during the Vietnam War. He also told me he was a homosexual. He and his special friend had served together in North Vietnam. Although he was assigned to Iran, his friend went to the United States." Mary wanted to know if Gus suspected that he was homosexual and he answered, "Yes".

"He recounted the story of a captured Air America pilot who was finally brought to Moscow for extensive questioning. The Viet Minh identified him because he was carrying an American lighter with his name engraved on it. They sold him to the Russians in exchange for a shipload of weapons. After he gave the KGB everything he had, they executed him. The lighter was the only thing he had left. Mongolian asked me to try and trace his name."

"Did you trace the pilot?" Mary asked. "What was the defector's name? What was the name of his special friend, the other homosexual?"

"I forgot to check. I knew Mongolian's real name but promised to never tell anyone. He did mention that his friend was transferred to Department S in North America. During my contacts and later during the defection, we didn't use any real names."

"Any more contacts?" Mary asked. "Did you ever inspect the Zippo? Could he have hidden something inside it?"

"The British handled him until Prague and no, I didn't look inside. It's in Boise at my grandmother's in the top drawer of my dresser; I took it home that summer on vacation just before my active duty period at Fort Leavenworth.

"Do you believe his story?" Mary asked.

"Why wouldn't I believe him?" Gus replied.

"If your Mongolian was trying to smuggle something into the west and not let anyone know, he would hide it in a lighter and have an innocent third party carry the contraband. Don't tell anyone else about the lighter, not even Papa." Gus raised his eyebrow causing

Mary to repeat. "Don't tell anyone until you have a chance to look in the Zippo. If the Russians find out, I believe they will assault your grandmother's house." Gus shut up since he hadn't thought it through.

"I'll fix us breakfast, and then you can shine your shoes. I'm going to spend the day on a final check of my dissertation. A headquarters clerk is meeting me to make Xerox copies for everyone on my Abschlussarbeit committee. I've written 90-pages and I had to buy a ream of photocopy paper to make five copies."

"I may leave on Monday morning to fly back to the states." Gus told her. "I'm going to try and get on the same Pan Am flight to New York Colonel Bankhead is taking. From New York, I'm going to Boise and take care of a number of things. I have to inspect the lighter. I want to drive back to meet you and Andy when you get to North Carolina."

Mary told him, "The earliest my committee will hold the verbal questioning of my dissertation is the 25th. Papa and I will then need a week to pack and say goodbye to my mother's relatives, so we can't get to Fayetteville before December the 2nd. Our household shipment will take another month or six weeks. By then I'll be in the Army."

"My birthday is the 6th of December," Gus said. "Maybe we can celebrate it together."

After breakfast, Gus changed to a dry pair of socks and got out the old ammo can of polishing gear. He set everything up next to the small stove in the workroom he had stoked before his morning run. Taking two old Kiwi metal lids, he put a few chunks of black polish in one empty lid and put it on the stove to melt. He carried the other one into the kitchen and put a few spoonfuls of water in it, and brought it back to the stove to heat.

He then took the new fine linen handkerchief from the package of three he bought yesterday and rinsed it out. Brushing all the dirt off his first low-quarter, he wrapped the white cloth around two fingers, dipped into the melting shoe wax and started swirling on a superfine coat of polish. It was hazy at first, but he buffed in the very thin coat rather than add more wax. He then dipped some water and polished the black wax. Rather than using a horsehair brush to polish his shoes he always kept his fingers moving in a swirling motion only adding a small amount of melted wax when it was necessary.

After 30 minutes, he picked up a round pencil and boned in a groove where his foot flexed between the toe and vamp. Setting the first shoe on a chair beside the stove, he started on the next. An hour later, while both shoes were drying out, he polished his tasseled loafers and then his work boots. Finally he renewed and water-proofed his running shoes. Getting out the three-ring binder with Title 18 of the US Criminal Code he started studying the hundreds of chapters. He had taken a class at West Point on the Uniform Code of Military Justice and most of those chapters were similar.

Mary came in wearing a robe, her wet hair wrapped in a turban. She inspected his new dress shoes. "They're still not very shiny." Gus couldn't help but stare down the gap when she leaned over. He told her it was only the first layer of a new base. He would have to put on at least a half-dozen more before he was finished.

Later that morning warrant officer Mitchell stopped by and brought them up to date. He first told Gus Colonel Bankhead would see him for an hour just before the start of cocktails at the dining-in ceremony. "Our two detainees are claiming diplomatic immunity and won't say anything else. The bearded one has documents that look sketchy."

After lunch, while resting his shoes, Gus brought in his laundry from the clothesline and started ironing everything, helped by a can of Faultless spray starch. Tonight he needed the spread collar white broadcloth and tomorrow he would wear the button-down white oxford cloth shirt. He continued by pressing his underclothes and new handkerchiefs.

Mary was in the process of collating and binding the newly xerographed pages of her dissertation. She said, "I'm absolutely amazed you also do household chores." Gus explained he had done his own laundry since he went to college. "I learned to iron my underclothes as a plebe."

Taking out his tuxedo and trying it on, he then hung it up for a brushing. He installed the miniature metal combat infantry badge, and below it an unofficial CCN badge from MACV-SOG the military's Studies and Observation Group. Nobody in Germany had a set of SAS Ibis wings.

With Mary coming in and out, Gus mumbled quietly, "When I get to New York I need to go shopping for some clothes. I left most of my work clothes and half-a-dozen dressier outfits in Iran. I don't have much at grandmother's house." Mary had not said a word. Gus realized she wasn't listening.

So Gus asked, "Mary, I have to buy some replacement clothes when I get to New York. I was thinking. Should I also buy a tuxedo?"

"Yes you should," she responded. "Christmas is coming up and I would like you to escort me to any formal parties."

As Mary went back to her thesis, Gus went over to the Special Forces pistol range. Ammunition was free so he emptied and reloaded all his magazines with military target loads. He shot the standard NRA 25-yard targets on the regular pistol range. He fired a box of 50-rounds of standard velocity .22 LR through the Ruger followed by another box of 50 with his 9-mm ASP and finally 50-rounds of .45-ACP.

Gus was surprised when he added up his totals, 1420 out of 1500. Less than half the holes were in the X-ring with the rest 10's and 9's, no flyers. Shooting his target pistols he usually didn't score much higher.

14

J ust before it turned dark Gus drove the black Suburban up to the officers mess. Colonel Bankhead was staying in one of the visitor's double rooms, and he asked him into the adjoining sitting room. He mentioned that his old sergeant now chief warrant officer, Dean Mitchell had told him about some of the things that were happening.

"Tell me about your background from the very beginning at the Point; why did you join the Special Forces?" as he pointed at Gus' class ring with a questioning look.

"I was a rising junior in 1962. General Yarborough came up from Fort Bragg to talk to the plebes and upperclassmen about the new Special Forces on Acceptance Day. President Kennedy had authorized their wearing the new Green Beret less than a year previously. I was just over halfway through my studies for an engineering diploma and the general reinvigorated me. Instead of wanting to quit, I wanted to join the Special Forces. There were a hundred cadets interested in the new unit, but I was one of the half-dozen who knew more than one foreign language." The colonel nodded for him to continue.

"As a freshman I had exempted the Department of Foreign Language requirements by getting a superior rating on the test in French, German, and Russian. My grandmother was a PhD college professor of foreign languages who had taught me for years and made me speak, read and write in each of the three different languages every week." Gus explained.

"During our meeting after his presentation I mentioned my multi-language proficiency and the fact I was a Forest Service smoke-jumper with almost a hundred jumps. General Yarborough wrote down my details and promised he would get me to Fort Bragg next summer after sending me to Ft. Benning for airborne training." The colonel nodded in understanding.

"Looking at my name he suddenly asked me if my father had served in the Army? When I answered he was a West Point officer killed in the Philippines he said, 'I was in the class of '36. In September of 1940 I had just come back from my first assignment with the Philippine Scouts and was working with the parachute test battalion at Ft. Benning. I'm the one who got your father assigned to start-up a parachute company in the Philippine Division.' The next day, I signed up for the new course in Vietnamese being offered that fall." Bankhead commented, "I've heard of your father and his actions with the Philippine Scouts."

Over the next hour, the colonel asked penetrating questions. In some cases, it was almost as if he was aware of a lot more than Gus was. Finally he said, "Even though I retired from the Army in '58, I remember General Yarborough mentioning your name in 1963 after your summer at Bragg. With President Kennedy backing him he was trying to get some future high-ranking officers recruited from West Point."

"Most of our officers including me had come up through the ranks although I became a special advisor to Richard Nixon through all of his elections. For the past four years I've been helping former Governor Ronald Reagan. Tell me about what's happening in Iran?"

"The President made a huge mistake three days ago," Gus said. "My contact in Ankara says he blinked and sent a mild and ineffectual appeal to Ayatollah Khomeini asking that he release the hostages on humanitarian grounds, instead of getting tough. My source told me three hundred mostly peaceful Islamist students were in the initial wave, however they were backed by almost six hundred armed pasdaran warriors. Khomeini was willing to release the hostages the next day but the impotent reply from the United States caused him to delay their release."

"Where did you learn the word pasdaran?" asked Colonel Bankhead. "It's new to me."

"It's a common term in Persian for a Guardian of the Islamic Revolution, in both Fārsi and Turkic although it's spelled slightly different. In other languages they are called Warriors of God or Mujahidin. They're committed Islamic terrorist warriors."

"Can you speak either language?"

"I speak both although I am more fluent in Fārsi since I learned it as a boy from my nanny. She was Jewish and also taught me some basic Hebrew. Both Persian and Turkic are written in and descended from Arabic. You do know that for the past few years, none of the CIA officers in Iran were fluent in any of the native languages. That includes the three captured by the militants." Gus looked at the colonel to make sure he understood the implications.

"I've also heard from some of my friends that the Army, Navy, Air Force and Marines are vying with one another to lead a rescue attempt although none of them have any experience in Iran. They don't have any idea how difficult it will be." The colonel agreed with Gus' statement.

"My friend Warrant Officer Mitchell told me you want to fly back to the states with me tomorrow," commented the colonel. "That's a great idea. You should fly with me on the courier flight to Frankfurt and on to New York on Pan American. I already told him to book you tickets, is First Class OK? I guess you've got the proper passport." Gus immediately agreed.

"I'm meeting on Tuesday morning with my old boss from the OSS, William Cassidy who is also helping with Ronald Reagan's campaign. Can you meet with us to discuss these new developments?" Gus thought about the colonel's need-to-know and then decided he would have to have some more information.

"I won't work for the CIA so I've been commissioned as a Special Agent of Diplomatic Security. Since the KGB has been trying to kill me, I now have the right to wear a pistol."

As he mentioned pistol, he lifted the corner of his tuxedo jacket exposing his concealed .45-ACP. "There also may be drug dealers after my ass so I don't want to take any chances. I think the Mafia tried to blow me up in Italy three days ago. You do know the KGB tried again last night. The officers in Ankara issued me an official shield and ID to go with my black Diplomatic Passport and I've been studying the US criminal code. The Deputy Director in DC will confirm my identity and authority."

"Just whom in Washington are you working with?" asked the colonel. "I was hoping you could keep the Reagan team up to date."

"I can never work directly for the Director of Central Intelligence. Someone has already tried to kill me and I believe the Russians got their information from either Turkish intelligence or the CIA. I'm working with the Station Chief in Ankara, an old OSS hand named Charles Metcalf. John Campbell the RSO in Turkey and Keith

Allison, the Deputy Director of the Security Office in Washington are just as interested in releasing the hostages in the embassy. They also want to discover any worms in the CIA apple. Although I have a problem with the CIA, I'll always help protect the United States."

"I know about Metcalf from the war. In France I worked with the Gaullist FFI and later during Operation Iron Cross, I worked with various Jewish refugees who were fluent in German. You do know I'm Jewish. In London I met Metcalf, and he would have nothing to do with the Free French or the Jews. He upset enough people that he was transferred to China. I don't know if you can trust either man in Turkey." Gus studied the colonel and then nodded.

"I've also reviewed the list of former Green Berets you gave to Mitchell and we need to discuss some of them. I've heard about a small group of rogue actors who have gained a reputation for smuggling drugs, guns, women and money throughout the world."

Gus then went into the details about drug smuggling by the Russians that Berke had given him followed by the limited information from Ed and Derek about the Silk Road smuggling. Finally he mentioned that he had heard the numerous rumors about drugs in Vietnam and later in the United States. "What do you know about these men, their banking and their Mafia connections? Do they work for the Russians?" Gus asked the retired Colonel.

"Richard Nixon started the War on Drugs and created the DEA. We discovered a lot about their banking transactions during his administration. Most of our money leads came from Howard Hughes and his Mormon bankers during the Glomar Explorer/CIA debacle. As soon as they discovered that Nixon was investigating drugs, someone started talking to reporters. The CIA uses a regular bank in Washington for their legal activities. They also have a parallel illegal bank with several branches around the world. It started in Australia early in the Vietnam War, although it now has its headquarters in

George Town the capital of the Cayman Islands. It has branches or offices in Europe, Switzerland, Bahrain and the Far East. It's called the Noggin-Sand Bank. Mike Sand served in the Special Forces and then handled drug shipments from Laos into Vietnam. Frank Noggin is an Australian with close connections to organized crime. Among its officers are a network of US Generals, Admirals and CIA men. Their legal counsel is a former Director of Central Intelligence. They handle most illegal payments for the CIA. They are also the bankers for at least four Mafia families and they're involved in a few illegal transactions for the Russians." As Bankhead listed some of the banking relationships, Gus wrote them down. "Why was this information suppressed?" Gus asked. "With his Watergate troubles a decision was made to cover up all this information. When the Democrats won the presidency in 1976 everything was hidden."

"I only have one more question," the colonel asked. "It's the same one Bill Cassidy from Reagan's campaign asked me earlier today. Why did a highly regarded and decorated West Point graduate leave active duty after four years and go to work for the CIA?"

Gus paused and thought for a moment before he answered. "In Vietnam I was also a sniper," Gus continued. "I was following the advice of my spotter and eventually best friend. You might have known him, he was a Master Sergeant named David Shiner and a dedicated anti-communist."

"I knew him very well," Colonel Bankhead said. "He was one of the founding members of my first team in Germany. We never talked about personal matters or political beliefs."

"He told me I could accomplish twice as much working undercover for the CIA as I ever could with the Army." Gus continued. "However, I must have a master's degree and be recruited as a career operations officer rather than work as a contract paramilitary officer. He then said, 'The CIA is our last hope for anti-communism. They are the future unlike the State Department or most of the other Executive Departments, all of which are riddled with socialist and communist. Also, just in case stay in the Army Reserve.'" Colonel Bankhead laughed when he heard Gus using the exact eastern European accent as David did.

"He had uncovered some information the South Koreans at their Da Nang camp next door were developing. This was before Tet in 1968. They captured a high-ranking Chinese observer to COSVIN and the Koreans weren't telling the Americans or South Vietnamese about him. I'm sure they were torturing him to get information. Apparently there was an internal dispute between the Chinese massive attack plan for Tet and the Russian plan to negotiate a peace."

"David heard that the success of Robert Kennedy in raising money and collecting endorsements were driving LBJ to accelerate his efforts. Johnson's Six Wise Men who were secretly advising the government, along with several State and Pentagon officials were holding secret talks with North Vietnam in Geneva, Switzerland. Johnson was expecting to easily be reelected in November. Within sixty days, his administration was going to withdraw all American troops and turn the south over to a UN coalition for joint admin- istration. In other words, they were going to surrender, just like they finally did in 1975."

"All the insiders working for Nixon suspected what LBJ was planning." Colonel Bankhead said. "There are a few I would like you to meet."

"Master Sergeant Shiner was killed at the end of the Tet Offen- sive in the spring of '68. By then I was disgusted with political actions, which were spinning the truth from the administration and high ranking Pentagon officers. The Pentagon wanted me to go to the Captains Career Course and I wanted to go to graduate school. I discovered that I could transfer to the Reserves and do both."

The dining-in that night included all the active and retired Special Forces officers and warrants from throughout southern Germany. Gus drank soda water on ice and kept his ears open. Everyone was speculating about what was going to happen in Iran and several men mentioned one planning officer from Germany who was at the Pentagon to start integrating the response from the Army with the rest of the services. Apparently there was a good bit of competition between an old assault group called *Blue Light* and Beck's *Delta Force* within the Army.

He overheard officers complaining that Navy SEAL's, Marine Force Recon along with Air Force intelligence were involved in making sure they were included in any plans. Colonel Bankhead had already mentioned that Tehran was within the new US Readiness Command's sphere of influence and not the Army, Air Force or Navy.

RedCom was in the process of organizing a Rapid Deployment Joint Task Force for Middle Eastern Operations under the command of a Marine Corps Lieutenant General. Every officer at the dinner had different ideas of what should happen. Gus kept his mouth shut about Iran and just listened.

Dean Mitchell joined them to talk about the list of soldiers Gus had given them, "Apparently the corrupt soldiers can be divided into two groups; those who started their illegal activities in the Asian Far East and others who were involved in the Bay of Pigs. Many were involved in both events. The two main actions occurred during the late '50s and early '60s. Some of these individuals will do anything to advance their own agenda." He watched Gus to make sure he understood what he was implying.

"Some offshoots are intertwined with organized crime in smuggling heroin into the United States. What originally started as transpacific routes using the bodies of dead soldiers have morphed into Mediterranean transshipments from Afghanistan and Iran through Turkey to Italy and finally to New York. Their newest product is cocaine from Central and South America through Miami, New Orleans and the Mexican border to the northern markets using Latinos from the CIA. These groups of former CIA cowboys are principally involved in gunrunning out of the US and drug transportation back in. Rather than smuggling product in through regular ports, they use private cargo planes and government surveyed routes that are radar-free."

That evening when Gus got back to Andy's, he was already in bed. Mary was listening to a symphony on the radio. Gus sat down and she snuggled right into his arms, kissing and hugging him.

15

Early Monday morning, Gus contacted Berke on the shortwave and told him about the Noggin-Sand Bank. "I've heard from two contacts at the eastern end of the Silk Road." Berke responded. "Each of them says that the Russians are going to invade Afghanistan by Christmas. Apparently the radical Islamic revolution is spreading east from Iran and it frowns on opium production or transportation. The Russians think that once Afghanistan becomes a reliable Marxist Republic, they could attack Iran from the east while Iraq comes in from the west."

Before the sun rose, Gus and Mary once again went for a run on the SF course. Later he, Colonel Bankhead and the pilot took off from Baker Army Airfield, lifting through the patchy fog and rain flying to Rhein-Main Air Base, which shared a runway with Frankfurt-am-Main Airport. An Air Force sedan carried them across to the International Terminal on the north side of the runway, and they walked up the stairs and into the main ticket lobby.

Gus thought, it's pouring and I usually wear an old cowboy hat or my full-brim Fibre-Metal hard hat to keep the rain off, but I abandoned both in Iran. The old black wool baseball cap was too ratty to wear with a tie.

As he shook out his trench coat he said to Colonel Bankhead, "My hair is soaking. I need to get a good hat for rainy weather." The colonel was wearing a dark grey beaver fedora that looked perfect. Realizing that Gus was looking at his hat, "I know where you can buy one of these dress hats in New York. It's a Stetson Imperial and they have them in the hat section of Brooks Brothers."

Walking down to the Pan American ticket desk, they went to the First Class counter where the colonel had return tickets. When Gus stepped up, he showed his black passport and the gold American Express card when she asked for his papers. Inspecting his diplomatic documents, she glanced up and inspected him, his blazer and colorful tie.

Taking out the leather case with his badge and his DS identification, he got them ready as she asked his status. He declared, "I'm an armed special agent carrying a diplomatic pouch."

Diplomatic couriers were not normally armed, so she looked up at him as he opened his DS badge and ID. "I'll call the gate and let them know you are flying armed. The captain will want to interview you since they no longer assign armed sky marshals on our flights. Both of you can wait in the Clipper Club for the flight to be called."

She printed the invoice, ticket, and boarding pass. While Gus signed the payment slip the ticket agent checked-in his Gladstone and duffle. "I've put both of you upstairs in the dozen rows on the top deck, rather than down in the nose. There's also a lounge up there for 1st Class passengers as well as the piano bar downstairs. Our hostess will escort you to the club."

As they were led down the concourse it stopped raining and the sun came out flooding the floor to ceiling windows with light. Several groups of stewardesses wearing brightly colored uniforms walked past chattering in various foreign languages. The cheerfulness was a relief after years of drab people behind the Iron Curtain and in Middle Eastern countries. A half-hour later the Pan Am captain came into the club and greeted both men. After Gus introduced Colonel Bankhead, he moved into a private room with the captain. "Let me see your ID. Is your firearm safe?" the captain asked.

Gus showed him the badge and ID." The pilot said, "I don't see many of those badges. They usually don't send an armed DS special agent even with highly classified material." Gus then showed him his pistol. "It's a Colt Commander with a round in the chamber, but the hammer is resting on a safety block that only moves when I pull the trigger, cocking the pistol and firing a bullet. It's loaded with hollow point ammunition."

"I assume you know how to use it? Why does the barrel stick out and have a crosshatched fitting over those threads," the pilot asked in curiosity.

"The threads are for a silencer. I have one in my briefcase." His answer dumfounded the pilot. Gus ignored the question about his competence.

Going aboard with the first group, they walked up the circular stairs and through the upper deck lounge to their seats. He was sitting in the right hand aisle seat of the upper emergency row, with its expansive legroom. Seatback trays would be too far forward to reach so the seats duplicated the first row with armrest trays. The colonel had a window seat on the left side two rows up.

The entire upper level of the 747 was decorated with a bright nautical theme while the seats were red and blue leather. Their perky stewardess came down the aisle in her military looking tan uniform and asked if she could help them with their overhead baggage. She glanced at his blazer, trousers and silk tie before looking down at his polished work shoes.

Gus had both Halliburton aluminum briefcases and the longer diplomatic pouch, with his extra firearms, suppressors and his shotgun broken into two parts. He thanked her and said, "I can take care of this myself. Please make sure other passengers don't try to use this overhead. Is there anybody sitting beside me?"

"The ticket agent is trying to make sure your companion seat is empty."

The upper deck filled with passengers, mostly comfortable German businessmen, although there were a few attractive young ladies among them. An Air Force Lieutenant Colonel took a seat on the other side of the emergency row and slid over to the window.

Major Boris entered the dark granite main entrance into the KGB headquarters, the Lubyanka in Moscow just before noon. He was having lunch with his father in a few minutes. The Major General's conference room was just down the beautiful parqueted third floor hallway from the Chairman's suite. All the principal offices overlooked the square and statue of Felix Dzerzhinsky, the Polish nobleman who became head of the Cheka. Making his way through two security checks, he met his father in the small conference room adjacent to his slightly larger office. The general was in charge of the Second Chief Directorate; active measures, counter-intelligence and internal political control.

"I was with the team from our embassy in Ankara when we recovered Georgi and the bodies of the rest of our men in Tahir Pass. It was handled covertly since the Turks furnished the trucks and allowed one of our planes to land at their nearby airbase."

"I'm assigning you an additional dozen men. I want you to handle the entire Silk Road Operation. With the extra money earned by your brother from the cocaine now coming up from South America, we are completely paying for the annual cost of running the KGB. In

1973 with the drawdown in Vietnam we lost our most lucrative source of income and we're just now recovering." Boris nodded his head in understanding. Americans bought drugs and the profits helped assure their own destruction. Capitalism would fail from greed.

"What are we going to do about this former American spy?" Boris asked his father. "Our turncoat in Ankara said that the small American counter-narcotics team working out of Tabriz had intercepted some chatter from my men about the encrypted documents copied by Konstantin Garin; they called him Mongolian. They reported to our man that Gus Smith might know something. I had my Mafia contact try and eliminate the problem in Italy. Ed Warren and his mentor were both killed; unfortunately Gus Smith survived. The girl is the only one from the original team still alive. Should we kill her too?"

"I'm sending your number two to the US today to kill Smith," the general told his son. "He's meeting with the top Cuban assassin in Miami before they intercept our target at his grandmother's in Idaho. I'm leaving the backup plan to your brother in New York. If there are some mythical encrypted documents, it will take the Americans years to decrypt them."

The plane took off at 10:30 and the flight was uneventful. Gus spent the time studying his three-ring binder filled with criminal statutes. The rest of the passengers were watching the movie, *Apocalypse Now*. It gave him a few flashbacks and a lot more laughs at the stupidity of Hollywood. He knew the real officer portrayed by Marlon Brando playing Colonel Kurtz.

Rather than be pinned down by the retractable tray, he extended the one in the next seat and ate his lunch, one dish at a time as he continued to read. The plane was scheduled to land at JFK airport.

He thought he should call Keith Allison as soon as he cleared customs. His appointment with Colonel Bankhead and William Cassidy wasn't until tomorrow morning for breakfast. This afternoon he could go to Brooks Brothers and shop for clothing. He would take the Eastern shuttle from LaGuardia to DC on Wednesday morning, meet with Allison and be back that evening. His new suits should be ready by then.

The 747 landed and taxied up to Worldport where he and the colonel were in the middle of the disembarking pack of 1st Class travelers, clutching their immigration and customs forms. Waiting in the official lane, Gus stepped up to the immigration kiosk when it cleared.

The senior officer inspected his diplomatic passport and said, "This is a new passport, there're not many entry or exit stamps and it was issued in Ankara last week." Gus first showed him his badge and ID from DS, and then took out his civilian passport, the one with 72-pages.

He said, "I often work undercover and this is my other passport. You can see I escaped from Iran last week, the day the embassy was seized."

"Are you armed? Is that a diplomatic pouch you're carrying?"

"Yes and yes. In addition to several additional weapons, I'm carrying top secret-eyes only information." Gus watched while the officer pressed a button under his desk. A customs official hurried over and the immigration officer told him, "He's an armed Diplomatic Security special-agent with an eyes-only pouch. Please escort him through."

Once he cleared the quarantine area, Gus called Keith Allison in Washington and reported in. He said he would be on the early shuttle Wednesday morning. Allison interrupted and said, "I'll meet you for breakfast in New York Wednesday morning. I don't want to talk about this in DC."

He then met the colonel outside baggage claim and they shared a limousine to the Hilton New York on the Avenue of the Americas. It was raining outside, a steady drizzle. Most of the overpasses hadn't been painted since the Eisenhower administration and the metal was scabby with huge patches of rust. Everything was coated with graffiti, not only the roadway but also every subway car and bus. Every vacant patch of land had high weeds.

After checking in, putting the diplomatic pouch into a safety deposit drawer, he followed the bellhop with his bags to the room. He washed up and walked the twenty floors downstairs. He asked the doorman if he could borrow an umbrella to walk to Brooks Brothers main store. He was wearing his trench coat and the now polished Wolverine 1,000 mile half boots. They did a great job shedding rain. The doorman offered to hail a taxi, but he wanted to stretch his legs with a brisk walk. "It's almost ten blocks walking, you need to plan on taking a taxi back if you buy anything." Gus thought ten blocks is only a mile.

The Brooks Brothers doorman directed him to the elevators under the clock. The gentleman's suit department was on the 3rd floor where a really nice older man asked if he could help, noticing his trench coat, blazer, slacks, and silk tie along with the work shoes.

Gus decided to try for some sympathy, "Last week I had to leave almost all my clothes behind, when I fled Iran. I only have this outfit I bought in Switzerland a few days ago. Can you help me?" Gus realized the clerk was making notes, so he continued.

"I need several complete sets of new clothes including shoes and accessories. I'll also need a tuxedo to wear tomorrow night. We may need to alter standard suits rather than custom tailored ones. Can you finish the suits in time? I also need a suitcase and a garment bag."

Gus realized that he was speaking too fast and his thoughts were running together.

The older man was scribbling notes as fast as he could. Pausing, Gus then mentioned that he wanted classical clothing, not the most current fashion with pointed collars, wide ties, or this year's color.

"If we combine standard tux components, we can finish a dress outfit by tomorrow." The clerk explained as he crossed the letter t. "The tuxedo set we have on sale comes with a summertime white dinner jacket in addition to its light-weight black one. Our fall rack suits are medium weight jackets and trousers and some of the blue and gray colors include waistcoats. The ready-made suits can be altered by Wednesday noon; the custom tailored ones will take a few weeks. Everything else should be at your hotel later today."

Gus had just nodded OK when he remembered the backless vest of his rented tuxedo interfered with his pistol. "Can you make sure the tux has a couple of cummerbund sets?"

The gentleman led him to the fitting area where they asked him to remove his trench coat, and jacket. He was still wearing his Colt pistol in the waist holster and the ASP in his ankle holster. The clothier was a little surprised when the trousers waistband were so small and his chest was so large; he said, "You definitely need a custom tailored athletic cut. The only thing on the rack that's large enough for your chest is the tuxedo set and a solid navy blue suit without a waistcoat. I can also fit you with a sports coat. Your jackets are much larger than your trouser waistbands, like a tall quarterback. You should order a second medium-weight dinner set that fits better, probably some business suits as well. I can make all the custom tailored jackets with enough room on the left and right for a pistol in either a shoulder holster or a strong-side belt scabbard."

After reviewing styles and then material he started to try on different custom suit parts. They included blue and gray three-piece suits with subtle pin stripes. There also was a Lovat tweed three-piece made with olive green wool. It was Scottish looking with its thin oxblood under-pattern. While he tried on suits, the clothier sent a porter over to a nearby luggage shop to buy a wood framed leather Pullman suitcase and a leather and nylon garment bag.

After fitting the suits they went downstairs to pick out shirts, ties and several pocket squares. They then went to the shoe department where he suggested a pair of handmade cordovan oxblood wingtips after Gus told him, "I have new pairs of black dress shoes and tasseled loafers but I didn't want to get them wet."

They rounded out his purchases with socks, underclothes, belts, and braces. A few years ago, Gus had gotten into the habit of wearing both a belt and suspenders to help carry the extra weight of his pistol and spare magazines.

The store promised to pack everything but the tailored items in the new suitcases and send them to the hotel. They would have the tux ready by tomorrow evening. The rack suit and sports coat would be ready by Wednesday.

Gus snapped his fingers and said, "I almost forgot. Colonel Bankhead suggested I get a few fedoras' here for rain or snow. I guess I need an umbrella too since I'm borrowing one from the Hilton.

The clothier asked, "Will you always be wearing your khaki Aquascutum or will you be buying a dark overcoat."

Gus answered, "I'll normally wear the khaki. Do you think I need to order an overcoat?" He was surprised that the fitter knew the brand of his trench coat. As the fitter whipped out his tape and measured Gus' head he said, "Yes, you need a below-the-knee length one." He showed Gus several choices in black, charcoal and navy.

"In addition to a dressier overcoat you need several Stetson Imperial hats. Your hat size is big, a 7-3/4. I need to check our stock.

One should be silverbelly colored, another should be a black-on-black and then you'll need two more. A taupe one and another that's mink colored, both with wider black grosgrain ribbons. Since your suits are dark colors, they will work well with a dark overcoat or the Khaki trench coat. Why don't you go ahead and also order a summer Panama fedora. A supreme quality Montecristi will take six-months to deliver. I'll include a dressier black wool overcoat in addition to a dark maroon, grey check and a new plaid scarf."

"Get me a double breasted overcoat and include the scarves. I'll also need to add gloves," Gus said.

"Do you need extra gloves, maybe thin cabretta driving/shooting ones? Some of the items may take several weeks. Do you want us to hold them or deliver them?" Gus said to go ahead and include a thin shooting set and some warmer gloves with cashmere or fur lining.

"I'll call you about final fitting and delivery," he said.

Gus always liked to scout any city where he was staying for main streets, bridges, trains, buses and airplanes. During his years in college further up the Hudson, he knew his way around NY City but he used the trip to the clothier to walk around Grand Central Terminal and then back to Bryant Park where he took the F line up to 57th Street and over to the hotel.

As soon as he got back he called Idaho and talked to his uncle, discovering he was going to be at the governor's announcement tomorrow night. He would pick him up later to fly back to Boise.

That evening he and the colonel went out to a new west coast seafood restaurant just down the street where he had a green salad, sautéed fish, and asparagus but no potato or bread. After dinner, he unpacked his new clothes, removed the tags and pins and then sent everything out for laundering. He immediately fell into a deep sleep since it was now 4:00 am in Germany.

16

G us woke early and walked downstairs to the exercise room to use the various resistance-training machines, ending with a 5-mile jog on the treadmill. It didn't feel as good as natural exercise. Upstairs he called a friend in Pakistan to confirm his information about Afghanistan.

By the time Mr. Cassidy arrived from his office just four blocks south, he was ready for their breakfast in Colonel Bankhead's suite. He was surprised when two more men joined them. Cassidy introduced them as Colonel Edwin Messer, the governor's campaign Chief-of-Staff and Richard Allenby his national security consultant.

"Colonel Messer is in the Military Intelligence Reserve and has a top-secret clearance. So does Allenby who served as the senior advisor for Nixon and Ford's National Security Council. I understand the Governor and his wife Nancy are upstairs in the Presidential Suite working on his speech for tonight."

Cassidy then asked Gus to introduce himself and give everyone a brief summary of his training and experience leading up to the action in Iran. Gus started with his background.

Throughout his fifteen-minute exposition, he had to stop and answer numerous questions. In particular he had to explain why he left the active army for graduate school and then joined the CIA as a covert agent. Their second area involved questions about the Halloween Massacre and why the CIA released him.

They then discussed the events that occurred in Iran and the Russian reactions in Turkey and Germany. They were also puzzled by the Italian bombing, asking what he knew. No one could understand why the Mafia was trying to kill him. Was someone high up in the CIA working with the Russians and the Mafia? Was there more than one turncoat?

Allenby finally asked, "What's in it for Governor Reagan? How can we use this information?"

"There are several different issues," responded Gus. "One involves the traitors within the American government and the second is the hostages in Iran and our exploding problems in the Near East. Colonel Bankhead knows both of my contacts in Ankara. I've already told him the president blinked when he politely asked Ayatollah Khomeini to release the diplomats on humanitarian grounds."

He went on to explain that unless the government came up with a successful rescue plan, the hostages wouldn't be released until the next president takes office and it wouldn't be the former Governor of Georgia."

"Based on what I know about the CIA and Pentagon planning, their rescue plan won't be timely and it will probably be too complicated to be successful." Gus continued with his explanation. "The Israelis successfully planned and executed the release of 100 hostages during the Entebbe raid just over three years ago. It took them less than a week. None of the ultra-liberals in this government will use the Israelis to help solve the problem." As Gus looked around the room, he realized all four men agreed with his assessment.

"We have a much bigger third problem that nobody is aware of; I believe the Russians are going to invade Afghanistan before the end of the year. The result of this mess will be a huge problem for the current Democratic administration."

No one said a word for a few seconds; suddenly everyone had questions and something to say about Gus' revelations. They discussed these issues for another half-hour. Finally Bankhead said, "What about your first problem with the Russians and the CIA?"

"I'm meeting Keith Allison tomorrow morning here at the hotel," Gus said. "I'm going to have to work with Diplomatic Security or the FBI since I won't work with the CIA directly. Unfortunately, the Diplomatic Office of Security can't let the Secretary of State know what they are doing since he's an anti-war dove. Allison can't even bring me to Washington as long as someone might find out."

Richard Allenby then said, "You can probably trust the current National Security Advisor who is almost the exact opposite of the Secretary or the other peaceniks within the Democrat administration. Have your uncle contact him. Richard Knowles is one of our top financial supporters, although he also gives money to selected democrats. He'll be here tonight for the kick-off speech."

"Why don't you come up to the pre-speech reception with your uncle," said William Cassidy. "I'll introduce you to the governor. All of us are going up for lunch where we'll talk to him about the hostages, potential CIA turncoats and your new information about the Russian plans for Afghanistan. Will you keep us in the loop as far as future plans?"

Before he left, Colonel Bankhead took him to the side and said, "I've talked to the Pentagon about Sergeant Major Johnson's daughter. The residency program at Ft. Bragg's Womack Hospital is in Family Medicine. They have a much more appropriate residence fellowship at Walter Reed Army Institute of Research leading to a second doctorate, a PhD in Infectious Diseases, Tropical Medicine and Epidemiology. There is only one opening at a time and the current MD fellow won't finish until this coming June. I then talked to the commanding general at Walter Reed. He had already studied her resume and was planning on contacting her before this summer. When I told him about her connections and the fact she was joining the Army in January, he said he would be pleased to accept Dr. Mary Johnson as their next scholar when she graduates from her basic medical course at Sam Houston." The colonel wrote the name of the personnel officer and his number on a Hilton pad and then added a second number. "It's for the general at the Forest Glen Annex near the Capital Beltway." Gus wrote down the number and asked a few questions.

"I've also talked to Colonel Beck and he is expecting you at Fort Bragg as soon as you can get there. I wrote down his home phone number. I don't know if you will be working out of New York, DC or North Carolina but he and Dick Mead are expecting you to give them all the information you have. You are the only former NOC who's still sober, knows Teheran and the embassy, has knowledge of northern Iran and also knows the language."

"I've been warned by the station chief in Ankara to be very careful in passing information on to the Special Forces operation at Fort Bragg," Gus warned. "Apparently most of the various administration officials are arguing against using facilities in Turkey or troops from Israel. Even though the Israelis have the most experience in releasing hostages held by Islamists. Of course the navy wants to fly everyone in from the Indian Ocean, and the Air Force is insisting that everyone use their airplanes. Senator Glynn and the Marines will probably insist on everyone arriving in spaceships."

"There's a real disconnect in the Near East sections of State and the CIA between Israel and the Muslim countries." Colonel Bankhead admitted. "Some Americans support the Jews and other *Oil Men* support the Arabs. I've even heard we have one group that supports Black September and the PLO against the various Israeli paramilitary units. I suspect your CIA person in Ankara does not work well with Israel. I'll talk to some of my contacts including the former Secretary of State and get you some names in Israel. They know more about Iran than anyone in the United States. In the meantime tell Colonel Beck what he needs to know. I trust him."

Walking down to his regular hotel room, Gus called Mary in Germany and brought her up to date without using any of the words that might spark an international listener to eavesdrop. When she heard about the position in DC she asked his opinion.

Gus said, "Andy will always be welcome into the SF retirement community at Bragg, however you need to think about what you want for the future, family medicine or research in infectious diseases and tropical medicine." He gave her the name of the personnel officer at the Pentagon.

The weather had cleared overnight and it was a beautiful late-fall day; sunny, windy with the temperature just hovering above freezing. He thought he would walk down to the far end of Central Park, loop down the west side to the Battery and back up the east side. Maybe he would stop and buy a book to read. Afterward he might eat a salad.

He changed from his blazer outfit into blue jeans, black turtle-neck, SAS commando sweater, trail-runners and the trench coat. He still wore his backup 9mm ASP and his .45-ACP. Since he was walking through several sketchy neighborhoods, he also carried his Randall knife in its small-of-the-back sheath. With no shirt pocket he put his badge case and ID in the inside pocket of his trench coat. Going downstairs he firmly fixed the comfortable, but ratty black cap on his head. The only fedora Brooks Brothers had in his size was a dressy silver-belly Stetson so he left it in the room.

As he walked, he tuned his mind to his old training about moving through a foreign city, recalling in bits and pieces almost everything he had been taught about defensive observation. He was starting to see, hear and smell everything occurring in front and behind him as he walked. He noticed at least a dozen NY cops looking him over and deciding they didn't want to ask him questions. He was too big, too muscular and most likely in law enforcement, causing them to ignore the telltale signs he was carrying more than one weapon.

The few obvious criminals and one gang of youngsters almost always turned around and walked in the opposite direction. Gus realized his hat was doing more than keeping him warm; he looked like he was undercover. Even though his stubble-beard was growing out and filling in the space between his chin, sideburns and mustachios.

When he got back, he walked up to the room to pee and drink a glass of water. His blazer outfit and tan trousers had been picked up for cleaning. A tailored tuxedo and dress shirt was in a bag on the bed along with a heathery Harris Tweed jacket and light-brown slacks. The store had dry-cleaned both before sending them over. New clothes that hadn't been cleaned usually had sizing chemicals present that made him itch. The attached note said his tailored blue suit would be finished tomorrow morning.

It was their best tuxedo assembled from standard components. The notched lapel coat was an extra-large size and there was more than enough room for his pistol and extra ammo in the large cummerbund. Of course the trousers had a much smaller waist and long inseam. It included two bow tie sets, a solid black and a maroon polka dot along with an onyx/gold stud and cufflink set. He already had a few other sets at his grandmother's. He picked out the black cummerbund to wear with his fresh dress shirt tonight. He didn't want to garner attention so he wouldn't wear any weapons to the Grand Ballroom. After eating a small salad, he called Boise to confirm his uncle's arrival, 6:00 pm eastern time. The reception started at 7:30 so they wouldn't have time to go to dinner.

Gus polished his low-quarters and then read some in his new book *Shibumi* by someone named Trevanian. It was interesting, although somewhat amateurish in its depictions of international spy craft and improbable in the Japanese/Russian/American plot. He just wished he could be as accomplished as Nicholai Hei-the main character, was with women. At 6:30 his uncle called.

Gus went up to his uncle's room a few minutes later. He and Richard talked while he was changing for the reception. First, Gus gave him a copy of the code number for the safe deposit box in Zurich. "I already explained the difficulty of what to do about the gold and cash we got from the Shah," his uncle Dick started to explain. "None of the executives at MJ wants it back in the US. They're giving it to the two of us so we're going to use the money and gold for other projects overseas. If anything happens, we're responsible. They agree we need to set up a company in Europe with you owning half while I own the other half, maybe through a family trust. We'll talk more in Boise next week."

His uncle agreed to postpone his appointment with the National Security Advisor since he didn't want to interfere with anything Director Allison was planning. He would fly down to Washington Wednesday morning and stop back in the afternoon to pick up Gus and fly back to Boise.

Upstairs, since Gus wasn't wearing his Army decorations, he didn't attract attention. He could pass for a tall waiter wearing his plain tuxedo. While his uncle circulated, talking to half-a-hundred important guests. Gus stayed in a corner with his soda water on ice.

William Cassidy and Ed Messer came over and took him and his uncle to meet the Governor with the proper whispered explanations as to who-was-who to both Governor and Mrs. Reagan.

She talked to him for a few minutes. Gus could see she had a much better grasp of what a unique opportunity he represented for them attaining the presidency. By the time the speech and post-activities were over, it was past 11:00 pm so Gus excused himself and jogged up the stairs and went to bed.

17

The next morning he was up at 5:00 am and went for a full speed 10K run around the perimeter of Central Park and then back to the exercise room for a half hour workout. Gus felt great after the exercise. Weighting in after the full resistance progression, he was at his target.

He was aware that a car with two men followed him all the way, stopping every few hundred meters to allow him to draw ahead. They were obviously agents in an almost new radio car. To help them, he ran with the traffic going out Central Park West and returning on 5th Avenue.

Gus dressed in the grey slacks and his black leather blazer, with both firearms. As he went up the stairs, he recollected, "My camel-skin black leather sports coat fits perfectly, no longer a little tight, it's broken-in and twice as comfortable in cooler or windy weather. In Boise I have some fatigue jackets and a leather flight jacket. Of course I also have the trench coat and new overcoat for really cold temperatures.

He had arranged to have breakfast, coffee and juice in one of the 33rd floor executive meeting rooms. There was a knock at the door and Gus let three men into the suite. Two of them had followed him this morning, so he greeted them first and turned to the third man saying, "Hello Keith. We haven't seen each other since 1972 when we both worked for the CIA." Pointing to the chafing dishes he offered everyone breakfast.

"Let me introduce two of my special agents in New York," Director Allison said. "They assured me you ran around Central Park faster than anyone else out exercising this morning. The taller one is Diplomatic Security Special Agent Derek Lambert and the second is FBI Special Agent Kenneth Cox. They both work for a covert counterintelligence section here in New York keeping an eye on UN spies." Gus explained how he was open until afternoon, but his uncle was flying back to Boise with him later.

There was another knock at the door and Allison motioned for one of his men to open it, "I would like you to meet the DEA Assistant Administrator for Intelligence-Narcotics and Transnational Crime, Don Reilly. I believe you already know Dedee Anderson who actually works for the State Department Bureau of Intelligence." Allison introduced his counterpart and the girl accompanying him. "They flew up on the shuttle after me."

"There was a four-person section working out of Tabriz," Dedee started to explain. "We suspected that Russian KGB agents were escorting opium along the old Silk Road from Afghanistan to Turkey and on to the Mafia in Sicily so we moved a small intelligence electronic monitoring station into the old consulate. Ed was a former DEA agent who trained and then transferred into the CIA's Narcotics Intelligence Unit while Derek was the DS Special Agent with authority overseas. I represented State Department Intelligence and John was an electronic specialist from the National Security Agency.

All four of us spoke Russian in addition to other languages but we sent everything electronic we scooped up directly to the satellite. We were also watching you at the Khoda Bridge jobsite since you were just across the river from a twelve-man unit of KGB Spetsnaz who usually escorted opium shipments through Azerbaijan and Armenia. Several years before we had been given a brief heads-up by MI6 about Russian drug documents promised them by their defector called Mongolian; we had been told his Russian name was Konstantin Garin. Almost two weeks ago some Russian couriers mentioned the microdot film.

Allison then started to explain why he had brought in the special agents from New York. "Their joint section evolved from the old Venona Project, a thirty-seven year effort to decrypt, decode and exploit messages sent by Soviet Intelligence agencies. It includes mostly FBI agents, a few of my men, a couple of CIA and some DIA officers and more NSA agents. My men are responsible for counter espionage at US embassy properties overseas, however we are also responsible for protection of UN and foreign dignitaries here in the United States. The FBI is responsible for counterintelligence in America, while the NSA and DIA helps us decrypt coded messages. The CIA's second largest secret facility is in the Post Office tower across from the World Trade Center but I've told no one there what's happening." He paused waiting for Gus to indicate that he understood.

"Yesterday, I met with the Directors' of the FBI and DEA. Later I got together with the Vice Admiral commanding the National Security Agency. I got all of them to approve this mission. The NSA Director called the Assistant to the President for National Security Affairs and got his verbal go-ahead. The President's man wants copies of anything we develop to cross his desk."

As he paused, Gus motioned with his hand and stated. "I remembered the object that I have. I believe it's what the Russians are trying to get their hands on it."

Allison stopped and stared directly at Gus saying, "Go on."

"The Russian defector I knew as Mongolian gave me a Zippo lighter just before I escorted him across the Iron Curtain. It supposedly belonged to an Air America pilot who was tortured and executed by the KGB. I don't smoke and never checked it out. It's in the top drawer of my grandmother's in Boise."

"Get the number," Allison said to Cox as he went over and picked up the phone taking a booklet out of his jacket. Calling a new number, he handed it to the director. "Is this the field office in Boise? I want to talk to the Special Agent in Charge. I don't care what time it is. I am the Director of Diplomatic Security. How many men are in the office right now? I see, have the SAIC call me at this number immediately," reading the number off the table pad. "I'm in Suite 3305."

Turning to Gus he asked him to write down the house address where the lighter was now. "The special agent in charge works out of Salt Lake City. There's only one man in Boise right now, so I'll send some men from the FBI's Salt Lake field office to keep an eye out."

Turning to Lambert and Cox he said, "You two fly out to Boise and guard the house." The phone rang and Allison picked it up, "I know what time it is in Salt Lake. The director has put me in charge of this operation. You will immediately get someone in Boise over to 1121 North 8th, use the State Police if you have to. Cover the front and back."

Listening for a minute he continued, "Our agent's grandmother and her companion live there so don't bother them. But be aware, there is a potential for Russian assassins to show up. Her grandson and two of my special agents from New York will be there as soon as they can. In fact I'm sending my two men from here on the next commercial flight. Pick them up in Boise and have an extra car or two for them. The grandson will follow on the MJ corporate jet later today. He's the only one I want to go into the house. What do you mean bullshit, our agent has already killed eight KGB officers in the past week."

"You know I didn't kill all eight Russians," Gus said as Allison hung up the phone.

"No, I understand Berke Demir says that he only wounded two and you killed all of them with head shots. In addition, two days later you killed another two terrorists in Italy, don't forget the sixteen Iranian terrorists. I heard you killed twelve of them."

Turning to the two special agents who were listening with great interest, "Get out to LaGuardia and catch the next plane. You'll probably have to go through Salt Lake to get there. The three of us are going to stay here and review the various Federal laws our newest special agent needs to know. He already knows twice as much as you two do about shooting, unarmed combat, and spy stuff. In fact I suspect you're just like me, you've never shot anybody in combat."

Gus called downstairs and talked to his uncle Dick about how he was going to rush the tailoring. Could he fly him to Boise instead of Washington?

18

L ate Wednesday afternoon, the large Grumman Gulfstream II landed at the Boise airport and taxied to the MJ hanger. Gus and his uncle were among the dozen construction men flying back from the east coast almost filling the fourteen seats.

MJ used its two jets and four multi-prop planes to fly back and forth to most of their North American construction sites and none of them had fancy interior finishes. Waiting outside the terminal office were a 15-passenger yellow-brown van and a white Suburban. "I see executives don't have to drive mustard colored vehicles," Gus said to his uncle.

On the drive north into town he thought about his grandparents, Gus and Heddy who had met and married in Paris during the First World War. Since his grandfather was away at the Second World War when he was born and his grandmother was a college instructor, his aunts' and his nanny raised him. Rachel was a Jewish refugee from Persia sponsored by his grandmother.

After the war his Aunt Jane married Dick Knowles and Aunt Gay married a JAG lawyer who was now sitting on the Idaho Supreme Court. Gus had six cousins, three from each aunt.

Grandmother Heddy still lived in the large 1889 two-story house on 8th Street, accompanied by her companion and friend Rachel. It was originally one of the rural clapboard farmhouses with pastures out back in the north end of Boise. The developing neighborhood ended up a part of Hyde Park just up the street from the Fort Street Marketplace and only a few blocks from the high school.

Gus commented to his uncle as they crossed the Boise River, "There's snow on the mountains to the north, overlooking the city. They look like they're on fire with the orangey-yellow setting sun reflecting off them."

The station wagon dropped his uncle at the main offices and then took Gus on to his grandmother's house. He noticed a plain green Dodge four-door was parked just down the street with Cox, the FBI man. Waving, he assumed someone else was in the back alley.

Grabbing his bags and skipping up the three steps to the wide front veranda, he went in and shouted for his grandmother and then for Rachel. Both came out of the front library, the room his grandmother used as an office. It had books spread everywhere and a small coal fire was burning in the fireplace.

He kissed her first and then his old nanny. Both of them were gushing with questions. "I'm here to visit for a few days. First I have to go upstairs to the bathroom and then check something in my room. I'll be back in a minute, why don't you start a pot of coffee on the electric stove."

He specified the appliance since there was still an original Victorian cast-iron cook range in the kitchen in addition to the twenty-year old electric stove. They probably had a fire going in the range for the heat on this freezing November day. The whole house was normally heated with steam from an old coal fired furnace in the basement. Its huge brick chimney rose through the middle of the staircase along with the steam pipes, completely enclosed within plaster walls. There were another four fireplaces along the perimeter walls. The house was rectangular with two-and-a-half stories above the full basement. The two main floors had four large bedrooms and two smaller rooms on either side of the stairwell. There was a full height extension in the rear housing the country kitchen, scullery and pantry on the ground floor with a fifth bedroom, bathroom and closets above it on the second. Firing-up the old furnace and fireplaces called for constant fuel replenishment. The furnace must not be working since it was drafty and cold in the house.

Running up the wrap-around Victorian oak stairs and then the attic steps, he walked into his room and opened his dresser drawer. There was the full-sized zippo lighter with its engraving cutting through the plating into the brass base. It said Hampton Cudbow in cursive, followed by block script underneath saying Flying Tigers.

Pulling the lighter apart and studying the insides he realized most of the felt was replaced with tightly rolled strips of small film. He went across the workroom to use the water closet and washed his hands and then his face in the freezing water of the small lavatory.

Back downstairs he led his grandmother and Rachel into the library and sat both of them down while he explained why he was there. He didn't mention any of the dangerous events that had recently occurred. After answering dozens of questions Gus changed the subject.

"Do you still have a friend in the photography section of Fine Arts at Boise State? Could you call and ask him to pick me up and make copies of these microfilms? Maybe in 30-minutes, I really need to do this tonight." He showed them the tightly rolled film as he explained.

Then he asked, "Grandmother, could you go next door to call? Someone could be listening in on our phone line."

"Does it have anything to do with the policemen who have been outside for the past few hours," Rachel asked. "I've seen local cruisers, the state police and several unmarked cars changing shifts every four hours."

"The Russians and certain traitors will do anything to get their hands on this film," Gus told them. "I asked for the FBI to protect you. I'm not sure I can trust some of the people I'm working with, so I want my own copy. When I get back from the university I want to talk with both of you about my future plans. I'm going up to change into something warmer and less noticeable."

In the college lab as they started to inspect the three rolls of films, the professor told Gus, "These rolls of 35mm negatives were filled with microdot images and then processed. There are multiple pages on each exposure. There must be over 6,000-pages of documents. I'm going to have to print three reams of photocopy paper with the multiple images on each page. Even then you'll need a magnifying glass to study each document."

"Can you make me four copies of the actual photographic film?" Gus asked. "You keep one. Sometime next week you can make me individual paper copies all six thousand images."

The professor answered as he studied the images through a loupe, "The original three film rolls are 35mm acetate and it looks like they are slightly deteriorating. Look it's stamped TACMA along with what looks like Cyrillic characters. I should make the copies using the more modern Kodak polyester which is much stronger." Gus didn't say anything but he knew Tasma produced black & white film at Factory No. 8 in Kazan, Russia.

167

After making the film duplicates the art teacher started making contact copies. As he looked at each sheet spitting out of the processor, Gus said to the professor, "There's a coded page that is almost always followed by several pages of unencrypted top-secret American documents. The code is all numerals, grouped into six digits, a pause followed by another group of six until the end of the message. Most of the pages are a few dozen groups, however there are a few multiple page messages."

The professor was studying the same documents and said, "Notice all of the earlier American documents were originally photos taken with a small camera like a Minox, although the second and third roll are mostly photocopies. Someone has then reduced them to micro size and transferred the pages to the photographic film. Only specialized equipment can reduce a page this small."

That night he slept poorly in his extra-long single bed. He remembered when his grandmother got it. He was fourteen and had outgrown his regular length single.

Around three in the morning, something woke him. There wasn't a sound from around the house even though the window was cracked open an inch for ventilation. It was below freezing outside but the wind wasn't blowing. He started thinking the Russians knew almost every move he made; maybe they knew he was in Boise? The last commercial flight from Salt Lake had gotten in just before midnight.

He got up and dressed in warm field clothes, including his guns and knife but instead of work boots, he put on his German trail-runners and then his worn leather flight jacket. As he exited the front door, he quietly locked it behind him. He silently moved to the sidewalk and peeked down the street. He could see smoke flowing out the slightly opened driver's window and then the glow from a cigarette.

Turning around he flowed like a ghost around the house and back to the garage. He whiffed a hint of tobacco smoke. Unlike the Marlboro's both agents smoked, it was acrid and pungent. It smelled almost like the Turkish-Balkan blend that Berke smoked.

Gus reached under his jacket, unsnapped the knife from its sheath and held it gently along his thigh, like a sword. There was no sign of movement from the car in the alley so he stepped cautiously onto the gravel, causing the first sound.

Abruptly a form swept out of the shadow and an arm tried to cross his chest and sweep around his neck. He spun into the grasp, twisted and rolled, using his left hand to elevate the shoulder facing him.

He immediately attacked thrusting straight at the man's exposed side causing a deep wound and then a second and third just under his ribcage. His quick jabs were just like a boxer.

His Randall Model 2 dagger had a double-edged 5-inch blade but he couldn't seem to get it thru the leather jacket all the way to his enemy's heart.

Without pause, he dropped to ground and spinning off his left side, he swept his legs into the opponent, knocking his feet out from under him, a jujitsu move.

He scrambled over to stab him again. Then, rising to his feet he heel stomped into his throat, and dropped on his chest with a knee. He then drove the razor sharp blade directly into an eye socket.

The assassin was dead, but there might be two. Replacing the dagger, he drew his shoulder-holstered .45-ACP and slipped the suppressor over the interrupted threads and screwed it a quarter-turn to seat it.

He moved in the shadows as he went to check the car down the alley. Its window was broken and DS agent Lambert was bleeding down the front of his white shirt. It looked like a knife wound on his cheek and maybe in his chest. He must have tucked in his chin to protect his throat.

Gus tucked the long pistol into his belt, leaned in and grabbed the mike keying the transmit button as he quietly called, "Anybody listening on this channel."

Speaking slightly louder, he repeated his call and paused for a reply from anybody. Hearing squelch break he transmitted, "A special agent is down with a serious knife wound in the alley west of 8th Street. One suspect is dead and I'm looking for others."

"Who is this station?" Gus heard the dispatcher transmit.

"I'm wearing gray pants, a leather flight jacket and I'm armed so make sure responders know I'm out here. Also, there's an FBI special agent over on O'Farrell Street." Immediately the radio started blasting, "11-99 officer down."

As Gus turned, FBI agent Cox ran into the alley.

Gus told him, "Put a bandage on his chest until help arrives, I going to check for more bandits."

Gus ran to the house checking the back door before pausing to think. Anybody approaching the alley probably came from the south. The other three directions were residences. He either parked in the Fort Street Market or further south at the high school. He glanced down the alley and saw nothing unusual.

He ran back out beside the body lying in the gravel leading to the garage door. Something was strange about his appearance, he though he knew him. Gus squatted to look at his face.

Suddenly there was the sharp whizz of a bullet and crack when it passed where he had just been standing followed by a metallic thump as it embedded itself into one of the garage doors. It came from a gunman down the alley, almost halfway to the next street.

He was firing a suppressed pistol and it sounded like a smaller rather than a larger caliber.

Gus alligator crawled back to the corner of the garage as he drew the silenced pistol out of his belt.

Following the first shot was another one at FBI agent Ken Cox that ricocheted down the alley.

Moments later there was a third shot shattering the garage window above his head and then another down the alley. They were all slow and deliberate shots.

Gus took aim but couldn't see the assassin, he had taken cover behind a tree about 25-yards down the alleyway. Gus peppered the edge of the tree and gravel to force him back, firing seven shots in rapid succession.

He paused to change magazines and the ambusher used the respite to head south toward the Fort Street Market, dodging over to 9th and running down the sidewalk at full speed.

Gus stood and started after him, pausing only to look left to make sure Cox was OK. He ran after the shooter slipping the empty magazine into his rear pocket. At each intersection he checked to make sure no one was waiting to ambush him. They passed the closed and shuttered market and continued on south. The assassin cut across the Catholic Cathedral parking lot to 8th Street. Gus was running in easy strides, although he was aware that he could charge into a new ambush so he was slower than the fleeing triggerman. Gus arrived at the State Capitol building and paused.

Looking catty-corner across State Street at the parking lot entrance, a car caught his attention. It was just starting up and a plume of exhaust was coming from the back of the dark sedan. Gus could see a hazy silhouette in the driver's window.

He dropped into a squat and duck-walked to a tree at the entrance to the Episcopal Cathedral. A few cars were parked along his side of the curb across from the Capital. He could hear a siren in the distance behind him.

Looking at the warming car he saw the indistinct head turn both dark eyes in his direction. They seemed to widen as the car accelerated out of the lot in his direction. There was an abrupt increase in the sound of the motor, and the suspension bottomed across the gutter but there was no squealing of the tires. The driver was a trained professional.

Rather than running, Gus stepped into the street and extended the long pistol toward the moving car. He assumed a two-handed Weaver stance.

Locking the front and rear sights into a single plane, he fired a shot at the driver, followed by the recoil and recovery, picking up his rigid alignment for his second shot, and third, and fourth, and fifth through to the seventh.

Rather than signaling his intentions, Gus was prepared to dodge left or right at the last minute, but the driver lost control by the fourth or fifth shot and careened to the north crumpling into the traffic light pole.

Gus quick changed to his last magazine; he had been counting each shot and he still had a round in the chamber and seven more in his fresh magazine.

Running over, he tried to open the jammed door and finally broke out the window. He felt for a pulse before realizing the man was dead with holes in his upper chest, neck, and lower face.

The car had Idaho plates, but it looked like an airport rental. The front windshield had a softball-sized hole where his rounds had hit and there was another strange sticker, partially pierced by several of the .45-caliber holes. It looked like a Hertz sticker.

Popping the trunk lock with the can opener from his Swiss knife, there were two small suitcases inside. He ran back to the alley carrying them, arriving just as the first police car pulled in, followed by an ambulance.

Gus walked to the back door and put both cases inside. You couldn't fly around the country without some type of identification, but you would never take it on a job with you. It must be in the suitcases.

He removed his leather jacket so everyone would see he had a shoulder holster over his OD sweater and walked back into the alley. His memory seemed to click as he remembered where he had seen the first dead assassin. He looked like one of the KGB officers from the Khoda Bridge in Iran. He must be one of the missing Spetsnaz officers from the dozen men with Spetsgruppa Alfa.

The first plainclothes detective was just hurrying up, so Gus pointed out the dead body beside the garage and said, "I checked south to the Capitol and there's another dead guy with his car crumpled against a traffic light standard. Somebody still needs to look in the other three directions."

The cop looked at him strangely, moving his hand toward his pistol. Gus warned him to stop what he was doing and pulled out his folder with its badge and ID. He identified himself, the wounded agent and FBI Special Agent Cox. "Do you know the dead guys?" asked the detective.

"Yes and no. This one is definitely a Russian KBG assassin and I'm assuming the other is also an assassin or a murderer for hire," replied Gus.

"Is that a silencer on the end of your pistol?"

Replying, "It's a sound suppressor, I didn't want to wake up the neighbors."

The detective turned and Gus followed him back to his car where he got on the radio and said, "Wake the chief, he needs to get over here. You'd better call the sheriff too."

Gus walked down the alley to talk to Ken Cox and said, "I found the microfilm inside the lighter, but you guys were already off duty. We better let Keith Allison know and get it to your offices."

"He already made arrangements for a F-111 from Mountain Home AFB to fly it to McGuire in New Jersey and then by chopper to our offices, maybe three hours tops. I need to get to a secure landline." Gus told him to use the one in the kitchen.

The Boise police chief arrived, followed by Sheriff Handle of Ada County. Gus knew Chuck Handle who was several years behind his father in high school. He was first elected sheriff a dozen years after he came back from Korea and his Marine service there. Handle recognized Gus and the house they were standing behind. He pulled Chief James Church to the side and started whispering to him.

Both senior elected officials, combined they must have almost 80-years of experience, walked over and greeted Gus asking if he had anything more to tell them.

"I can't really tell you much, it's way beyond top secret. However you two should know the assassins' local transportation is wrecked against a pole just down from the Capitol parking lot. The dead partner is inside and it has a broken trunk lock. If both of you come into the kitchen, Rachel will fix a pot of coffee while we inspect the suitcases that were inside. You'd better not tell Washington how we got access. I guess you'll have to get an official warrant and then tow the car, discovering what's there later. The dead men won't complain."

His grandmother was inside with Rachel and Ken Cox waiting while the coffee was percolating on the electric burner. The cast-iron range was cracking and popping with the growing heat from the firebox. Gus took a three-cell flashlight and inspected the entire periphery of both suitcases looking for wires or traps.

Finding none, he picked the lock on the first case and discovered two sets of documents along with a round trip ticket from Miami to Boise and back to south Florida continuing on to George Town on Cayman Island. A light bulb went off and he started inspecting the lining of the case.

Pulling out his Randall, he realized it was still bloody. He rinsed it in the sink as he got a kitchen knife instead. Hidden in the lining was a third set of documents including a US passport and a CIA ID card, from the office in Coral Gables. Both had the assassins picture and the card listed him as special agent Miguel DeMiguel.

Opening the second suitcase, he discovered a complete set of false identity documents and a US passport showing the Russian had flow from Rome to Miami two days ago. His ticket also showed he flew from Miami to Boise last night but his return was to JFK in New York. A piece of notepaper was tucked in the corner listing an address on Brighton Beach Avenue, Brooklyn. "It's a transient hotel on Cony Island." Ken said, "Mostly Russian immigrants stay there."

Gus showed the documents to the FBI agent, the sheriff and the chief. Church commented, "I see what you mean, I don't want to touch this with a ten-foot pole." Cox didn't say a word. You could see he was thinking. He was also worried.

"The CIA card is probably fake," said Gus. "As are the passports. You're going to have to do a complete autopsy and fingerprint set on both men. They obviously flew in from Miami and they were splitting up when they finished. I want to attend the autopsy later today."

Turning and nodding to the special agent, "Ken Cox and maybe the FBI agent from here in Boise can go with me. Send any fingerprints through the CJIS at the FBI and find out who this Miguel

DeMiguel is. I've worked with the other man for the past two years along the Russian-Iranian border and I doubt his prints are on file. He's a trained KGB Spetsnaz officer. Be prepared, as soon as you send in the fingerprints, alarm bells may start going off."

"This investigation will draw in the Department of Defense, the Central Intelligence Agency, and of course several competing departments within my FBI along with the DEA," Ken Cox finally said.

"What are you worried about?" Gus asked Ken privately as he poured him a cup of coffee.

"Before we flew out here Derek called in to the New York Counterintelligence Division and told them where we were going. Last night as we were going back on duty, he told me he had called in again and told them that he thought you had found the lighter, but you hadn't given it to us. Someone leaked our location. Why else were the assassins trying to get into your house through the alley?"

Gus wasn't saying a word, just starring directly at Cox. "Some of us believe a team of KGB wet boys is working out of Brooklyn." Ken lowered his voice and said, "There may be others in Florida and California. For the past few years we've been getting hints the Soviets are basing wet teams in the United States. The Mafia is giving them cover. What if another group is following the first team? What if your lighter has information about these covert spies? What if there's an entire clandestine network of them?"

Returning to the kitchen Gus said to Sheriff Handle, "Give me a set of fingerprints for the Man from Miami and the Spetsnaz officer. I'll have them hand processed through my alternate contacts at the Department of Defense. I'll send both of you a copy of the results as long as you let me know if you find out anything here. Ken Cox is worried we may run into some resistance from competing federal agencies so maybe you should contact the Idaho State Police colonel and have them help. He's also worried that the Russians may continue to try and eliminate me."

"What are you going to do now?" asked Sheriff Handle.

"I guess I can skip my morning workout. I have to go see my friend at the Ford-Lincoln dealership and find out about ordering a handicapped van. Later this afternoon I want to go to the autopsy." Turning to his grandmother he asked, "Can I borrow the convertible for my errands?"

Grandmother Heddy had been listening to everything said and was almost bursting with her desire to speak. "General Motors doesn't make full size convertibles anymore. Your uncle Dick just bought me a Cadillac Eldorado Biarritz and had a custom coachbuilder turn it into a convertible. It's in the garage, and the keys are on the hook."

Gus interrupted and said, "I've got to drive one of my cars to North Carolina and get there by Monday morning for a special meeting. Then, I'm flying back here for Thanksgiving. I think I'll take the Corvette since it's a very warm coupé in the winter and it has a 37-gallon gas tank. With fuel injection it gets pretty good mileage, although it needs super-premium. It has street legal exhaust pipes after the two cutouts for racing. I guess I better stop by and tell Jose to fill her with fresh gas, change the oil and check the pressure, seals and hoses; maybe install new tires too."

"You'd better tell your man to get you a case of octane booster," Sheriff Handle said. "They've changed the octane formula and tetraethyl lead is no longer in almost all premium gasolines. With the president's *Drive 55* campaigns almost no filling stations still have super-premium pumps." Gus took the sheriff to the side and got him to agree to keep protection around the old house, even if the federals pulled out.

19

G us drove the maroon Cadillac convertible several blocks over to the garage his grandfather had purchased in the fifties. A Mexican couple now looked after it, living rent free in the old house next door with their four children. José did yard work and snow shoveling for his grandmother and worked around town for others. He also took care of the house on 8th Street and the stored cars. His oldest son answered the door. "I'm Gus Smith, how are you doing?" as he shook the teenagers hand. "My name's Juan and I'm a freshman at Boise State," the young man replied. "Your grandmother helped me get a scholarship."

In addition to watching after his grandmother's six stored cars; his father looked after Gus's vehicles, his grandfathers Thunderbird and made sure the new Eldorado had its oil changed. In the back of the shop was a winterized 26' *Overlander* he had bought in early 1957 to tow to sports car races. There were twin beds in back and the front gaucho style davenport folded out into a wide bed while it was loaded with rough camping features like septic holding, pressurized water, tank and filter, and a dual 110/12-volt electric system. The two butane tanks supplied the range, oven, space heater and hot water while the taller refrigerator was an icebox electric unit. The back of the original four-wheel drive pickup carried an electric power generator, a Lincoln welding machine and an air compressor along with tools. The trailer was up on jacks and the tires were stored. "As soon as I got my licence, I started driving one of the 4-wheelers with the travel trailer or Brian's pulling race cars." Gus remembered.

After he came to the door, Gus asked José to check everything on the Sting Ray, change the oil and put on new radial tires before Friday afternoon. "Should I put in new plugs, points and check the timing?" José asked. "Yes," Gus answered.

His uncle had told him his friend Brian now owned the local Ford dealership, his next stop. Brian Wood started as a dirt-track racer who became a sports car driver, working for Ferrari and later both GM and then Ford. Until Gus bought the new Corvette, his grandfather bought Brian's used racecars.

He met Gus as he came in the door, slapped his back and asked what he needed. Gus realized his teenage driving instructor was showing his years of fast women, hard drinking and wrecked cars.

When he mentioned a handicapped van to take to North Carolina, the dealer took him back to his office as he asked when do you need it? "Next Friday or at the latest by the following week," Gus answered.

"Most of the van conversion companies are in the Midwest, in Indiana or Michigan. They usually have hand-control models with hydraulic wheelchair lifts in stock and they just finish the inside to what you want. If we call in an order today, Thanksgiving holiday next Thursday will probably interfere so they may be able to deliver one at their factory by Monday the 26th. I've got several conversion vans here on the lot, let's go and look at options. Anything else?"

"Yes, I want to get a really fast coupé for my birthday next month with enough room inside to cross the country, smooth suspension and air conditioning. I would love to have a top speed of over 150, a European touring car. I'm taking the Corvette south this weekend because it's a better winter car than either of the Cobra roadsters and quieter than the Mustang convertible." Gus then turned to his driving mentor, "Brian, the Corvette is sixteen years old, hot as hell in the summer and rides like the racecar we ordered in late '62."

They discussed various options and looked at numerous sports car magazines before Brian called a friend in Greenwich, Connecticut. Although retired Luigi was still one of Enzo Ferrari's best friends. For a couple of years in the late 50's-early 60's Brian had his own team and drove a factory car for the North American Ferrari importer. Fiat now imported the brand.

Before noon, Gus had ordered a custom built van for Andy from a converter in Indiana and a new red Ferrari 512 Berlinetta Boxer. Luigi's friend Dick was in the process of modifying one of the handbuilt Italian aluminum imports in Danbury, Connecticut to meet the American DOT and EPA specifications. It would be ready by his birthday in December.

Going back home, he exercised upstairs in the workroom alcove and then ran for five miles. While he ran he reviewed all his options. The autopsy was scheduled for 4:00 pm. For supper, Rachel was fixing a pot of chili and cornbread muffins. He hoped the two didn't interfere with each other.

On Friday he wanted to go shooting and clean his guns. Tomorrow night he was taking both his grandmother and Rachel out for their weekly restaurant dinner. So he had tonight, and Friday night to study the documents from the lighter. He needed to get more information about Miguel DeMiguel.

As he finished the run, he was breathing much easier. He felt good. A front was approaching as he ran back to the house. There was still no snow in Boise and this early in the winter it would probably rain.

Next week, after Thanksgiving at the Knowles, he was going hunting for two days with his oldest cousin and his uncles. He'd have to shoot one of his grandfather's old double-barrels or change the barrel on his Model 12 shotgun, replacing the 20-inch cylinder bore with the 28-inch modified one. For his birthday in 1960 his grandfather ordered a takedown Pigeon Grade shotgun from the Winchester custom shop fitted with two barrels, an English style straight walnut stock and a red rubber butt plate. Both barrel sets had a matted solid ribs and he had taken the shorter one to Vietnam. The men were going to the Long Valley just south of McCall for pheasant, chukar, quail, grouse and partridge. Mule deer and elk were in season, but nobody had drawn a permit this year. Maybe they should try and fish for some fresh trout.

In 1948 while building the Payette River dam to form the Cascade Reservoir, Grandfather Gus bought two full square-mile sections, an old ranch originally settled by two brothers. The old farm portion was losing 40-acres of bottomland to the inundation. The new homestead included a small house, barn and outbuildings that they now leased to a tenant farmer who cropped wheat on the rolling farmland.

In a wooded area overlooking the lake his grandfather had built a hunting cabin using logs from trees in the future lake bottom. During the long summer furlough between his sophomore-junior year, Gus earned enough money working as a smokejumper out of the McCall Base to pay his grandfather for the Corvette he ordered and got at Christmas. During his days off-duty he lived at the log cabin and studied by the light of a Coleman lantern since there was no electricity. He built an enclosed lean-to beside the cabin for the Dodge power wagon. He also built a 3-foot roof overhang on the back and side to protect a winter's worth of firewood that he split over the summer from standing dead timber. Grandfather Gus left the 1240-acre farm to his three offspring in his will, so Gus now owned a third and the families of Aunt Jane and Aunt Gay each owned the other third.

At 3:30 there was a honk and he stepped to the curb. Gus got into the green government car and Ken introduced him to the Boise agent, "Chester Adams. He wasn't there last night since he had finished a double shift earlier." Although tall and slender he seemed rather old for fieldwork. He smoked like a chimney and must be within a year or two of the mandatory retirement age of 60.

At the morgue Adams introduced Gus to the ME, "He's the special agent who killed both assassins." The doctor responded, "I've got everything they were carrying both in their pockets and in the car over on the side tables. I inspected their documents under a microscope and agree they're false. This morning one of the detectives went to the airport and searched all newly rented lockers, but he came up empty."

As the doctor escorted all three, they walked to the pedestal type autopsy tables and inspected both bodies. "You can see from their teeth that both of them were heavy smokers and the Cuban was a coffee drinker," the medical examiner remarked. "I've never seen the type pistol he was carrying." He stepped over to a stainless worktable and picked up a tube.

Gus took one look at the pistol shaped like a bicycle pump and said, "It's a Welrod. An assassin's pistol built by the British SOE during the war and used by the CIA and the SAS ever since."

Removing the magazine Gus twisted the knurling at the rear and cycled the manual action ejecting a shell as he continued, "The caliber is .32 ACP and it looks like there are four shells remaining. It's very quiet but not very accurate beyond about 10-yards."

"The Russian was wearing a leather jacket reinforced with a strong wire mesh; I think it's tightly woven titanium wire rather than steel encapsulated by an inner felted matt backing up the wire that is unusual since it doesn't melt. I've never seen anything like the fiber before but I think it's a form of Kevlar. The jacket is finished with black nylon fabric lining." Gus picked it up and started inspecting it.

"The jacket looks like a black copy of a US Army field jacket except it's made from leather. You can see where your knife thrust to the body didn't penetrate very deep although several ribs are broken and there are a half-dozen cuts in the leather." Gus realized the jacket must be bullet proof.

An hour later as they were getting ready to leave the morgue the ME said, "It seems your bullets were highly frangible. Three out of your seven shots broke up on the windshield glass, scattering pieces of lead and jacketing all over the car. What were you using?"

"Super Vel 190-grain hollow points," Gus responded. "That reminds me, two of my magazines are empty. I have a couple of boxes of metal-case Hi-Way rounds in my closet. They're for piercing thick car bodies with a submachine gun. A hotter load; they have a stronger jacket to penetrate light armor.

That evening he, his grandmother and Rachel had a bowl of tomato based chili con carne, a green salad and cornbread muffins. "I made the Mexican stew really mild since both your grandmother and I have trouble with spicy food," Rachel said. "I sautéed some venison, beans, hot chilies, spices, onions, and garlic for you to add to your bowl. If you look, you can also see that some of the muffins have red and green peppers in them. Do you want an ice cold beer to go with the chili?" He had to explain why he no longer drank alcohol in any form. You could see that both of them were secretly pleased from the huge grins on their faces.

Gus started his part of the conversation by stating, "Yesterday the furnace was cold and no one had touched it since I cleaned out the clinkers during my summer leave. I had to drain and refill the radiators before firing up the boiler to eliminate any water hammer. There's more than a ton of coal in the basement, so how are you two keeping warm. Has anybody been taking care of maintenance since grandpa fell off the ladder fixing the gutters? Uncle Dick told me he was never the same after he broke his hip."

"We've been sleeping on the sitting room couches," his grandmother admitted. "It and the kitchen are the only downstairs rooms with cast iron stoves. José stops by several times a week when it's cold and brings in firewood and coal."

"Why don't I hire José's son Juan," Gus said. "He can stop by every day before and after class to check on the furnace and water level in the boiler. I'm tied up with a few secret projects, but they should be over in a couple of months. As soon as it gets warm, I'd like to renovate the house."

"Do you think that we are in any danger from the Russians?" Grandmother Heddy asked.

"I think that the KGB is getting first hand information from someone who is reporting everything I do." Gus said. "Since I sent the film on to the east, there is no reason for them to try anything, but they may not know that. Besides, if they want anybody it's me. Not the two of you. However there are officers watching the front and rear. I've been promised that someone will be keeping an eye out through Thanksgiving weekend."

After some more small talk he mentioned he had met a girl in Germany that he really liked. They both hushed and then it was like a dam burst. They had a hundred questions. After answering dozens, he asked if he could bring Mary and her father Andy out for Christmas. They both insisted he start making plans.

After dinner he went up to the finished garret space in the attic. His grandfather had modified the existing large workroom of the Victorian house rebuilt by his great-grandfather. There were long dormers on both sides almost doubling the attic space. In the central room a grouping of mission style furniture surrounded a railroad station agent pot-bellied stove that was giving off a lot of heat. Almost five-feet tall it was a dull black with nickel trim, foot-rails and a mushroom top. The legs rested on a thick slab of stone inset into the golden oak flooring.

Along either dormer wall were worktops, one made out of thick maple butcher block and the other out of a soapstone laboratory worktable. His room and a guest room were located at the back, both formerly occupied by servants. The plaster covered chimney rose through the center of the main stairs and exited through the front ceiling so his grandfather had added a water closet/lavatory on one side and a secure storeroom where he locked his firearms in the other front attic space. The front and rear attic gables had windows for light and ventilation.

Gus kept his, his father's, grandfathers, and great-grandfathers guns locked in the closet. The poorly heated storeroom had a long reloading/cleaning table under the triple windows in the front gable. First on the worktable was the shooting case with his target pistols. Just behind them were several green cardboard boxes of .45-ACP metal-piercing ammunition along with dozens more target wadcutters and yellow boxes of Super Vel's in two calibers. Taking them to the wooden bench, he reloaded three of the matching magazines with the Remington Hi-Way Master solid bullets. First thing at the range would be to check the sights on his pistol using the new bullets. He then planned to reload one or two of his combat magazines with the rounds. He already knew that their weight and speed almost matched the Super Vel's so they should strike near each other rather than substantially higher. He then brought out the shotgun and changed to the longer barrel. Next Gus brought out range bags with custom-made sniper equipment and put together a kit to take east. He went back and picked out a short olive Cordura rifle case from among the dozen that held a special bolt-action rifle broken down into three pieces. This was the long-range rifle he would need if he went into Iran. When he got back, he would clean everything before loading the car. He already had two-dozen boxes of hand loaded unmarked covert ammo for the Haskins/Weatherby so he put a hundred rounds in the kit. He always handled this ammo wearing thin shooting gloves to avoid leaving fingerprints.

That night Gus walked with his grandmother and Rachel to their favorite Chinese restaurant for Friday dinner. They were creatures of habit, either going to the Chinese or the local German Hofbrau & Beer Garden every other Friday for the past twenty years. As she got older Rachel became more orthodox and didn't ride in cars or cook after sunset on Friday, on Shabbat.

On Saturday morning Gus warmed up, stretched and then ran for five miles. It was cold and black; it would be a new moon in two days. There was still no snow at the lower elevations as he ran up to Jose's house. Before he went up the steps, Jose came out and said, "I knew you would be here before 6:00."

Handing him the keys, he walked across the courtyard and opened one of the garage doors. The silver Sting Ray looked ready to run. Gus got in and pulled down the street, stopping at his grandmother's. His two bags of clothes and weapon cases were waiting just inside the double door. Rachel came into the hall and said, "After you load the bags, come back and have a cup of coffee and a slice of cheese bread. You have to say goodbye to your grandmother."

Gus changed into his trail-runners, blue jeans, western style shirt and old leather flying-jacket, along with his usual set of combat weapons. His beard was growing longer. Within another month he could dye his hair and pass for a native Turk or Iranian. He felt his chest pocket to make sure he had his badge and ID. After he drank a cup and ate a slice, he said, "I'll see you when I fly back on Wednesday," as he kissed both ladies.

As he left town he headed across southern Idaho on the interstate highway headed toward Wyoming. He was planning on stopping for food and gas, with only a few short catnaps during the 2500-mile drive. He wanted to be in Fayetteville by Sunday night.

For the first 300-miles he averaged well over a hundred miles-an-hour since he knew the State Police in Idaho and Wyoming were aware he was coming and what he was driving. He stopped for a late lunch in Rock Springs, Wyoming where a state trooper said, "You're making good time. Have a nice day." He didn't need gas yet since he was getting over 600-miles per tank. Jose had put a case Lucas octane booster in small bottles on the floor of the passenger side.

It was too warm with the heat flowing back from the engine, so he pulled around back, took off his leather jacket and changed to the cotton field jacket. His pistol was digging into his hip in the tightly fitted leather seat with the racing safety harness so he changed from the hip holster to the shoulder rig. Of course he kept his ankle holster as backup.

It was daytime and he couldn't hear any music using the old AM radio, so for the next five hours he mentally reviewed each chronological section of the American part of the top-secret information the traitor had given to the Russians. The other 75% of the encrypted pages seemed to be unbreakable. On Thursday and Friday evening, he had been studying everything using his grandfather's old glass magnifier that rotated out of a two-inch round leather case. He remembered a lot of the broad detail on the usable 1,500 pages. Occasionally he slowed and studied his notes.

He had the Zippo lighter in his pocket, and when he changed, he took it out and put it on the tray between the seats. In addition to gun cases and luggage in the small back area on top of the racing gas tank, he had to stuff the rest into the passenger foot well and seat. Every few hours he got a coffee when he stopped for gas and to pee. Somewhere between Nebraska and Illinois he lost his connection to the State Police. It was turning dark so he couldn't spot speed traps.

Jimmy Carter was enforcing his 55 mph national speed limit and Gus had to keep his eyes peeled. He told himself he was going to buy one of those Fuzzbusters Brian had told him about. Twice he had near misses, with a divided highway helping him in one instance and his pulling off for a coffee for the next. When the policeman came back to the diner, Gus was calmly sitting there with his badge and ID beside his napkin. The officer took a good look at him and then his identification. Saying, "Drive carefully."

He entered Kentucky in the middle of the night, knowing he was going to have to pay tolls to use the unconnected parkways from the middle of the state to West Virginia. He kept his speed below a hundred throughout picking up speed across the mountains and into North Carolina. He stopped in a mountain town for a few hours sleep and parked in the town square, just across from a closed café. The sheriff's office was in the courthouse but no one was on duty.

Gus arrived in Fayetteville early Sunday evening and checked into a Holiday Inn near the base. Following his training he went to a pay phone down the street and called Colonel Beck at home to report his arrival. "Dick Mead knows you. He'll pick you up at 5:00 am and bring you in for breakfast. We always exercise before we eat, are you ready? Bring a change of clothes."

Gus decided to keep his mouth shut until he found out who was who. He would give them some of the things they needed to know about Iran, but nothing about Russians, CIA turncoats or drug dealers. He called Mary before it got too late in Germany and then studied his documents for the next hour. Mary and Andy were still coming to Bragg in two weeks, but she said she was probably going to take the fellowship in Washington in April.

Going back out to a new pay phone, he called Keith Allison at home and checked in with him letting him know about his meetings tomorrow. Gus didn't ask him about rumors from Russia.

After that he called Dedee Anderson at her apartment in Washington and asked if she had gotten any warnings that Russia was going to invade Afghanistan. She asked him for a clean number so he gave her the one from the first booth. She called him from her own sterile phone booth and they talked for a half-hour.

20

G us was waiting at the entrance door when Dick drove under the porte-cochere to pick him up. Wearing his trail-runners, black shorts and a plain old olive drab tee shirt beneath his dog-eared black sweats, he was cold in the creeping mists of 5:00 am. He had his Gladstone bag with a change of clothes and a selection of his pictures and papers from Iran.

He also had both his backup and main pistol in their holsters on top. "I haven't seen you for eleven years. I thought you'd retired." Gus said to Dick Mead as he hoisted himself into the passenger seat of the pick-up.

"I did. I just make twice as much now as a private consultant."

At the main gate, the guards waved them through, and after more driving they arrived at the old base stockade where there was a second fence topped with barbed wire. Dick asked, "Are you armed?" and when Gus answered, "Yes". He said something to the guard who held out his hand. "They keep a shelf of lockboxes with all the weapons. Any firearms inside the compound have to be issued by the armorer." Gus thought to himself, that's stupid; if I brought in a kill team all the unarmed people would be easy targets.

Inside, between two of the buildings, there were a hundred men assembling for the morning exercises. Gus could see some older men who were probably assigned to desk jobs, but most were young warriors in their middle 20's. About half wore shorts and tees while the rest wore sweat pants and long sleeve shirts. Dick said, "Some of our fighting men are down in Florida. We're going out on the 10K cross-country course with exercise stops every klick. At the finish everyone runs the obstacle course." Gus nodded that he understood.

"You might not have noticed, but the men are divided into shirts and skins by their outfits. You're a skin so you'll have to take off the sweat clothes. Everyone leaves in timed pelotons of ten men each. Although we time every group, you're only racing against the other nine men since the fastest man in each platoon is also carrying a timer."

Gus thought it's exactly the same as the 10th in Germany. One must have copied the other. He didn't know if he could beat the younger men, however he knew he had to finish before any of the more senior runners, well into the top 10 or 15 percent. Two clerks with multiple stopwatches started each group after shouting out their name.

Gus pulled to the front of his *Turtles* on the way to the first stop, the 40-yard low crawl. It looked like his group included some staff officers and clerks. He crawled like an alligator and finished it perfectly.

Continuing on to the next stop, by the third kilometer he was running with the timer. Three other men from his group were over 100-meters behind. Gus later discovered the lead man was a slender 30-year-old marathoner who was the colonel's radio operator.

The next stop involved the 150-yard man carry and he slung the timer over his shoulder and took off for the distant stake. Coming back, the lighter runner had trouble carrying his almost 200-pounds. The operator immediately started for the fourth marker with Gus just behind.

By the end of the 10 kilometers, Gus and the marathoner were close, with the smaller man finishing just a few strides ahead of him. Both of them made short work of the obstacle course, helping each other across several of the high barriers. By the time everyone finished, Gus discovered he finished 14th overall. Colonel Beck and Dick Mead observed rather than participated.

Everyone showered and changed for breakfast. Once again Gus had Cheerios, fresh pears and black coffee. The milk machine only had regular so he just dampened his cereal, with no sugar. Many of the men were eating thousand-calorie breakfast with eggs, bacon, biscuits and the beef and gravy called SOS.

After eating, several of the operations planners met with him in a conference room. Most of them were army captains but the group included an Air Force major along with Dick and the colonel. Colonel Beck introduced him with an abbreviated history and then turned the meeting over to Gus.

"I escaped from Iran exactly fifteen days ago. A day earlier my survey team had a run-in with a dozen pasdaran Revolutionary Guards who were trying to take us hostage. We discovered they were planning on seizing the US Embassy and both consulates the next day. I tried to contact Teheran and Mashhad but someone was jamming their frequencies. I did get in contact with the CIA operative at Tabriz and his people evacuated across the Turkish border with us." Gus explained how MJ used the old military MARS network of civilian ham radio operators.

"My office in Idaho called Langley, the State Department and the Pentagon warning them about the next day's assault plan." Gus paused as Colonel Beck asked, "Where is this CIA operative, and what happened to the Iranians?"

"He was killed by a terrorist bomb in Italy while we were trying to get the information back to the states. The answer to your other question is we killed all twelve pasdaran at our compound and then another four during our escape." The colonel started to ask another question and Gus waved him off.

"Let's not get sidetracked about information you don't need-to-know. I want to give you four critical pieces of information. There are several other issues, which are strictly classified as need-to-know, SCI." Gus stared at each man sitting around the table until they nodded in understanding.

"The first item is about the embassy compound in Teheran, I've been there dozens of times. The most recent was last month. I have some knowledge about what's in each building, and it'll probably take us a full day to discuss." Each of the planners was making notes and no one interrupted.

"The second is about infiltration and exfiltration across the Turkish border." Gus explained that it was still open and it was how they got out.

"The third is about the environs around Tehran including the new International Airport construction site south of the capital, a huge swath of now unoccupied land but with a few empty buildings, power and water. It's just off Highway 7 to Qom about half-an-hour out of Tehran." He knew that they must have been reviewing all options for laagering and resupply so he wanted to give them his two-cent opinion.

"The fourth is speculation on my part but you need to know what I suspect." Gus paused to catch his breath and to gauge the reaction from the listeners. He was also building up their suspense. "The Russian Army is going to invade Afghanistan within the next four weeks."

The entire room quieted and everybody looked at Colonel Beck. Russian interference could make a huge difference. "I believe the invasion will happen on Christmas Day." Gus realized they must have been planning a rescue attempt, maybe sometime within the next month.

"If we start with the embassy compound, we can move on to conditions on the Turkish border and finish up with any additional questions in the morning." Gus started to say.

Colonel Beck interrupted him and said, "You've got to tell me everything you know or suspect about Russian movements in Afghanistan? Where did you hear these rumors?" Gus looked at the waiting staff and the impatient colonel before he answered.

"I have three sources, the first from Afghanistan and the second from Turkey." Gus explained.

"I knew Spike Dubs before he was killed in a terrorist attack. Before the incident Spike sent the nephew of the Afghan President to me for safekeeping, since he wouldn't go to the US or Europe." Gus paused to consider he next words. "Zahir Kahn had recently graduated from university with a BS in Civil Engineering so I gave him a false name and trained him as an engineer on the Khoda Bridge dam for almost a year. He's one of my sources even though he now works in Pakistan. I talked to him more than a month ago and again last week." Gus answered several questions about Zahir from a captain who introduced himself as the intelligence officer, the S-2.

"Do you have any more information?" The colonel asked. "Why haven't you talked to this source more often?"

"He's being watched by Pakistan's ISI and unless you meet or call him at a safe location it's too dangerous for him to talk." Gus answered.

"My other source is my assistant from Iran. He's a Turkish army officer working with National Intelligence, the MIT. He started getting warnings from moles within Soviet Azerbaijan and Armenia that the Russian army was going to invade Afghanistan before the end of this year. He told me even though the PDPA, the communist party of Afghanistan has taken control of the government, the Russians aren't happy with their Islamic stance about Sharia law, alcohol and narcotics. Ever since the Russians lost their source of illegal opium from the Golden Triangle to the North Vietnamese, they've been cultivating sources in Afghanistan. They are going to seize it and merge the country into Russia." Gus looked directly at the colonel.

"I confirmed this information yesterday from an agent with the State Department Bureau of Intelligence." Colonel Beck didn't say anything at first. He then said, "I need to get more information and some photo reconnaissance. Continue with your ideas."

"Tomorrow, we need to review some of the uninhabited areas outside Teheran." Gus continued. "I'm leaving the next morning to fly home for Thanksgiving. Next week I'm bringing a handicapped van for my friend, retired Sergeant Major Andy Johnson who's flying in from Germany."

Turning to the colonel Gus said, "We need to find him a ground floor apartment while his daughter spends four months at the basic officers courses in Georgia and Texas."

Gus saw him nod he would take care of it. He must remember Andy from his time with them while he commanded MACV-SOG.

"You need to have all your questions ready by next week, since I will probably have to go to DC for the other issues." There was a knock at the door and the Sergeant Major escorted a soldier in with a tray of refreshments.

As everyone rose to get a fresh cup of coffee Gus whispered to the colonel and his civilian advisor, "Everything I do is passing across the desk of the National Security Advisor. I am working with specific officers at State, Justice and Defense, however the CIA is being kept in the dark. Don't tell anybody in DC what I'm doing. Also, I need to get some information from your Sergeant Major and have him process two sets of fingerprints."

"Whom are you working for in Washington?"

"The National Security Agency. I'm also working with the FBI, DEA and the Director of Diplomatic Security."

"I know Keith Allison the DS Director, he was the CIA's coordinator with the Joint Personnel Recovery effort during Operation Ivory Coast at Son Tây in 1970." Dick said.

The colonel motioned for his senior sergeant to join them and nodded for Gus to continue. "I killed two assassins in Boise on Thursday. I recognized one body as an officer with the Spetsgruppa Alpha who had been keeping me under observation in Iran. Here's a package with the fingerprints, autopsy photos and both sets of identification papers."

"You'll notice the second man had a CIA ID showing that he was called Miguel DeMiguel. There's also a newsletter from the Brigade 2506 association, the Cuban exile organization for survivors of the Bay of Pigs. His unused ticket to the Caymans leads me to suspect he may be working for Frank Noggin and the Noggin-Sand Bank there in George Town. Can you get more information?"

For the next two days Gus got full cooperation from the Combat Applications Group Detachment at Fort Bragg. He exercised with them the next morning, finishing 8th before flying back on Wednesday through Atlanta, Salt Lake and finally Boise.

At Thanksgiving in Boise there were fourteen for dinner. They ate at the sprawling house on the 18th fairway of the country club where uncle Dick and Aunt Jane had raised his three younger cousins. Uncle John and Aunt Gay lived just four streets over and raised three more cousins in their rambling split-level. In this northern section of Boise some streets ran almost uphill and the higher houses overlooked the golf course and the older city down in the valley.

Rachel and Marta, José's wife, were helping in the kitchen, although Marta was going home to fix dinner for her four kids before noon. Rachel counted the guest and knew she would have to eat with the families rather than staying in the kitchen. Gus came into the kitchen and said to Marta, "Tell José that I'm bringing my girlfriend out for Christmas. He needs to clean up all the cars and trailers in the shop."

His oldest Knowles cousin Dick-Junior was an engineer for MJ Civil working on a job in San Francisco while both of his younger and still unmarried sisters lived at home, although the older one was semi-engaged and her future husband was a guest. She was studying for her PhD and the youngest was an elementary school teacher. Of course his uncle John Allen was a judge and his oldest girl was a stewardess for TWA, his middle son was a captain in the Air Force and his youngest girl, an unexpected surprise, was in her sophomore year of college.

After a traditional dinner almost everyone was stuffed, although Gus only ate turkey and vegetables. He skipped the bread, stuffing and desserts. Richard asked Gus and Judge Allen to join him in his sanctum. His library-office had room for bookshelves, a desk and leather couch for napping.

He nodded to his brother-in-law John and said, "I can't tell you what Gus has been doing for the past few weeks, but you know he has been working overseas for MJ on many of our government related projects. He is one of our two employees with a Top Secret-SCI clearance." With a shrug from his uncle, Gus explained the various Top Secret clearance levels including Special Access Programs-SAP and the highest Secure Compartmented Information-SCI. "It usually calls for a current full-scope polygraph every two years to keep the SCI classification." Gus said.

"I've talked with the senior executives here at headquarters," his uncle Dick said. "We think Gus should set up a specialized construction company in the Washington, DC area. We want the new company to chase the Top Secret work for various government agencies. Most of his employees will require high security clearances, so they'll need to hire some new people. MJ can't let US government classified-jobs interfere with our worldwide commercial customers. We'll need to find an available company name that implies something Top-Secret or Covert." Uncle John had several questions about working overseas for other countries. Uncle Dick explained the arrangement with the bank in Switzerland and how they had deposited so much money.

"If Gus' overseas corporation holds 45% of the stock and MJ owns another 45% we would be left with 10% to distribute to politically connected individuals on the board of directors," his uncle continued. "We need at least five who are powerful, have a lot of contacts, but they've retired from the federal government."

John Allen responded, "You'll probably need seven board members. Explain why one of the owners has to be an overseas corporation?"

"We both agree the American parent corporation needs to be more than 40% and less than 50% owned by an international company," answered Gus. "If an offshore corporation owns a substantial share of stock in the US Corporation, we can leave some of the profits in low-tax jurisdictions for reinvestment overseas. There's no requirement to repatriate overseas profits and a number of jurisdictions have no corporate tax. Also, the international corporation can issue all subcontracts with foreigners. That will legally isolate our American parent corporation from lawsuits while we hold the prime contracts with the US government."

"I can see you'll need someone from the Senate, the State Department and the Pentagon." Uncle John commented. "Why don't you ask retired Senator Len Jordan here in Boise to be the Chairman? He's a conservative Republican and despises Idaho's Frank Church—LBJ's protégé and our socialist Democrat. Jimmy Carter is going to lose next year and the ultra-liberals will be out of power for a decade. Senator Jordan will protect MJ's interest in the new company. You'll probably need a couple of retired generals from the Pentagon, one from the intelligence side and the other from the Corps of Engineers. I'll talk to Len and ask him if he'll take the job, and see if he has any recommendations for other people, Dick needs to be a member of the board, you too. If you increase the number to seven, add an outside lawyer or an accountant, either with government experience."

"Gus, you know where I expect you to come up with half the capital to start the new company," Richard Knowles winked as he said it to him. "MJ will definitely put up $2-million in capital. That let's us start with $4-million."

"Can you handle the US incorporation," Gus asked his uncle. "Maybe in Delaware. With the right directors we could probably get our first real job by late summer."

Richard replied, "I suspect we can get our first job much sooner. The current administration has some critical problems with OPEC oil deliveries that have to be solved by next month."

Since they were finished talking business Gus said, "Sometime next summer, when it's dry, we need to renovate Heddy's house. Neither she nor Rachel can handle shoveling coal anymore so the furnace and chimney needs to be removed along with the steam radiators. We should install a gas-hot water system and an air conditioning system. We also need to replace the plumbing and electrical in each room. The house still has knob-and-tube wiring from 1905. Of course nothing is insulated and the house needs to be caulked and painted. It also needs a new roof. I went ahead and hired Juan, José's son to come in twice a day and keep the place warm."

The next day all five men were flying up to the McCall airport and then going down the valley to their tenant farmed section to hunt for upland gamebirds, spending the night in the log cabin lodge. Gus thought, I renewed my sportsman's license last week and fired a box of target loads through the Model 12 shotgun, but I haven't shot gamebirds for a few years. I may also take grandfather's lightweight 20-guage Parker side-by-side for the chukar, quail, partridge and grouse. Since we may fish for trout in the Long Valley, I think I'll take his old Orvis Battenkill bamboo fly rod, wicker creel and tackle vest.

21

The smaller MJ Learjet left Boise at 5:00 am mountain time Monday morning carrying Gus for drop-off in Indiana. The Vice President of Engineering and three of his personnel were heading on to Ohio for a meeting with a client there. At the small Kokomo airport there was only an old Checker taxicab to carry him out to the van conversion facility on the main highway. While he was gone, the sheriff and police chief had promised to have each shift drive by and check on the ladies.

When Gus went in, they still needed a few hours to finish, but he inspected their progress and was satisfied. Sitting down, he pulled out the now 6,000 full pages from the microfilm and started reviewing them once again. Last weekend and again two days ago he had checked in with Keith Allison in Washington and there was no new information. He continued to maintain a back channel with Dedee Anderson of the State Department Bureau of Intelligence and Research.

Last week Dedee called him in Fayetteville from a sterile pay phone and warned him that he should be more careful when he used

AT&T long lines. Since her small office of narcotics and trans-national crime had few contacts within the CIA, he assumed that her warning was coming from either the State Department or the National Security Agency. He already knew that Turkish intelligence was monitoring most phone calls there. Was AT&T listening in on calls within the US? She also mentioned that her office hadn't gotten a copy of the microfilm from the Zippo, so he sent her one through the Army courier network.

He was now carrying a special device made by a friend Pete, a former AT&T electronic genius fired by the Company during the Halloween massacre. Gus called him in Seattle and had him build it last week. He called it a "Blue Box" and then explained it was a multifrequency tone generator. Using the device Gus could bypass all central office attempts to discover his call location. Pete swore the Russians and the NSA recorded and tracked every long distance phone call.

Holding the small blue box to the mouthpiece of a regular hand-set or a pay phone, Gus could duplicate the sounds of all the tones, even coins dropping into the box. His friend taught him a series of code tones to divert calls throughout the AT&T network, including to and from communication satellites. It would work with most US routing and all international calls. He gave Gus a list of tone sequences for dozens of countries including the Bell standardized systems in Turkey and Iran.

As he sat there in Kokomo he thought, even if they discover who's giving the Russians information from the CIA, they might not tell me. They may secretly follow the man for the next five years trying to discover his contacts. I need to find someway to get more information for myself.

Gus decided to wait and call Washington from North Carolina, hoping he could disguise his location. It was after lunch by the time he left so he decided to drive all night with a few catnaps. Both front seats of the new van swiveled around 180 degrees and the rear seat folded down to form a single bed. There weren't any middle seats only floor latches for a wheelchair, although there was a work counter all along the side opposite the hydraulic lift and a double handrail along the raised roof on either side. The engine hump had a very useful wooden tray with cup holders and storage recesses. A Coleman steel cooler kept food and drinks and a porta-potty was under the bed. There was even a 12-volt coffee percolator. He'd have to stop at a hardware store and get a Stanley stainless vacuum bottle for coffee on the road; the wooden hump tray had a cutout for what looked like a quart thermos.

In Fayetteville on the 27th, his first call was to the sergeant major of 1st SFOD-Delta. The senior enlisted man for Delta told Gus, "I'll pick you up in a half-hour. We have an appointment with a crazy old retired sergeant at his cabin south of the reservation."

During the hour long trip the sergeant major explained how the shit hit the fan when he submitted the fingerprints of Miguel DeMiguel through DOD. Luckily the Pentagon was protecting their special unit.

"The CIA definitely flagged the fingerprints and they know the name, he must have been an agent. We're going to talk to an old Special Forces hand, Guillermo 'Bill' Diaz who's been talking about conspiracies for the past two-dozen years. Bill is a Cuban who had just finished his second year at the University of Miami in June of 1950. He enlisted in the Army and served as an airborne trooper in Korea."

"Later he became a Special Forces sergeant. Because of his background he was seconded to the CIA as a trainer for the parachutist of Brigade 2506 in Guatemala. Through the rest of the '60s he served mostly in Laos with Operation White Star, later transferring to the Paramilitary section of the CIA. He is absolutely sure the Russians and Cuban communist have riddled the various CIA operations starting during the Cuban Revolution."

After taking several roads, each one less improved, the went down a rough dirt road for several miles ending up at a frame cabin backing up to a slow moving stream, almost a swamp. It had a junk filled front porch and a screened one in the back overlooking the water.

A bearded swamp-rat came out and greeted the sergeant major. He introduced Gus to Bill without mentioning his CIA experience. Showing Bill the picture of the dead Cuban and the documents he was carrying, Gus also went into his run-in with the KGB and Spetsnaz.

"That's him." Bill Diaz said. "I've known the man you're calling Miguel DeMiguel under several different names since 1961. He's definitely a Cuban-Soviet wet-work specialist. The funny thing is, he was born and raised in Columbia and they joined Castro in 1958. He and his brother were recruited into the CIA's Operation 40 in early 1960 and became two of their assassins." Bill then explained everything he knew about OP-40.

"I first started suspecting them when they were supposedly captured during the Bay of Pigs, numerous Cuban patriots claimed Castro handled them with kid gloves. DeMiguel was involved in a lot of plots in Central and South America during the early 60's and later he showed up in Laos working for the CIA. He maintained close contacts with his brother who had become a drug smuggler working close to several organized crime families. During the 60's he regularly met with certain Italian-Australian groups who were closely connected with the Sicilian Mafia."

"Did he work with Frank Noggin or Mike Sand," Gus asked.

"Yes, in fact he's been working for their bank for the past few years," Bill replied. "He's their traveling enforcer and killer. He also maintains contacts with the New York and Miami Mafia families for the bank. What about his brother Rodrigo, he's much more dangerous. He's Frank Noggin's personal bodyguard. You do know the Noggin-Sand bank is not only the official bank for the CIA, it's also the chief banker for the KGB and several Mafia families of American organized crime."

Bill Diaz did not have much written proof, only personal testimony and his conspiracy theories. Gus started to worry when Bill started claiming both DeMiguel brothers were Castro's main people in the JFK assassination plot. They were the actual shooters and Lee Harvey Oswald was a patsy set up by the Russian KGB.

That night Gus went apartment hunting. The colonel had recommended the real estate agent wife of a retired sergeant to look at various units. They were both friends of Andy and they knew Mary from several joint assignments. Gus finally narrowed the pick down to two different units he would show to Andy when they arrived.

He was going to drive his new Ferrari when it was finished so he decided to teach Mary to drive the old Corvette and send her off to Fort Benning and Fort Sam Houston in the modified racing car. The seat could be slid up and the steering wheel telescoped forward for her smaller frame.

Gus called Mary after he drove back to the motel. Before he could say anything, she said, "The movers are coming to pick up our household goods tomorrow and we're flying into Fayetteville from JFK the next day, on Thursday evening."

"That's great. I got a couple of apartments for Andy to look at and I have several other surprises. I'll get motel rooms for the three of us for a few nights."

The furniture won't be here for weeks," Mary said. "We have the whole month of December to travel around. Are you free?"

"I would love to show you and Andy around, where do you want to go?" Gus answered. She started talking about Key West, Washington DC, New York, and then the West Coast, maybe San Francisco and LA.

"Whoa down. You need to go to DC and visit with the general at Walter Reed to build a firm relationship. Then I would love to take you and Andy to Boise to meet my uncles, aunts, cousins and especially my grandmother. I told her about you and she insists I bring you out to meet her. Maybe we could drive west ending our Christmas touring in Idaho. My grandmother would like to invite you and Andy to join the family there. When do you report for duty at Benning?"

"Wait a minute," Mary said. Gus could image her holding up her hand. "Where do we go, how many guests will be there and what do we wear in Idaho? I have to be at Fort Benning on Sunday, January 6th to start my orientation and I finish in San Antonio on April 19th. I report to Walter Reed on April 29th. Now answer my questions about Idaho."

"The family gets together with my grandmother and Rachel at the old family house in North Boise at noon, after church. Both of my aunts, their husbands and all six cousins usually join us. Sometimes a few friends in town or from overseas projects are invited. Usually the ladies wear slacks or skirts, shirts and sweaters inside the house while the men wear wool or corduroy trousers, shirts and sweaters or jackets. We're not too fancy. Grandmother always wants all the Catholics to go to sunrise mass at St. John's Cathedral."

"After Christmas in Idaho, you may want to go to Key West for a week or two before you report to Benning."

"What about your work?"

"I found the item we talked about and sent what was inside to the experts. I kept a copy for us to review, but I'm stumped and need your help. I think we'll have to use frequency analysis, the same kind of statistics you use in Epidemiology." Mary interrupted and said, "I've moved on to other Bayesian probability models like regression analyses or even better I've developed a new Monte Carlo algorithm. I've written a computer program in UNIX for minicomputers and adapted it to IBM 370 system mainframes."

"Let's talk about what we can do after you get here," Gus said. "I can take the next month off, my first real vacation in seven years. Maybe we should buy one of the new minicomputers?"

"They're picking up the phone tomorrow, so you won't be able to talk to me until Thursday." Mary ended their call by saying how much she missed him.

On Wednesday morning Gus went back out to the old stockade where he spent the next two days answering hundreds of specific questions about everything. Delta had the "As-Built" drawings from the original embassy and the official additions over the past few years.

They had made an extra copy for Gus to use making changes with a red felt marker. He showed the things they had changed locally. He ignored his instructions and gave them a lot of specific information about details inside the classified sections like the door swings and locks, ventilation systems and the top-secret spaces on the upper floors.

Dick and the colonel asked him into a SCIF that had been built inside the office complex and reminded him of his Top Secret-SCI obligations.

"I'm going into Iran under the cover of an Irishman next week," Dick told him. "I'm flying in with Joe, a retired CIA man and we're going to meet with an Iranian who retired from our Air Force and is now married to a local. We're calling him Fred."

Gus said that he had never heard of Joe. "Whom did he work for?"

"Although, Joe never worked for the Special Operations Group he was trained as an intelligence agent and worked with SAVAK in Iran for more than a dozen years. The CIA has promised we will make contact with some local Iranians who were also formerly with SAVAK. They have also promised we can rent a warehouse and some stake-bed trucks in Tehran. They're still trying to identify remote locations for staging helicopters." Dick continued.

"The CIA has warned us away from any contact with Turkish or Israeli intelligence." The colonel said. "We've got to plan on operating with a mixture of Air Force planes and Navy helicopters through Egypt and Oman."

"You do know I don't trust any former SAVAK personal," Gus responded. "They've either joined the revolution or they're dead. I don't trust the CIA either. If you're smart you'll also work on a backup plan from northern Turkey. Don't let anybody in the CIA know what you're doing." Gus was carefully watching both officers.

"I suspect you had an early attack plan," Gus continued. "I'll bet you are waiting to see if the Russians do anything. I called one of my sources yesterday and they tell me the Soviets have moved their entire 40th Army to staging areas along the border. He also told me there is a Soviet airborne battalion already acting as the presidential guard in Kabul along with several hundred KGB agents throughout the country. They are definitely planning an invasion." Gus paused for any comments and then continued. "I was told that during the Christmas holidays designated Spetsnaz units will seize critical communications while their KGB Alpha unit assassinates President Hafizullah Amin. Within hours the 103rd Guards Airborne Division will parachute into the air bases. More divisions, regiments and brigades will follow them from the Turkmen and Uzbek SSR's."

"We know," said Colonel Beck. "A blackbird flight took side scan pictures last week and the Russians are definitely building up their combat units along the border. The plane also took a number of pictures of your abandoned International airport site and the MJ construction facilities, which is the reason we're talking to you."

Gus had brought copies of the original preliminary drawings and plans for the new international airport south of Tehran. Of course he also had progress drawings of the abandoned hanger-like structure, warehouse and buildings that were located next to the WWII gravel airstrip they were reusing. No work had been done on the new airport other than some early grading. The American design/construction joint venture abandoned the site a year ago, and the nearest Iranian resident was now almost 7-miles away. It was a perfect staging and exfiltration site.

"We may have to use the old MJ construction facilities since there are almost no other good alternatives. We'll need a Special Forces trained experienced CIA-SOG officer to lead the separate mission. He must speak the language and pass for a native. You're the only man who meets those requirements. You will know nothing about the rest of our plan, just where you have to be and when you have to be there. Will you take the mission?"

"Yes," answered Gus. "I need to develop a plan of what we need and how to get it into and back out of Iran. When I came across the border three weeks ago, there were at least three flatbeds with army trucks waiting to cross into Iran. MIT, the Turkish intelligence agency may help, but any drivers I recruit need to pass for native Farsi speakers, maybe some with Turkic. I would be very careful about using any Muslims, even from Turkey. First I would try and find Iranian Azeri Christian or Jews who speak Farsi."

"In addition to your thoughts about trucks and drivers, we need you to set up an alternate refueling point for helicopters," the colonel commented.

"We love your idea of bringing completely sterile trucks in top operating condition across the border to wait for our strike team," Dick said. "An alternate plan is exactly what we need. Your trucks would be a back up to the CIA plan."

"I still need the rest of December and maybe January to neutralize the CIA turncoats who are reporting to the KGB. Let me give you a single example of what we are facing."

Gus pulled out his stack of documents and fanned through until he reached the section about Operation Ivory Coast, the Son Tây prison camp raid into North Vietnam. He knew Dick Mead had led one of the assault groups. "These are from the actual KGB microfilms although we still haven't decrypted the Soviet lead document." Gus showed them the half-page coded document.

"On June 10th 1970, a planning group known as Polar Circle met at the Pentagon to discuss the possibility of a raid into North Vietnam to free as many as sixty prisoners-of-war at the Son Tây prison camp." Gus suddenly had their full attention, so he paused for a moment before continuing. "Actual tactical planning didn't start until August 8th. Of course you know no prisoners were present when the raid finally occurred on November 21st." Dick Mead was nodding in agreement.

"Here is a Soviet copy of the original Polar Circle task order sent to the KGB on June 11th and the initial tactical plan which was sent to them on June 20th."

"We haven't decoded the Soviet side of the transmission yet, but I'll bet you in order to protect their agent in US intelligence, they recommended the North Vietnamese move the prisoners. The entire Ivory Coast task force was attacking an empty compound." Dick

Mead was astounded. The blood had drained from his face. He couldn't speak. "You can't tell the CIA your real plans," Gus concluded. "Or at least all of your plans."

"Neutralize this threat to our mission before you go back to Turkey," the colonel ordered. "I'm putting you on the payroll as of last week as a special consultant. We're building a mock-up of the compound and buildings inside a hanger at Eglin AFB. You can come down at the end of January to make sure we have included everything?"

"It would be safer for me to stay away from anything you are planning. If I don't know anything, nobody can get information out of me. On the other hand, if no one knows what I am planning, nobody can interfere, so don't tell anyone especially the CIA. I just need two things: Complete cooperation from the 10th in Germany for flights into and out of Turkey and a contact with the Israeli Mossad or better yet their military intelligence directorate, Aman since Mossad talks to the CIA daily. I need to recruit some Persian Jews or men from the Armenian Christian Church to drive my trucks. You do know that the Armenian Patriarchate is in Jerusalem." Gus explained both groups of Farsi speaking men had been flying into Jerusalem for the past two years.

The next day, Gus left the compound at 5:00 pm to go to the Fayetteville airport and meet the flight coming in from New York.

22

G us stood next to the door in the glass walkway, projecting out from the single level terminal. He watched as each passenger came down the integral back stairs of the Piedmont 727. Finally, two porters manhandled Andy in a narrow transport chair down the built-in stairway to the ground. Mary followed him although both paused when one of the baggage handlers unloaded his real wheelchair from baggage and helped to transfer him into his own device. It was dark on the tarmac, but well lit when they came through the door. Gus moved over to Mary and gave her a big hug and then a kiss. Taking the handles of the wheelchair, he started pushing Andy to the terminal.

"I brought the new van so you can drive if you want," he said to Andy who declined. "After you check into the motel, we're going to dinner at the local Mexican joint to meet with a dozen active and retired Special Forces sergeants and their wives."

At the van he showed Andy the ramp controls and had him push the button to open the door and lower the aluminum device. "You then roll on and push the second button to raise it to entry height." Gus pointed out how to swivel the front seats and how he could grab the overhead rail after locking his wheelchair into place. Although he was tired from flying all day, he started appreciating his new independence when Gus showed him the folding bed, cooler, porta-potty and 12-volt coffeemaker along with the long worktable-desk and other features. As Andy got into the passenger seat, he had dozens of questions about operating the hand controls.

"First thing in the morning," said Gus. "We're going to look at apartments. Tomorrow afternoon one of the retired sergeants promised to take us out to practice with the new van on a remote part of the base. I was thinking I would take Mary with us to teach her how to drive the Corvette. Since it's a semi-competition car, the clutch, steering and brakes are more difficult to master."

"That's my other surprise," Gus told his old friend, making sure Mary was paying attention. "I've ordered a new car. I was thinking Mary could drive the Corvette to Benning and then on to San Antonio. If she doesn't take the Corvette, it'll remain parked most of the time while I drive the new car." He waited for some kind of negative response from Mary, but apparently she wanted to drive a true sports car.

"We could drive up to DC on Saturday," he continued. "I want to see the museums and galleries. Monday morning, both Mary and I could check in with our respective bosses. We could take both your Ford van and the Corvette."

Andy replied, "I may want to stay here and visit my old friends. You and Mary can go, as long as you reserve separate rooms."

The next day Andy looked at both apartments and said he liked the second one. He told Gus he wanted a month-to-month lease. With Mary now going to Walter Reed, he wasn't sure he wanted to

213

stay in North Carolina past this coming May. He might like Washington more.

"I was very uncomfortable last night with all the wives and particularly the widows of old friends hovering around me like helicopters." Andy told both Gus and Mary, as they got ready to go out and practice driving.

"I haven't said anything to you two," Gus responded. "But, MJ is backing a brand new company in the Washington area that I will run as president. I'll also be a part owner. It'll specialize in jobs for the various government agencies requiring design and construction workers with high security clearances."

"Next week I'm touring potential building sites and reviewing the preliminary drawings. For the next few months I'll be busy as a consultant to several agencies in DC and then I'm working for our old friends here at Bragg. By this summer, I want to be working full-time on building the new business."

He paused and turned to Andy asking, "Would you go to work for me, my first employee? Forget North Carolina and move into a furnished apartment in Washington with enough bedrooms for Mary and an office. We can store your household belongings until you choose a permanent place to live. We can reinstitute your Top-Secret SCI clearance. One thing though, you may have to go armed and carry backup weapons in your van and the apartment."

Andy accepted, "I've wanted a real job for the last few years."

"You need to follow me up to DC tomorrow in the van, Mary can ride with either of us. I'll drive the Corvette. We can park them and look for new apartments. This afternoon we need to go out to the local gun emporium and buy several pistols, a shotgun and whatever else you're comfortable with."

Andy interrupted and said, "We don't need to go and buy guns. I'll call the colonel's wife right now and ask her to poll the widows.

She can find out if any of them have custom firearms they want to sell. I'll bet we can get a fine selection of guns from them."

While they were learning to drive the cars, Mary discovered the lighter on the tray between the racing seats. When she asked if it was the item he had mentioned on the phone Gus told her about finding it and then mentioned the incident in Boise and the "Man from Miami". "Can I keep this and study it?" Mary asked.

Gus replied, "I have a copy of the film that was inside. You can study it too."

The two car convoy left at 5:00 the next morning and got to the suburb of Tysons Corner for lunch across from the mall. While they ate, Gus explained, "I think we should build a new facility near the Capital Beltway. Somewhere between Custis and George Washington Parkways into downtown." He turned the map around and used his ballpoint to point out the various locations. Searching through his field bag, he got out a notepad and started sketching.

"The basement and ground floor needs to have secure storage, warehouse racks and shipping." Gus told them. "It's a constant problem to get secure materials to a job site in a timely fashion. We should buy and fill our own shipping containers, keeping records of where we store everything. At the jobsite, the containers can be stacked into quadrangles making a warehouse for secure material storage. The rest of the new building could be for designers, engineers and project pre-planning."

Turning to Mary, he said, "If we're on the Beltway, it'll be less than 18-miles across the I-495 bridge to the Maryland side and around to the Forest Glen Annex north of Silver Springs. Let's check into the Hilton and use the van to drive around in. All of the museums are open tomorrow and we can spend the day on the Capital Mall."

215

"I want to take this lighter to a tobacco shop at the mall," said Mary. "They must have one since it's the biggest shopping center in the America. There's something not right. I think it may be counterfeit. Also I noticed the name has thirteen letters and Flying Tigers has twelve. There are some strange scratches around the duplicate letters. A really good alphanumeric code can be built using twenty-five different letters." Gus was flabbergasted. He had never considered the name and reference to either the WWII unit or the later airfreight line might actually be a code.

"Did you ever ask if anyone in the military or the Agency used the name Hampton Cudbow," asked Mary. "Who did you give your copy of the fingerprints from the dead Man from Miami?" Mary made Gus squirm when she reminded him of things he should have asked or he had forgotten to follow up on.

"More than a week ago, at the colonel's recommendation, I gave a package to his Sergeant Major including both assassins' fingerprints, the name on the lighter and a request for information about the Noggin-Sand Bank, which started in the Far East. The Sergeant Major and I followed up earlier this week, although I haven't found out about the name on the lighter." Gus looked over at Mary to make sure she approved.

"I did find out about the Man from Miami, our Miguel DeMiguel. A retired sergeant at Bragg knows him and claims he is definitely a Russian agent. DeMiguel and his brother work for the Noggin-Sand Bank. He also told me the bank moved to a new headquarters at George Town on Grand Cayman Island a few years ago, and they opened a second branch in Switzerland. Of course Mike Sand started in MACV-SOG and went on to work for the CIA before moving over to the bank branch in Switzerland. Frank Noggin in George Town was the Australian always affiliated with shady activities in

Southeast Asia. Many people thought he was affiliated with the Mafia."

"Here's the plan," Mary said. "Gus, go and get us three rooms and make sure two of them open onto a parlor suite where we can lay everything out while we work. I'm going to take Papa into the mall and look for a tobacconist; we'll meet you at the hotel. Skip the idea of going touring tomorrow; we can do that later in the week when it's less crowded. As soon as you get to the room, call the Sergeant Major at the compound and find our what he has. It's Saturday but he's probably still at work. If he has a packet of information, get it up here to Dulles on the next flight out of Fayette-ville." Mary remembered the only money she had were German Marks so she asked Gus for some cash.

The sergeant major did have a dozen more pages of information Gus needed to review. Nobody named Hampton Cudbow ever served in the Army, the CIA or Flying Tiger Airlines. He also had another dozen pages on Miguel DeMiguel. He was a contractor for several CIA front companies throughout the Caribbean, using at least four different aliases. The Agency released him after his name came up during the Watergate investigation. He would send a sergeant up with the information this afternoon. "Meet him at the fixed base operator on the private side of Dulles. He'll be there by 5:00 pm."

He then called his uncle Dick in Idaho and asked about the status of the new company, first telling him about his hiring Andy. Dick Knowles said, "The enterprise is officially organized in Delaware as Enigmatic Inc. You can sign contracts and documents as the new president. The new name means mysterious or unknowable. I sent you a packet of information about the directors along with new checks for the bank account, letterhead stationary and a minicomput-er." He then explained how the computer specialist at the MI offices in Virginia was waiting for their call. He would set up the computer at their hotel this afternoon. It was a German made IBM machine compatible with the 370 series used by MJ.

"Of course I'm the CEO and Len Jordan is the Chairman," uncle Dick continued. "The others include a retired Ambassador and two retired generals from the Engineers and Intelligence. Since you're on the board, we'll need a lawyer or an accountant as the seventh member. Each board member gets one percent of the stock and the rest is reserved for future bonuses. There is a mandatory buy-back clause for the board."

"What about my other roommate, Ari Goldman." Gus asked. "He's both a lawyer and CPA and he certainly knows his way around Washington."

His uncle told him to wait a week or two before talking to Ari, "I need to poll the other board members." Dick Knowles continued, "UBS in Zurich registered a holding company in Liechtenstein with the same name, Enigmatic$_{AG}$. It owns 45% of the stock in the Delaware Corporation. Your other uncle recommended that we not use mine or his name so half the stock is in your name and the rest in a family trust run by your grandmother." Gus asked enough about the stock ownership to answer his questions.

"They are extending two million in credit," his uncle Dick told him. "You need to get to Switzerland and sign the various official papers. You can change some of our hard assets into more liquid ones they can transfer internationally. The information is waiting at the MJ office in Rosslyn; call them right now to start things. On Monday they'll set you up with a local architect and a real estate agent."

As Gus was hanging up, there was a knock at the door. It was Mary and Andy. "The lighter is an expensive counterfeit Zippo. The maker reversed the location of the registration mark at the end of the word Zippo and the manufacturing location of Bradford, PA is also misplaced. He also left off the period. The chrome plating is too thin and the engraving cuts into the brass case." Mary brought it over and showed Gus what she was talking about.

Using his magnifying glass Gus could see there were light scratches adjacent to several of the duplicate letters. "Hampton Cudbow and Flying Tigers actually spell out Hampvqx Cudbow and Flying Tkjers." Mary said. "If I use the light scratches there are 25 unique letters. Let's start working on the code."

23

By Monday morning, Mary had broken the two-digit code where every message was transmitted in blocks of six digits. Starting with the most recent message, she was finished with about a hundred pages. The minicomputer was set up and the printer was spitting out decrypted pages of simple code. Dedee Anderson had joined them in their code breaking efforts.

Unfortunately, over 4,000 messages were in different codes.

Each of the twenty-five letters was represented by two numbers with the rest of the pairs of numbers always representing phrases, end words and sentences. Another common double was used to start and stop numbers.

Of course the most recent message was sent just days before the 1977 ambush in Austria and the first message was in 1962, fifteen years before. The CIA turncoat working for the Russian was never identified, but there were tons of information about various rogue operations that were outside official purview.

Andy was guarding the suite where Mary was working on the decryption. Gus was beginning to get the hang of converting the numbers to letters since these messages were written in English and the accompanying American top-secret documents were unencrypted.

On his Sunday morning run with Mary, Gus noticed a local gun shop so he went back after it opened and bought some cleaning equipment and extra ammo for the inherited firearms the widows in Fort Bragg had sold them. They now had three fully automatic submachine guns, two with suppressors, a 9mm pistol with a suppressor and several more pistols and revolvers. Also included was a 12-guage riot shotgun similar to the Winchester Gus carried but it was a six-shot Mossberg Cruiser with an aluminum receiver and pistol grip which kept the gun light and short for use from a wheelchair.

"You'd better call Keith Allison from Diplomatic Security and hand over the lighter," Dedee said before she left Sunday night.

"Are you going to tell him how much we've already decrypted?" Mary said Monday morning as she glanced at Gus to make sure he understood the danger of giving the bureaucrats too much information. He replied, "I need to call him and our MJ office to set up meetings," as he excused himself to go next door and get the various phone numbers.

When he got back Mary had already poured him another cup of coffee so Gus called the MJ office in Washington and arranged to meet with the architect and real estate agent later in the morning. He then called Keith Allison's phone number and told him he was in Washington. Allison said they were making no progress on decoding the microfilm, however they were trying to figure out who had access to the various pieces of information. Apparently he didn't know Gus had his own copy of the information.

"When Ken Cox took the microfilm to the airport to meet the F-111 he left the lighter with me." Gus told the Deputy Director who was listening quietly. "I have since followed up and nobody with the name Hampton Cudbow ever served with the US Military or with the Flying Tigers, either the WWII outfit or later with the freight airline. I just had the lighter checked out and it's a high quality counterfeit Zippo, not made in the US."

"I need to pick up the lighter as soon as possible," responded Allison. "Since you shouldn't come here, where can we meet?" Gus suggested he come out to Tysons Corner as soon as he could. He would be waiting outside the Cigar Tobacco Shop on Leesburg Pike in an hour. After Gus hung up, Mary asked to use the phone.

"I'm going to call the Walter Reed Annex at Forest Glen and make an appointment for an official visit tomorrow. We'll use Andy's ID to order me a full set of uniforms from the military clothing store there at the PX. They'll have the fatigues, hospital whites and probably a standard Army green uniform, but I may have to order a dress blue uniform, and probably even dress whites. I'll ask at the annex. I'm not sure if I should have patches sewn on my field uniforms or just use subdued metal rank and branch insignia?"

"You probably won't need your Army Greens until the graduation ceremony at Fort Sam Houston. You can have patches sewn on later."

When Allison arrived in a black government Suburban with two agents in the front, Gus walked up to the back door and said into the opened window, "I want to point out a few discrepancies after we go into the store and you check out the Zippo's in their stock. Then I want to ask a favor?"

Allison got out and went inside with Gus. The shop owner knew what Gus wanted to show so he pulled out a magnifying glass and they looked at the bottom and then the engraving cut through the chrome and into the brass case. Gus pointed out the scratches, which seemed to change a few of the duplicate letters.

As they walked back out Gus explained, "I'm now a special consultant to the Combat Applications Group, 1st Special Forces Operating Detachment-Delta. I'll be going back to Europe and then working in Turkey and finally somewhere else for the next few months."

He paused while Keith Allison nodded his head in complete understanding. "I need to keep my diplomatic passport and identification as a Special Agent for Diplomatic Security for at least the next few months. However, I promise to keep John Campbell, your RSO in the loop. I won't be able to let him know any classified details, but I will let him know if I use the credentials."

Allison agreed, maybe too readily since Gus was sure the special group in New York just wanted him out of their hair. He reasoned Allison probably thought the proposed action in Iran would solve their problem of "what to do about Gus".

Going into the office in Rosslyn, Gus met with the architect and real estate agent and went down the street to a famous New Orleans style restaurant for lunch. When Gus lay out the design he was contemplating, the architect was interested in why he wanted certain features. The real estate man didn't seem to care. Finally Gus told them, "I want sensitive compartmented information facilities-SCIF's built with cast-in-place concrete walls on each of the upper floors." He explained that he couldn't discuss things further until the design team got their own clearances. I've already applied for you to get clearances through Diplomatic Security.

Turning to the Realtor he continued, "I also don't want anyone to rent an adjacent space or be able to watch our movements." He didn't tell him he was worried about line of sight angles. He listed the warehouse requirements and the other spaces. "I'm taking my friends to New York this weekend so we have to select the property before then. In addition I want the preliminary drawings finished by the middle of January so we can start on the underground construction."

After lunch they drove to a half-dozen listings for vacant land just off the Beltway between Arlington Boulevard and Georgetown Pike, the last commercial exit on I-495 before Maryland. The architect and Gus narrowed the selection down to two pieces of property, but the designer wanted to get some geotechnical information before he would approve a final choice.

Gus told the real estate man to get all the listing for nearby condominiums and apartments and come back tomorrow; he would pay him a commission even on apartments. That night Dedee came back over. She and Mary continued to decode more of the documents.

On Tuesday while Andy and Mary went over to the annex, Gus went looking for someplace to live. The first apartment complex was east of the Beltway on Dolly Madison and had numerous three-story buildings with one, two and three bedroom apartments. Gus liked the look of the complex.

It had an exercise room and a game room near the pool. In addition, at the back there were several townhouse pods, with two-story townhouses sandwiched by end units that were double-width single-story handicapped apartments. Each of the handicapped units had three-bedrooms and all the units backed up to a park. Across the parking lot were dozens of rentable single garages.

The townhouse was a standard two-floor design on top of an unfinished basement that included the laundry. The handicapped unit on either end was designed to mimic the center townhouse units but the two floors were side-by-side on a concrete slab. Since there were no stairs, there was a windowless middle office/bedroom in its place. Rather than a half-bath down and two upstairs there were just two full bathrooms. The kitchen was slightly bigger, and it had a side-by-side front-loading washer and dryer in the pantry.

"The units are unfurnished," the rental agent said. "We can always provide rental furnishings, mostly tired old stuff. However there are several furniture companies that will completely decorate and supply everything for both units. In addition, nearby places like Sears and K-Mart have almost everything else you need."

"What about the garages?" Gus asked.

"There's an added cost each month but they're standard size. If you want to store anything you have to install your own shelves. I understand you have a van with a side ramp. It'll fit just fine but you probably won't be able to extend the ramp inside. The reserved parking in front of the one-story has a doublewide handicapped space."

They went back to the office and Gus signed the paperwork for three units, a handicapped one plus two townhouses, along with garages for each. They could put their own lock on the garages and start storing things immediately.

Gus went back to the hotel, ordered a salad and pot of coffee from room service and started to read every encoded message sent to the Russians, along with the American top-secret documents included with each message. Dedee called and said that she was meeting with someone from counterintelligence and wouldn't be in that evening. Four hours later, when Mary and Andy got back with their bags of army clothes Gus said, "Let's go visit our new apartments."

As he pushed his good friend around the handicapped unit he said, "You can make the third bedroom into an office and workroom, each of the other two bedrooms has its own bathroom. I also rented two townhouses next door, I'll take one and Bill Williams and his wife Jan will live in the other. I'm bringing him in to supervise our office construction." As they went out on the patio, Gus pointed to the trail running throughout the park behind the units, and how there was a half-hidden gate just a hundred feet away. He also mentioned the exercise room, recreation room and pool complex. He then walked across the parking area to the garages and opened one to show Mary where she could keep the cars, mentioning to Andy that the van would have to remain out unless Mary put it in the garage.

Back at the hotel Gus asked both for advice before Andy got out of the van. "Do you want to keep the furniture coming from Germany? Your bedrooms and the upholstered living room furniture is pretty old and worn, although there are a few nice pieces. We can mix rooms, rent some and buy others. Even if I get a different place later, we'll probably continue to use these apartments as temporary housing for construction personnel."

"What do you mean, a different place?" Mary asked.

"I'd like to buy a house in the woods overlooking the river. I was thinking about something with about ten acres, a pool and a dock. Maybe even a farm further out in Loudoun County. We'll need a small annex or house for Andy."

"You know a place like that could cost a half-million by the time you finished."

"I know. That's why I'll take some time to get the business going first."

As they went in, Gus whispered to Andy, "I want you to read the marked paragraphs in the Zippo documents while Mary and I go shopping for furniture and household items. Order in something to eat from room service, we'll get something while we're out.

24

On Wednesday morning, Gus and Mary drove the full van to the apartments. The computer expert was moving their equipment into the third bedroom office of the handicapped apartment. They stretched in the exercise room and then ran out the back gate and did four circuits of the trail through the park.

"Measuring my stride, I think each lap is just over 1.5 miles around." Gus said as they cooled down by walking a fifth lap. "Let's unload the van into Bill's empty garage. He and Jan won't be here for a few weeks. All we have is some office furniture from MJ. Most of the rental furniture will be delivered later today, and we can move all of it into the apartments. I think I'll ask the hotel for a late check-out."

As they unloaded the van into the third garage, they started talking about their upcoming trip to New York on Friday through Sunday. Gus said, "My friend Ken Cox has already made reservations for my birthday dinner at his special chop-house near Grand Central.

He says it's the best in town; although, he also said that the cops go there to stare at the Mafia hoods. I want to stay at the Hilton near the theaters. Of course on Saturday we're picking up my new car. I asked him to get us tickets for the Saturday evening performance of *Evita*. Should I get two or three? Is Andy coming?"

"I thought your birthday was tomorrow the 6th," Mary said. "I'm not sure Papa will go to New York. He wants to make a list of everything he thinks should be in the new building. He also wants to talk to you about our Zippo documents. He's waiting to have breakfast with us in the living room of the suite."

While Mary went to shower and change, Andy said, "I found a single mention of Miguel DeMiguel, a dozen citations for the Noggin-Sand Bank and more references to Mike Sand, Frank Noggin and Rodrigo DeMiguel. There were scores of mentions of other shady characters, many of whom I thought I knew." Gus was nodding his head in understanding.

"Our principal turncoat was sending two to three messages and top secret documents a week for fifteen years." Andy said. "There was a slowdown between 1971 and 1973 and the type of attached information changed in 1975. A lot more information came from state and not as much from the CIA. He was banking with Frank Noggin out of George Town in the Cayman's, and he collected over a couple of hundred thousand a year."

"Apparently the KGB is fully aware the DeMiguel brothers worked for the bank." He paused and looked at Gus. "The only way you're going to stop the Russians from trying to eliminate you is to expose their agent in the CIA or make him so uncomfortable he tells them to stop. If you kill Frank Noggin and Mike Sand it will force all the cockroaches to scatter like a light turning on in the kitchen. They won't be able to go on the offensive for months."

"I've already thought of that," said Gus. "I've never been an assassin or killed anyone who wasn't at war with me. However much these two tempt me, I can't kill them. Even though Noggin has already threatened my grandmother, there's no way his assassin DeMiguel could know the lighter was in Boise unless someone in the New York CIA group warned him through the bank. I believe Noggin passed a message to the Soviets and then sent an assassination team from Miami. The Spetsnaz officer was the only man who could recognize me, so they sent him to help." Gus paused as Andy nodded.

"Maybe we could do something else to take off the heat," Gus said. "First, I would have to confirm one of them is in the Caribbean and the other is at the bank branch in Lucerne." Gus continued. "Second, I've been trying to think of a way to get into the Cayman's undetected and then get from George Town to Switzerland before anyone knows I was there. Everyone at the CIA is going to shit if their main secret bank suddenly implodes, but I've got to make the players back off without letting them know it was me. They're bankers, we need to strip them of all their illegal assets."

"I know how to get into and out of the Cayman's," said Andy. "But, I won't tell you unless you let me set it up and go with you."

Gus thought about it and then said, "You can go. Start planning but don't do anything until I give you the final go-ahead. How are you going to get me in and out?"

"I have two friends who run a charter sailboat out of Fort Lauderdale," Andy told him. "Both men are former SEAL's who served in the Maritime Operations group at MACV-SOG. You might have met them at C&C Da Nang. Barry Norton is about your height and looks like a blond surfer while Paul Rodgers is much shorter, muscular and going bald, although he has a full beard." Andy paused while the waiter delivered breakfast. He knocked on Mary's door, and then wheeled himself back over.

"I don't want Mary to know what we're doing so we can't act until she goes to Benning on January 6th," Andy said. "We could then sail to the island using false ID, probably Canadian. It'll take about five days to round western Cuba and go past the Yucatán Peninsula."

"You take care of business while the rest of us distract any watchers and then go straight to the local airport and catch the 7:30 morning plane up to Montreal. Since Cayman is a crown colony and Canada is a commonwealth country there's no visa check between the two." Gus asked for more specifics. He didn't realize that Andy had researched the details.

"Getting into Montreal-Dorval at one o'clock you would have a several hour layover before catching the afternoon Air Canada flight to Zurich. Arriving just before 6:00 am CET you could catch the early train to Lucerne. You should be at Sand's villa well before sunrise at 8:10 am the next morning."

Mary came in to have breakfast wearing a towel turban and her bathrobe. When she got up to pour more coffee, Gus said to Andy, "Go ahead and start setting things up." He then asked about the New York trip and Andy said he had too much to do in DC.

Andy said, "I don't want to drive all around the country, besides your new car only has two bucket seats. Based on what you said last week, I've been thinking about everything we need to do. At the end of next week, Mary should follow you in the Corvette and leave it in the parking lot at the Atlanta airport. You two go on west from there and tour the west coast. I can fly from here to Boise and meet you in Idaho. We can all fly to Key West after Christmas. Later Mary can fly back from Florida and drive the car down to the post at Fort Benning."

Gus agreed with the plan telling Andy, "You can stay here, work on your issues while Mary and I tour New York. I'm going to pick-up the new car in Danbury on Saturday and drive it back down here on Sunday." He looked over at Mary to make sure she understood what he was proposing.

"In the meantime, I'll call the architect and the home office in Boise. Today we can move things into the new apartments and tomorrow I'll go to Alexandria and discuss the two properties with our designer. I also need to call Brooks Brothers and let them know that I'll be in town later this week to pick up the clothes they've been holding."

"On Monday the 10th I want to spend a week with the architect here along with a team from the main office. The new company needs to make an offer on the property and start conceptual drawings. Having studied his sketches I trust the man's ability to give us a good-looking building, however we may need the architects and engineers in Boise to complete the working drawings."

By Thursday morning the two apartments were occupied, however they still needed to fix them up. Gus and Mary went to the exercise room, lifted weights and stretched. They then went out for another six-mile run in the park. That evening Dedee came over and Mary fixed a special meal of veal wiener schnitzel in the new apartment and finished the birthday supper off with a German chocolate cake covered with candles. Dedee reported that she was collecting a lot of new information. "I met with James Jesus Angleton's replacement at the CIA and he swore that he has vetted the income of every potential suspect. I am supposed to check the spending habits of a dozen people who have left the Company for greener pastures."

On Friday morning, Andy drove Gus and Mary over to National Airport and they caught the Eastern shuttle to LaGuardia in New York. Ken Cox who had parked his official Ford at the curb met them at the gate. "I'm now a special consultant to the Department of Defense on another project," Gus mentioned on the way into Manhattan.

He then casually asked, "How's it going with decrypting the coded messages. I know the lighter helped, however have you guys discovered the identity of the Russian agent in the CIA?"

"The lighter?" Ken asked. "You mean the Zippo with the prisoner's name; we don't have it." He changed the subject to let them know they had an executive two-bedroom suite at the Hilton and tickets for *Evita* were waiting with the concierge. Don't forget your reservation tonight at Sparks; our SAIC had to pull some strings to get you in. He called in a favor from one of his contacts. You do know it's a mob hangout although it has a reputation as the best chop house in the city.

"Do we need to take a cab or can we walk," asked Gus.

"Let's take a cab there," said Mary. "I'm wearing a short silver lamé dress tonight with a black cape. The weather is beautiful, so maybe we could walk back. I can bring a pair of comfortable black flats I could change into and wear back to the hotel." As they got out of the undercover sedan, Mary handed Ken a piece of paper.

Going inside she said, "I gave him the letters engraved on the lighter and their corresponding numeric code numbers."

25

Dropping their bags in the suite, they went to Brooks Brothers for a final fitting and arrange delivery of his tailored clothing. They then spent the afternoon at MoMA, then the Guggenheim, and finally at the Metropolitan, until they had to dress for dinner. Although early December it was a beautiful late fall day, almost like early November. It was in the high 50's, sunny and mild. Back at the hotel, Gus showered and dressed for his birthday dinner. He was wearing his new tuxedo, the highly polished low-quarters and his ankle holster. He wore the dotted burgundy tie and matching cummerbund set. He wore both a black leather belt and a set of buttonhole braces to support the pistol, suppressor and extra magazines. Looking in the mirror Gus realized that although he looked like a waiter wearing the black accessories, in burgundy he looked like a piano player.

Everything fit comfortably since he was now down to his best weight. His hair, beard and mustachios were getting much longer; he hadn't shaved in six weeks, although his facial hairs were still too light-colored to pass for a native in Iran. Luckily he had stopped at a theatrical supply house and purchased some disguise items and hair color.

At 8:00 they took a taxi the ten blocks across midtown to the restaurant. Mary was wearing the short dress with her stiletto heels under her cape and the only reason Gus looked taller was his black dress fedora, which had been waiting at Brooks Brothers with the custom suits.

Her legs shimmered in the light so she must be wearing pantyhose; the dress was so short garters and thigh-highs would show. "You look fabulous tonight," Gus told her as he realized he had finally met the girl he should marry.

Going inside, they checked in and the maître d' mentioned they could wait in the small lounge for their table. Gus slipped him a folded twenty. Without a pause, he pocketed the folded money as he looked down at the reservation sheet and discovered they were supposed to sit at the special table-for-two in the dark corner.

It was well away from the kitchen entrance. As the maître d' left their small table, one of a party of four sitting in the darkened corner booth moved his hand so he stepped close and leaned over listening to what the man whispered. He looked at Gus and then turned his head as he said something in a low voice, and then moved back to the front entrance. A few moments later, one of the men in the booth slid out and headed through the kitchen door. His jacket didn't fit well; it clumped up where he was wearing a pistol.

Studying the remaining three, Gus could see from their bulging lapels at least two more were armed. He thought he recognized the speaker in the corner and tried to remember who he was. In the meantime he was talking with Mary and fielding questions about wine from the sommelier and a description of the hors d'oeuvres from their waiter.

"Why aren't you drinking wine," Mary asked?

"I'm afraid one drink will lead to another," Gus answered. "For a couple of years I've been having a problem with controlling my consumption. I decided to go cold turkey."

He mentioned to Mary, "This place is famous for its food and the Mafioso who are regular patrons." Gus snapped his fingers as he remembered his picture from the International Herald Tribune. "Peter Mangano, the number two man in the Gambino crime family is sitting in the corner booth."

A few minutes later, the mobster came out of the kitchen, sat down and leaned across to whisper to Big Petey who asked him some questions. A half-hour later, the four *Cosa Nostra* diners got up to leave, without paying for their food. As the four made their way to the door, Gus studied their movements. He leaned over, almost as if he were protecting Mary from their sight.

"What's that all about? Why were you studying those gangsters?" Mary asked. She was silent as Gus explained what he thought he had discovered.

"Colonel Bankhead told me the bombing in Brindisi must have been carried out by the Mafia after I mentioned that the men were Sicilian." Gus continued, "In Boise, Ken Cox told me at least one of the Mafia families here in New York has been building connections with the new Russian mobsters across the river in Brooklyn, mostly around Brighton Beach on Coney Island. He went on to tell me that during the late 50's and early 60's the Italian mob were closely connected with various Cuban organizations in an attempt to get their gambling operations back into Cuba. I know Miguel DeMiguel handled some assassination work for La Cosa Nostra in the Caribbean during the time period."

"Based on phone calls Ed Warren made from Turkey," Gus continued. "I was told he talked to someone at the CIA, a number at the Embassy in Ankara and I later found out to his Drug Enforcement mentor in Europe. One of them must be the Soviet agent or working for him. Someone wanted us dead and it looks like they hired the Mafia in Sicily to carry out the contract. We need to get back to the hotel, the safest way. We're too exposed getting into a taxi, there's no way to know who's driving." Gus stood to help Mary around the table.

"Before we leave, change your stiletto-heels for the flats," Gus explained after telling her his worries. "Then fasten your cape and scarf and be prepared to drop behind some cover if I say to. We'll try and face oncoming traffic since it will give us better protection."

They ducked out of the entrance and turned west on 46th jogging across 3rd Avenue. Gus planned to quickly move on toward Lexington and then Park. As soon as they left the restaurant, he pulled his Colt pistol out and held it by his side.

Stopping in a doorway and looking in both directions, Gus pulled out the suppressor and removed the thread protector as he screwed it onto the lightweight .45-ACP. To cover his white shirt Gus turned the notched satin collar of his tuxedo up, it was black wool felt on the back and had an old fashioned button. Gus fit it through the button loop on the back of the lapel.

"You carry the ASP just in case," he said to Mary as he stooped to draw his sleek backup pistol.

He was going to Park Avenue then turn north and head uptown. The north and southbound lanes on Park were divided and the wide plazas offered some space, so no one could get really close.

Their first problem was a block beyond Lexington where Park Avenue emerged from the viaduct under the old New York Central building. There were dozens of places where shooters could hide. They needed to get north before entering the open plazas and divided roadways of Park Avenue.

Gus led Mary one block north on Lexington to 47th and then continued west toward Park. When he got near the corner, there was a stepped plaza up into a bank with a 3-foot wide black granite wall.

Just as he suspected, somebody opened fire from the entrance lobby between the two viaducts with a fully automatic Uzi-submachine gun. It was noisy as hell and the shooter was firing in disciplined 5-round bursts. However, the gunman was more than 100-yards away. Most of the bullets were impacting into cars parked along the curb.

Gus grabbed Mary, pulled her across the low granite wall and down behind its protection. She had her purse and stilettos in one hand and the ASP in the other. Looking around he saw they were in front of Chemical Bank. His rough handling caused her pantyhose to ladder up both knees.

The shooter advanced backward to the other side of Park Avenue to get a better angle so they crawled along the wall away from him. A second later the assassin had to change magazines. During the pause, Gus and Mary dashed across some steps to get down behind a stone planter. Gus peeked around the planter and realized he had no choice except to return fire.

The assassin started up with his second magazine and the glass storefront to the bank shattered as the alarm went off klaxoning into the night. Suddenly two more gunmen were crossing the southbound lane to the median, both wearing dark leather jackets and pants.

As the gravel in the center parkway crunched under their feet, Gus took careful aim, bracing his arm on the barricade. He fired two shots across the intervening 60-feet into the larger man as the other man dropped and scrambled for cover behind a planter.

His first bullet hit him just below his nose and the second shot went into the center of his forehead. The smaller man raised and was starting to shout as Gus shot him in the roof of his open mouth and then followed up with a shot into his eye.

The *can* on the end of his pistol quieted the sound somewhat and the extra weight helped to steady the pistol back down for a quick follow-up shot. Both gunmen slumped into the ivy groundcover.

Gus peeked around the corner of the granite planter and saw the sniper with the short barreled Uzi was reloading again. The distance was now more than 150-yards so Gus aimed at the top of his head.

His first shot didn't drop him, and the ineffective marksman was bringing his machine gun into firing position, so he ducked back. The gunman fired his entire magazine of thirty rounds in two 1.5-second bursts, spraying bullets all over the area.

Gus looked back and fired three rounds even higher, hoping to hit his center of mass. The second and third shots were a lot higher than the first, a half-foot above his head and then a foot higher. Seeing dust jump from his coat he knew he had hit the man at least once.

Changing to a new magazine, he was ready with eight new bullets. However, rather than Super-Vel hollow points, this magazine was loaded with Hi-Way metal piercing rounds.

A van on the downtown curb started up and pulled out heading south. Gus held his fire until the van abruptly swung left starting a sweeping U-turn at the 47th Street crossover.

Gus started firing aimed shots at the driver's window and then the windshield. He could hear the higher pitched crack of rounds firing from his left. As the van started to waver, he changed his target and started firing at the passenger, riding shotgun.

Mary was firing the lighter but higher velocity 9 mm at the same van from his left. Her gunshots had taken on a more deliberate cadence but much sharper noise.

The thug leaned out firing a burst from another Uzi as Gus shot him with his last two bullets as Mary fired her last few also. The van crashed into the light standard just a dozen feet from them, but Mary didn't waver staying in her two-handed crouched Weaver stance.

Gus reloaded with his last magazine as he heard shouting from uptown. A foot patrolman was running down the middle of the northbound lanes, trying to draw his revolver and shouting at the same time.

"Put the pistol on the ground and sit down on the steps," Gus told Mary as he did the same with his .45. Pulling out his badge and holding it up he shouted, "Federal Agent."

After the cop called the badge number and ID to his precinct, Gus wandered over to look at the van and then the two bodies in the median.

Gus knew the larger man. He was one of the Spetsnaz soldiers from the Khoda Bridge crossing the Alma River. The soldier was wearing a duplicate of the leather field jacket worn by the assassin in Boise. Within 15-minutes they were surrounded by half-a-dozen policemen and the first detectives' arrived from Midtown North.

An older investigator approached and asked to see his identification. As he studied the badge and card, Gus removed his diplomatic passport and handed it to him. "I can't tell you anything, but you can call my New York contact," as he gave him the card from FBI special agent Kenneth Cox.

"You'd also better call the Counter-Intelligence squad and the Organized Crime unit since these Russian KGB assassins were sent here by Big Petey Mangano. I killed his associates in Italy last month. He recognized me at Sparks earlier tonight."

"Tell me what happened," both detectives started taking notes as Gus began reviewing his actions. A policeman came up and whispered to the detective. He turned and said, "The man near the viaduct is just wounded. I'm going down to ask him some questions until a bus gets here to take him to the hospital. Wait here for the senior officers to arrive."

Within the first hour, Gus and Mary were driven to 306 West 54th Street and separated into two different interview rooms. Over the next four hours the various detectives, officers and even the inspector in command of what used to be the old 18th Precinct asked Gus numerous questions.

FBI special agent Ken Cox came to identify Gus and they let him into the room. He said, "The wounded man was wearing a bullet-proof jacket. You hit it twice but your last round grazed him in the collarbone/neck at just short of 500 feet. You hit the rest of them in the head two or more times each. Whoever was shooting your ASP put all 8-shots into either side of the windshield and hit both men inside."

Assuming someone was listening, Gus said, "You know most of what they want to know is highly classified. In fact, I can't tell them where I've been, how I was made a Diplomatic Security agent, how I got a silenced pistol and I certainly can't tell them where I'm going next." Gus stared directly at Ken Cox.

"They won't like it but the fact is they have to give me back my pistols and suppressor. I'll need them when I go back into Iran. I'll also need some replacement .45-ACP rounds and more for the 9mm. I also want the biggest man's bulletproof leather jacket." Cox looked at him in alarm, then suddenly nodded in understanding.

"I did learn the NYPD has identified the crew that tried to assassinate you. They're from the Russian Mob," said Ken. "They usually work out of Brighton Beach. Their full gang includes around 10-gunmen who do outside wet work for the Gambino family."

"Bullshit! I recognized the big man as a Spetsnaz operative; he's in Spetsgruppa Alpha from their unit across the river at the Khoda

Bridge. Ken, can you investigate the four other Russians?" Gus asked. "They moved like trained Spetsnaz soldiers, not mobsters." As Ken left he said, "I'll talk to the CI inspector and the head of organized crime and ask them to release you."

Within 15-minutes he was escorted into the commander's office where he offered Gus an apology and handed him his badge, identification and both guns with the suppressor still attached to the Colt Commander. There were also full boxes of ammunition and both untouched leather field jackets.

"I understand you're going up to Connecticut to pick up a car and then you have tickets for a show later tonight. I would like to assign a couple of detectives to watch over you until then. They can drive you to Danbury."

The captain in charge of the Organized Crime unit and the CI Inspector were watching. "Get word to Big Petey Mangano," Gus said to the OC captain. "The contract he took out on me was bought and paid for by the Russian KGB."

It was almost 3:00 am when Gus escorted Mary to her room. "Do you want to go to the show tonight or should I try and sell the tickets?" Gus asked. Mary said, "Let's go."

"You're an incredible date, most women would run the other way screaming." Gus leaned over and kissed her on the forehead.

"Well, I've never had a date quite like this one. I'll probably have nightmares for a week." Gus smiled, looked into her eyes as he leaned over and kissed her the way he had been wanting to all night. Leaning back, he looked in her eyes and said, "You may not want me to date me anymore. I put you in too much danger."

"In more ways than one," Mary said as she took a deep breath.

Later in the day when he picked up his new birthday present, the dealer gave him several custom items including fitted suitcases, a

Ferrari team jacket, baseball hat and a picnic kit with a Ferrari labeled blanket. The car also had a bright red fitted waterproof cover with zippers for the mirrors and antenna.

Dick told them, "After it passed inspection I changed the American DOT approved headlights and fog lamps back to the more powerful European ones. I also hard-wired a Cincinnati Microwave dual band radar detector just above the mirror that picks up the X and the K bands." The fuzzbuster was now required for long range cruising since the president issued an order requiring everyone drive less than 55 to save the planet. Of course Hollywood donors with private jets weren't included.

"How much did you spend on this car," were the first words out of Mary's mouth when they were finally alone in the new sports car."

"It cost about $35,000 including the original import fees and duties. Of course there were additional costs for DOT and EPA certifications." He then mentioned that his grandfather had a 22-year old Ferrari GT California Spyder sports car and later bought a 1961 Ferrari Testa Rossa racecar from Brian his driving mentor. He had driven each for one or two seasons before selling them as used. They were both on trailers at the shop in Boise with broken parts so neither of them ran.

"Mary, I've spent less than a thousand dollars a year for the past fifteen years." Gus tried to explain. "All I've driven are crummy pickup trucks and I fly everywhere on military planes. I have ten-times as much in the bank as this car cost, including all its expenses. I wanted to splurge on a new sports car."

26

On Sunday, during the drive back to Virginia, Gus held the speed to below 60 mph to break-in the new twelve-cylinder car. At several different places he left the turnpike to drive through various New Jersey towns at much slower speeds. Although he told Mary he was breaking in the new car, he was actually checking to see if anyone was following them.

"Next week I'll change the oil and check for metal shavings in both the Ferrari and the Corvette before we leave for the west coast," Gus told her. During their Sunday afternoon excursion, Gus listened while Mary briefly talked about her lack of driving during undergraduate studies at Harvard.

"In Germany you can't get a learners permit until you're 18, even on an American military base." Mary started talking as they slowly drove past a park in Linden. "When I flew back to Cambridge to take up my scholarship at Harvard, I had never driven a car. In fact throughout my undergraduate studies I still didn't. There was no boyfriend to teach me to drive since I spent all my time studying and working." She glanced across at Gus to see if he had any questions.

"For the first few years I worked as a server and busser in the dining hall as a part of my scholarship. I made the track team in February and by late spring I had won a place on the '72 Olympic team in the 100-meter hurdles."

"I had no idea you made the Olympic team," Gus said.

"In Munich I didn't even finish in the top ten, the Soviet countries won all the medals. The Black September terrorist attack affected me deeply. I finally understood what my papa was doing in the Green Berets. By making the Olympic team I was awarded an athletic scholarship to go with my academic one. Tuition was included however I still needed spending money, so I became a Residence Assistant in one of the dorms, earning a pittance plus room and board." Gus asked her about free housing and Mary explained that women's teams didn't get dorm rooms or free food. There weren't many cash paying jobs.

"Because of Papa and another Special Forces sergeant, I began studying unarmed martial arts at a dōjō on the Harvard Square. As an RA I was responsible for the safety of the girls in my dorm."

Gus interrupted again and asked the name of the martial arts school. She told him it was Korean, teaching hapkido a modified aiki-jujutsu and he responded by saying, "I trained at the same dōjō when I was a graduate student at MIT. I lived in a studio apartment just off Massachusetts Avenue midway between the two schools."

"I'm still studying striking and throwing seven years later," Mary continued. "Although I am now a black belt, sandan degree. For the next two summers I worked as a server at Yellowstone National Park, taking the train out and back. I needed the tips. I did learn to fly fish while I was in Wyoming; there was nothing else to do. During my junior and senior years I worked as a waitress in a local pizza parlor where I made enough from tips to get by."

244

They were talking together in German and Gus realized it must be her native language. She confirmed, "Of course I speak, read and write perfect German. My mother was born in Bavaria and I went back to Munich for medical school."

"Why did you become a doctor," Gus asked in English.

Switching languages Mary continued, "Papa joined the Army when he graduated from high school in East Tennessee. His father was a farmer who struggled through the depression. His grandfather Johnson was a large animal veterinarian and Andy's great-grandfather had been a doctor during the American civil war. My grosvater on my mother's side was a surgeon killed at the end of WWII and his father had been a doctor, invalided during WWI. Taking care of the sick and wounded is in my blood. Growing up I always wanted to fix stray animals and my few friends with cuts." Gus was starting to understand her; his family had been engineers for generations.

"Because we moved all the time, I couldn't have pets. I remember living in Okinawa, Fort Bragg, Fort Benning, Fort Devens and at least two different posts in Germany. I made friends, but it was difficult to become close to anyone. All through elementary and junior high I was always taller than the other boys and girls. I loved school and always made perfect grades, to the consternation of the officers children in my classes." Gus felt her touch his arm.

"I was a Girl Scout and loved to go on camping trips and I won all the merit badges offered in medical areas like health aid, home health and safety, and personal health. Before I finished high school I earned the Gold Award. One major reason for my staying active was acceptance. No matter where my papa was transferred I would always be accepted on the new post as a Girl Scout with proof of accomplishment shown by the badges on my sash."

"I understand," Gus reassured her. "I joined the Boy Scouts to learn outdoor activities and make some friends."

"In high school I started swimming and track for the same reasons," Mary said. "When a new coach timed me swimming 100-meters or running the 100-meter hurdles it guaranteed I would be accepted into the new school's athletic program. I was already faster than all the other girls and many of the boys. Academically, during my entire experience in several countries and numerous schools, I made only one B+ in Home Economics." Gus was afraid to ask Mary about any boyfriends. He liked her so much he did not care; he just didn't want to know.

As they crossed the Delaware River at Trenton on the way into Pennsylvania, they continued small talk getting to know each other. Before reaching Maryland, Mary went into detail explaining the trouble she had in medical school once she became known as a pro-American hawk. All of her classmates and professors were dedicated anti-nuclear pacifist except for the few who were anarchist. After several incidents, she kept her head down and did nothing but study.

On Monday the 10th, Gus and Andy drove over to the architect's office in Alexandria where they were meeting the team of engineers and designers flying in from Boise. Bill Williams and his uncle Dick were coming in with them and they should be there by noon. They were having a working lunch buffet in the meeting room. Later in the afternoon Dick Knowles and Gus had a meeting with the National Security Advisor at the Executive Office Building, across the street from the White House while Bill and the geotechnical engineer visited the future site.

Last night he and Andy had reviewed his notes. Gus added several dozen additional items for the new office and warehouse and Andy had several more good ideas to secure the facility.

When they reviewed the plat of the property they were buying, Andy remarked, "If we move the new building closer to the boundary, we'll have enough room to build a second building beside the first some time in the future. There'll still be more than enough room for driveways on either side, a plaza in the middle and a courtyard in the back."

That afternoon, Gus drove Dick into downtown and through the entrance into the EOB parking. On entering both men had to show ID and Gus had to store his pistols. They went to the National Security Council section and waited outside one of the office suites.

"We're here to introduce you to the President's Assistant for National Security Affairs," said Dick. "I've been thinking he could give us a contract for a couple of oil loading-terminal projects within the next month." Gus remembered when two years ago they bid on a project for the Navy, but it was delayed.

"The first one should be just off the shore of Kuwait City and maybe a second one in Bahrain, Qatar or Dubai. He may have to talk to the Chief of Naval Operations."

Gus looked across at his uncle as he nodded at him. He realized Uncle Dick was saying maybe they could get several needed contracts issued this month. The new work would have to be done anyway; the Iranians had seized more than a dozen terminals.

"Sometime within the next year, the State Department needs a new embassy in Islamabad, Pakistan since the fire on November 22nd did significant damage. They'll also need a new consulate in Peshawar if the Russians invade Afghanistan at the end of the month."

The assistant came out to take them into the office suite. Dick introduced Gus to the National Security Advisor who shook his hand and then said, "I keep hearing unusual things about you. The most recent from New York."

"You know he had no choice," responded Dick Knowles immediately. "He was ambushed by the Russians. We think they were hired by our traitor in the CIA."

"I know," replied the president's assistant. "We're watching several suspects at Langley, but your turncoat may have left the Company and be working for a different agency. Someone got a call from a contact in our New York Counterintelligence office last week an hour before lunch. He was calling a blocked government number from a phone booth down the street that we were monitoring. There are very few phones numbers blocked from AT&T, usually only high officials and this one was in DC not the Pentagon, Arlington Hall or Langley over in Virginia."

"Have you narrowed down the suspects?" Dick Knowles asked.

"Immediately the man in Washington left his office," the APNSA recounted. "He went to a monitored phone at the ultra-exclusive F-Street Club and called the banker in the Cayman Island's just before lunch, reversing the charges. He could work here at the EOB, one of the government banks, at State or Interior, or the university. Within a few minutes, Frank Noggin called the phone at a known Mafia social club in New York and confirmed he would pay an additional $25,000 for your elimination; he used your full name and told them to use the photograph they already had. He then gave them information about your planned trip to New York and that the FBI was making reservations for you at Sparks."

"I'm a member of the F-Street Club along with some of our new board of directors," Richard Knowles said. "In fact I was planning on nominating Gus for membership."

"I've been there as a guest," the NSA said. "The President and VP are the only automatic members. It's so exclusive that not even the hundreds of members know who else belongs."

We'll go there after we leave here," Dick said. "Can I have the director call you to emphasize the importance of finding out who came in and used the phone just before lunch that day?"

"Yes." The NSA confirmed. "By the way, the FBI has definitely tied four of the five shooters to individuals who entered New York in 1975 using the Jackson-Vanik Amendment. All five were living in the same area of Brighton Beach that the man you killed in Boise had noted in his suitcase. Unfortunately someone in the NYPD Organized Crime section gave the Mafia your name and the number for the apartment in Virginia where you're living. They also said something about a red Ferrari with a dealer placard." His uncle looked to Gus to continue. He could see that he was livid with this new information.

"I withdrew from active pursuit of the information leak when I forwarded the documents I discovered in the lighter." Gus confirmed. "My girlfriend and I were simply in New York having a birthday dinner, picking up my birthday present and then a Broadway show. I was not tracking spies. In fact, I've been hired by a group at Defense to get a team of clandestine operatives ready to take trucks into Iran in support of a future rescue attempt."

"Hold on," the National Security Advisor nodded for his assistant to pull out a map of Iran. "Please explain what you want to do in Iran."

Gus reviewed the pictures and drawings from the old MJ hanger and buildings at the proposed airport site south of Tehran. He then explained how he wanted to modify the army surplus trucks and take them into Iran on flatbeds. He showed them photos of the traffic at the border crossing and talked about the old construction site, abandoned last year. Gus confirmed nothing would happen other than the purchase and renovation of the vehicles at Incirlik Air Base until they got the go-ahead.

Dick Knowles then talked about the new MJ joint company and what they could do if they had one or two contracts for marine facilities. Gus mentioned the Navy SEALs could work undercover on the new projects and be on standby for support action in the Persian Gulf when they were given the go-ahead. Gus warned the National Security Advisor, "You are aware the Iranian Revolutionary Guard may cross the gulf and attack any new potential competition."

"I've got to talk to the Chief of Naval Operations," the Assistant to the President said. "Since the president embargoed all oil shipments from Iran, we've got to scramble and immediately build several offshore loading platforms. I know MJ has done similar work around the mid-east. Naval Facilities Engineering Command may need to give you contracts for three or four of them. Can you deploy some men and get started before the State of the Union speech on the 23rd of January? I love your idea to bring in SEAL's posing as regular construction workers. We can marry them up with prepositioned equipment. If you can get started in time, we would be interested."

"There's a second set of contracts that we also need to issue," the president's assistant then continued. "The Air Force is planning a contract to rebuild all the Air Force barracks and facilities at Incirlik, Izmir, and Pirinclik in Turkey starting in January. The Turks kicked most of us out in '75 because of Cyprus and we're just about to sign a new agreement. I'm talking about giving your new company both the Air Force and Navy contracts. Can you handle them?"

Gus and his uncle walked the two-and-a-half blocks down to 1925 F-Street. "I doubt if they will identify who used the phone," his uncle said. "Everyone has to check in at the desk and they keep good time records. Let's see the manager rather than the receptionist, get your membership application started and then privately ask him to call the National Security Advisor. Membership names are extremely private."

After coffee, they walked back to the EOB parking with a list of two-dozen people who had checked in before noon of the day of the phone call. Gus dropped his uncle off at the MJ office and drove back to the apartments. He knocked on the handicapped unit and told Andy to put on a coat. Pushing him out the back gate into the park, he started discussing what he had just found out.

"Our spy is probably on this list of two-dozen high ranking individuals," Gus said. "I recognize at least ten who have worked closely with the CIA over the past few years. Membership in the F-Street club is really expensive and I was surprised to see that my old friend Keith Allison is a member. Let's ask Dedee to start researching the financial backing behind these men."

"How do you know it's a man and not a woman?" Andy asked.

"The voice on the phone was a man," Gus responded. "Someone's also looking for our Russian spy at Langley but we need to investigate the people in DC. I did discover that they're listening to international phone calls. They must be monitoring the mob in New York, maybe us here in Virginia. Finally they probably have a team watching the house and the bank on Cayman." Andy asked Gus what he was going to do?

"These guys are toast. I can't let them get away with endangering Mary. Let's go ahead and plan to take care of the threats in George Town and in Switzerland. We don't know whom the worm is or who's watching us here, but we should keep our eyes and ears open. What about fake ID's and passports, you mentioned it a week ago?"

"I have a friend who retired from Defense Intelligence," Andy said. "Frank now lives near Winchester in the Shenandoah Valley. For thirty years he manufactured false identities and documents for the Pentagon. He's told me he would make paper for our special group."

"I'm not giving you the go ahead but here's a new plan," Gus said. "You'll have to rent a place in George Town and keep an eye on our target for at least a week. I've got to know who's watching this

Noggin and where they are. I'll want a Canadian passport, driver's license and other paper showing me as a bank courier. It must have multiple entries into and out of Europe. I'll need a second set of Canadian papers for the flight from George Town to Montreal, no passport only a driver's license. Find out all you can about security, safes and possibly combinations. I want to strip them of everything they own."

"I'll need papers too," Andy said. "They probably shouldn't be Canadian, maybe British or one of the Commonwealth islands."

"Your SEAL friends may have to land, so they'll need false ID's, and they will need to get a few weapons," Gus said. "We may have to stake out the residence for a week or more so I can collect enough information about their security. I'll also need a Minox camera, document stand and strobe in case there are any books or documents.

"What guns do you think we'll need?" Andy asked.

"I'll carry my Colt silenced pistol and the backup," Gus replied. "You'll have to get one of your friends at Bad Tölz to leave me another suppressed pistol in a locker at the Zurich airport, either tell him to send you the key or hide it someplace safe.

"You're in charge of this entire plan. The attack in New York made me realize I love your daughter. Do I have your permission to ask her to marry me?"

That evening the three of them briefed Dedee Anderson about how to proceed.

27

G us and Andy went out to Winchester on Tuesday and then to meetings with the building design group for the next three mornings. Each afternoon, Gus and Mary went shopping and got things that they needed. Every evening Dedee met with them to bring them up to date with any new information. When she ran into roadblocks, one of them would help with suggestions about how she should proceed with her independent investigation.

On Wednesday afternoon Gus took Mary out to Laurel and the closed Beltsville Speedway. Tom the owner met them, complaining about the county sound ordinance. "Since I had to keep the Corvette in a garage well off campus I had cut-out butterfly-valves installed at the header flanges with the racing pipes still dumping just in front of the rear wheels but now with twin mufflers added to the rear exhaust system." Gus told Tom as Mary listened. During the next few hours, Gus taught Mary how to drive the Corvette at racing speeds. "I ordered it with the Z06 option, a 300-horsepower racing engine and large gas tank. I also got a Borg-Warner 4-speed transmission, racing brakes and a positraction rear," Gus told her. "General Motors charged us $5,300 in St. Louis and Brian Wood arranged for it to be delivered to Don Yenko Chevrolet in Canonsburg, Pennsylvania. They modified it for racing by changing the carpet for rubber mats, adding vents, deflectors and FIA racing lights. Finally they installed a quick-fill gas cap and exchanged the seats for these aluminum buckets and fitted a roll bar."

Mary picked up her new knee length white physicians smock followed by her Class A Green's with both a skirt and slacks during the week. On Friday she picked up her Dress Blues. Her commander at Walter Reed Army Institute of Research had already told her she would report to Benning with the rank of Captain and she should wear her caduceus symbol as a doctor sewn on her other collar since she would wear her fatigues every day while there, throughout the two weeks of orientation and the three weeks of jump school.

They kept the two sports cars in the garages but drove them every day that week. Bill Williams promised to drive the Ferrari back to Virginia from Boise, but he worried he wouldn't be able to bring his wife, Jan, until later.

The hand-built Ferrari had limited storage space under the sloping front bonnet with its V-12 mid-engine arrangement. It came with two custom pieces of leather luggage that nested into a fiberboard cover on top of the spare wheel. There were also several smaller cases and tool rolls in depressions around it. Gus would fill the smaller zippered suitcase and Mary the larger one for their western trip. Mary would pack the Corvette with her army uniforms and equipment when she left it in Atlanta.

The Ferrari Boxer had several other unique features the importer had installed in Connecticut, including the AM/FM cassette radio with a built-in CB. Gus took the Corvette out and had them change the old AM radio for one of the new multi-band units. Unfortunately, they couldn't sell radar detectors in Virginia so the Ferrari had the only one.

They were leaving before daylight on Saturday morning December 15th. Asking his uncle for a hotel recommendation, Richard knew it was French but he couldn't remember the new name. It had been built at the turn of the century and had a reputation as the very finest hotel in the south. It had been completely renovated and renamed in 1970.

Asking their architect, he commented that the Hotel Denechaud was now called Le Pavillion. Gus made a reservation for an adjoining suite in New Orleans, including a late arrival. They would tour the French Quarter on Sunday and leave early the next day. He thought carefully about what weapons to take in his new car, and what to give Mary, since she was supposed to get permission to carry a firearm onto a military base.

"I'm going to give Mary the five-shot .38-special—the S&W airweight Centennial," Gus said to Andy as they laid out the guns that had been stored in the basement of the townhouse. "By the way, how are you going to secure these guns while we're in Boise?"

Andy answered, "They're delivering a large gun safe tomorrow that fits in the closet of the spare room. I agree Mary needs the revolver, however I think she also needs a 1911 style .45-ACP. When officers qualify with a firearm, they can use a personal weapon as long as it meets army standards. Doctors qualify with pistols rather than rifles. She's a good shot with a .45 semi-automatic, better than I ever was." As Andy continued to bring out more and more weapons, Gus realized they probably had too many.

"I can give her one of the two pistols I won in a poker game in Vienna," Gus said. "They're an almost matching pair of Armand Swenson custom-built .45's, set up for combat shooting. They have really good adjustable sights." He starred at the guns as he asked,

"So, Mary takes the commander and I keep the full-length pistol. She carries handguns in the Corvette, what should I carry in the new car. It's kind of tight."

"Wear a shoulder holster with your Colt Commander and the backup on your ankle. There's enough space behind the seats to epoxy patches of Velcro loops to the back bulkhead and then glue strips of Velcro hooks onto a couple of gun scabbards. I think you should carry the Model 12 shotgun broken down into two pieces just like you carried it in Vietnam." Andy rolled over and picked up a Cordura briefcase, opening it to a sub-machine gun, magazines and a suppressor.

"Put this Ingram MAC-10 in the other scabbard. With a 30-round magazine in the handgrip, the control strap and the Sionics suppressor installed it should fit perfectly. Just below the gun keep this case with all four of its extra 30-round magazines."

"You'll need the extended suppressor to help control barrel rise and to keep the windows from being blown out by the explosion of sound. Of course, you know how to massage the trigger to keep each burst to less than 5-rounds." Andy sat patiently as Gus played with the short sub-machine pistol, aiming it at various points on the wall and unscrewing parts.

"You can't carry any full-length sniper rifles since there's just not enough room." Andy commented. "The seats are so form fitting you can only wear one shoulder-holstered pistol, and there's no room underneath the seat. When you get out and park the car, you need to unscrew the suppressor, zip it back into the briefcase, then slip it and the shotgun into the side pocket of your suitcase, at only 30-inches both will fit diagonally."

On Friday before breakfast Gus took Mary and Dedee to the indoor range to practice with the various guns. He gave Mary the snub-nosed Smith & Wesson pistol and the Commander length Colt.

Dedee was carrying an issue S&W Military & Police lightweight 38-special with a four-inch barrel. While Dedee had trouble keeping most of her shots on the target paper, Mary shot the center out of hers and changed three more times. She was almost as good a shot as Gus.

That afternoon, Gus got a call from Boise. The new Delaware Corporation, Enigmatic Inc. had received three new open-ended contracts from the Air Force to immediately start upgrading the facilities at their bases in Incirlik, Izmir and Pirinçlik, Turkey.

In addition, the Navy was issuing his new company a $10 million open-ended contract to build up to four offshore oil loading terminals, at cost plus the standard 15% markup. The home office would handle the initial startup and furnish most of the qualified workers.

Their principal subcontractor for the Navy jobs would be a local shipbuilding company in Bahrain. The first terminal would be at Mina Al-Ahmadi south of Kuwait City and the second at Mina Al Shuaiba another thirty-five kilometers south. The third and fourth would start a few months later and be at Sitra in Bahrain and Halul Island in Qatar. Everybody still in Virginia made plans to go out to dinner and celebrate the good news. Dedee met them at the offices before anyone left.

"I've narrowed it down to three potential Soviet agents who used to work for the CIA." She told them during a peaceful moment. "All three can't explain their extra income with all of them claiming the money comes from their wife's families. The first and least likely works for the World Bank and although he does oversee some currency movement, I don't see any current advantage for the Soviets from his position. The second is a senior advisor to the Council on Foreign Relations here in DC. He also advises the staff of the National Security Council. His wife is from Taiwan and I cannot prove that she has family money. The third suspect is your old friend

Keith Allison. His wife is from Paris and I'm getting mixed signals about her family wealth."

"Let's call my people at Fort Bragg," Gus answered. "The Pentagon and its specialist can run the three suspects through their databases to find out if they had any connections with the top secret information that was being transmitted. Although it's Friday, someone will be on duty although I doubt if we'll get a response before next week."

"Is anybody watching the suspects?" Mary asked.

"My entire section of desk-bound analysts is working four-on/eight-off following the three men," Dedee said. "I have no idea how we can justify the overtime."

"The Pentagon's Intelligence Command has an entire Field Operations Group called Blue Light designed for just this sort of thing and they have almost a hundred men at the Arlington Hall campus waiting for orders." Gus said. "I'll get them to take over surveillance later this evening. Do you think that any of the suspects are aware that we are interested in them?"

"It's always a possibility." Dedee answered. "Particularly since events in New York did not go as they planned. I can understand the actions that the Russians are taking to support their agent in place. I have no real idea why the Mafia is helping."

That Friday afternoon Keith was flying his private plane out of Hyde Field, just outside the Washington Beltway near Clinton, Maryland. He leased a hanger for his V-tail Beechcraft Bonanza between the runway and Piscataway Road at the far end of the field, away from the WWII Quonset hangers at the other end of the airstrip. His Soviet handler could drive down Piscataway looking for the proper sign on the back door, pull off the road and leave a message or have a short meeting. No one could follow since his driver could see over three miles of flat road in front and behind.

"What do you propose doing about this Gus Smith problem," Keith aggressively questioned the KGB diplomat from the Rezidentura. "Your New York solution failed miserably. I'll have to take care of the problem myself. Can you give me some support? If I take care of this problem will you pay me extra for it?" His contact was using the name Yuri.

"Of course. If you're compromised, you aren't much use to us. My driver today is one of our wet boys from *Spetsbureau 13* and he has a complete kit in the trunk. One of my men talked to the architect during lunch and found out that Smith and his girlfriend are driving to the West coast, leaving before daylight tomorrow. Their first stop is at the Le Pavillion hotel in New Orleans over the weekend." Keith had a dozen specific questions about the hotel and Soviet support in New Orleans.

"Whatever, we need to take care of Smith away from DC," Yuri said. "Our mob contacts in Louisiana are very strong. The police will not interfere; in fact they'll quash any investigation."

Keith had no intention of going back to old Main State building this afternoon. His wife had closed their Federal house in Georgetown and was already in Paris for the holidays and she usually went on to Morocco after New Years. In fact she could look after herself. If he had to run, he could always get someone younger. His emergency escape plan did not include Moscow; instead he had a completely separate identity in the Republic of Costa Rica on a ranch overlooking the Pacific.

He considered leaving this weekend for Central America, breaking all contact with the US and Russia. If either Smith or the Russians discover where he was hiding, they might kill him. New Orleans was 975-miles from Washington. Merida, Yucatan was another 600-miles with Liberia on Costa Rica's gold coasts another 745-miles. With just himself as pilot he could fly almost a thousand miles before refueling, since he had installed wingtip tanks. That morning he had left home carrying a small suitcase with a change of clothes and all of his personal valuables.

28

As usual, the Corvette started up instantly with a roar and then subsided into a deep rumble. The Ferrari took a longer cranking period with a false start before all twelve cylinders finally engaged and it started to idle, although some smoke came out the quad-exhaust during the process. Gus backed the Corvette out while the Ferrari idled and warmed up. He then backed it out, closed and locked both garage doors. When Andy flew from Dulles to Boise, he could take a taxi to the airport, leaving the van in the handicapped space.

At 6:00 am it was just hovering around freezing, but it looked like it would be a clear day when the sun came up. Gus wanted to get out of town before any traffic built up. Neither car would need gas until Greensboro, three hours south. Saying goodbye, they took off out of the parking lot and onto the Beltway.

After the sun rose, he put on his Ray-Ban Aviators. With the winter solstice only a week away, the glare from the southern sun would be brutal all day. Gus took the lead and rather than listening to music, he started getting used to the chatter on the CB radio, listening to channel 19—the trucker's channel. It seems they were making a splash; first by cruising more than a hundred in the left hand lane, and second by what the drivers of the towering rigs saw when Mary passed.

She was wearing high black boots and a short matching leather skirt. Her skirt must have risen above her knee as she operated the clutch. She was wearing a sleeveless white shirt, having removed the leather jacket because of the warmth inside the Corvette.

The wolf-whistles and catcalls caused Gus to start thinking about his feelings for Mary. In Germany they had kissed a little, but he was hesitant to go any further because of the respect he held for her. Besides, he was a guest of her father.

Last weekend in New York would have been his first chance to be alone with her. He had wondered how far he should try and go with someone he respected so much. Events intervened and nothing much happened.

Before he went to sleep every night, he thought about her. He wanted to introduce her to his grandmother and then ask her to marry him on Christmas day. He had no idea whether she would accept or not, maybe he should talk to her about it this afternoon as they drove together to New Orleans.

They stopped for gas and coffee in Greensboro and paid in cash with two $20 bills; the gas was $.86 per gallon for high test, three times as high as under Nixon. Three hours later they stopped again just outside Atlanta and left the Corvette in long term parking at the airport. There was only a single daily flight between Atlanta and Columbus and it was inconvenient for Mary's plans.

They were averaging a hundred miles an hour and the combination of advanced warning from truckers on the CB radio and signals from the radar detector allowed them to avoid the police. In Columbus, Gus showed Mary where to check-in at Benning when she returned in January.

As they crossed the Chattahoochee River they gained an hour from the change to central time so they stopped for lunch at a salad bar restaurant before pushing on through Alabama toward the gulf coast. During the long drive through central Alabama, neither talked although Gus wanted to. He didn't know how to break the ice. When they stopped for gas and refreshment on the outskirts of Mobile, it was more than an hour before the new CST sunset.

Crossing the piney woodlands of southern Mississippi, Mary finally said, "This is my first time looking down the twin tunnels of light created by the new headlights from the car and the trees beside the road. You can certainly see a long distance."

"In order to pass the US DOT standards, Amerispec had to install standard sealed beam lights in the popup units. The less powerful yellow tinted Carello fog lights stayed since there are no standards. I paid extra to have them exchange them again for quad Cibé Z-beams with halogen bulbs and polished quartz-glass lenses. They also replaced the yellow fogs with longer distance white driving lights."

As they barreled along the gulf coast on I-10, Gus hesitatingly started to talk about his feelings for her. He didn't know how to get started. She didn't say a word. He stumbled on finally blurting out, "I love you and want to marry you." He hardly had a chance to control the wheel as Mary leaned across and gave him a big hug. "The main reason I'm taking you to Boise is to introduce you to my grandmother and both aunts, Andy already approves."

"Hush up," she responded. "I've been waiting for you to make up your mind. I was sure the first morning when we went running together. You're the first man I've run with who is almost as good as I am and not self conscious about it. I was thrilled when you threw me over your shoulder and took off on the man-carry. Haven't you noticed any of the signals I've been sending you?"

After crossing Lake Pontchartrain they headed into downtown New Orleans. They pulled into the porte-cochère end of Le Pavillon on Poydras Street, and locked the car. "Get us a room with one bed," Mary said as she grabbed his arm and directed him up the three steps into the lobby. He had reserved one of the seven suites facing the river but the European Palace on the seventh floor was the only one with one bed.

The clerk said, "It has a huge double sized bathroom with Napoleon's bathtub and a king sized poster bed on the far side of the sitting room with its carved fireplace." They went back outside to transfer the shotgun to his suitcase and then disassemble the suppressor and extended magazine from the MAC-10, putting them into the fitted suitcase.

During this effort the doorman was watching while the bellman stood next to the cart. Gus held the doorman's arm as he pulled out his badge and told him, "I'm a federal special agent. The local police don't need to get all excited about my weapons," as he handed him a $20 tip. The doorman had already pointed across the side alley to a fenced parking lot where Gus could store the Ferrari, offering to valet the car. Gus asked him to wait until he came back down and helped secure the waterproof red cover.

It was almost 8:00 pm central time so Gus asked the older black bellman about dinner, as he lit the gas fire. "I can call my friend Paul Prudhomme and get you a table at his new K-Paul's Louisiana Kitchen, it's only about ten blocks." He walked to the phone dialed 9 and then another longer number, talked for a minute and said, "You have a table at 8:30."

Mary was whispering in his ear. Gus gave him two $20 bills as a tip and said, "She's going to change. I'll leave our clothes out in the hall, can you have them cleaned by tomorrow?" While Mary was changing, Gus went back out to secure the car and walk around the perimeter of the hotel; studying all avenues of egress.

Worried about intruders, Gus leaned the shotgun near the end of the bed and then installed the suppressor on the machine pistol and put its case in a chair on the same side of the of the bed where he planned to sleep, between it and the fireplace. Ever since the president's assistant told him the mob knew his address and the description of his car, he assumed they might be tracking them. Although he didn't say anything to Mary, he was prepared.

Freshening up, they changed and took the elevator down to the front entrance around on Baronne, and then a horse and carriage to the restaurant. There was more than enough foot traffic in the French Quarter to make his efforts to keep an eye out for shadowers ineffective.

The hostess sat them at a private table for two. Mary said, "Why don't you order me a German riesling since I'm having seafood. I know you only want water." Gus asked the waiter for a cup of strong coffee with his meal. As they finished their food, Chef Paul came out to the table to make sure everything was satisfactory.

Mary asked Gus if they could walk back to the hotel. They strolled hand-in-hand through the Vieux Carré window shopping and peering into the various nightclubs. Although neither of them had eaten a lot, she had finished most of the bottle of German wine.

Upstairs Gus unlocked the entry door, and they went into the foyer as Mary turned and hugged Gus with great passion. She removed his jacket as he pulled off her coat. Slipping his hands up her thighs he realized she wasn't wearing underpants or bra, only high stockings.

Another deep kiss and he drew the dress over her head as she hurriedly unbuttoned his shirt and then loosened his belt. The antique French Ormolu longcase hall clock struck eleven bells. By the twelfth second, Gus's pants were caught around his ankle holster and Mary clothes were almost completely off.

He sat on the floor and removed his shoes, socks and pants, then stood to take off his shoulder holster and disheveled shirt. She was naked as she ran across to the upholstered chair in front of the fireplace enticing him to follow. "What about protection?" Gus said as he pulled his last sock off.

"Silly, I've been taking the pill for the last month," she said as the fire flickered behind her. They made love on the oriental carpet in front of the mahogany and marble fireplace.

Later they took a shower together in the immense green marble bathroom and then moved over to the hand carved Carrera bathtub, made for Napoleon Bonaparte out of a single huge piece of white marble. It was near midnight when they made love a second time. They both slept nude in the four-poster bed, surrounded by a tapestry forming their private cave.

The next day, they ordered breakfast from room service and then dressed for shopping in the old quarter. They spent all day walking and looking at the architecture, the antiques, the art galleries, bookstores and boutiques. Mary really wanted to buy a house in Washington and decorate it in her own style, which seemed to be a mix of Federalist and French Revival.

They shopped at several jewelers, looking at engagement rings. Mary wanted a specific style, a white engagement ring that copied a tradition in the British Royal Family. She described it as a brilliant blue stone surrounded by smaller diamonds.

At one ladies dress shop, she bought a long red silk dress with the front cut almost down to her navel; it was kept from gapping by a gold chain. The back had a matching chain but was cut much lower. When she tried it on, Gus realized it also had a slit up the side almost to her waist. They went back to the hotel in the mid-afternoon and Mary went to the spa for a treatment while Gus made reservations for the next few days with the manager. He bribed him to confirm the same room for the week leading up to Valentines Day in February. Mary would finish at Fort Benning on the 8th and had to report to San Antonio by the 15th. Since the following week was Carnival season, with Mardi Gras on the 19th, he had to pay a premium for the same 7th floor suite from Friday through Thursday, Valentines Day. The manager promised to keep it a secret. All the suites were on the southern end of the building running from the third through the ninth floor, directly beneath the swimming pool on the eleventh. The single entrance to each suite was a double door centered at the end of the long hallway; the banks of elevators and the stairs were in the center. The outside wall of the northern end of the hall had a steel fire escape stairway surrounded by steel grating. Gus checked and the window to the escape was unlocked.

All through high school and during vacations while he was at West Point, Gus usually wore blue jeans and cowboy boots with western shirts and a farm jacket. After showing Mary where to report in at Fort Sam Houston, he wanted to take her to the main shop for Lucchese Boots just down the street from the main entrance to the old fort. He wanted them to make custom wooden lasts for both of them.

As he looked at the manager's map, they made reservations for one night at the five-star Camino Real Hotel El Paso and then again in Las Vegas at Caesars Palace. When he called, the manager confirmed a front booth at the second Frank Sinatra show at 9:30 Tuesday night.

Looking at the map, Gus was trying to decide whether to stay until Thursday. "Why don't you go and see the show at Circus-Circus and then drive from Vegas to the Biltmore Resort in Santa Barbara the next morning, maybe stopping at the Huntington Museum in Pasadena." The manager told him and Gus said it sounded like a great idea. "Go ahead and make reservations."

Gus agreed they could then take the Pacific Coast Highway north to Monterey before cutting across the Santa Cruz Mountains to San Francisco on Friday. He wanted to spend the night at the Fairmont and visit with his cousin. They would leave Saturday morning, December 22nd to drive across the Sierra Nevada Mountains to Reno and on to Boise.

The dealer in Connecticut had already warned him that the drive over the Sierra Nevada's would be dependent on the weather in the Donner Pass. A winter storm and any snow would require 4-wheel drive, chains, or studs. The special wide Ferrari tires were not available with any of these options.

Gus was upstairs getting ready for dinner at Commanders Palace. After brushing his teeth, he realized he needed to trim his neck and upper cheeks to make his beard look neater.

In the closet were his three nicer outfits. Of course, tonight he would wear his tuxedo and once again in Las Vegas, changing to the black accessories. He would mix his navy suit with his blazer wearing one or the other every night. He had two pairs of trousers, both a taupe and a grey along with light blue and white shirts and his polished black shoes. His clothing was much bigger and heavier than Mary's and he had the smaller of the two suitcases, so she had a lot more clothes.

For driving he wore his black camel-skin sport coat, tan cargo pants or blue jeans and one of two light colored trail shirts. They both had double chest-pockets and epaulets. If it got cold he could add a wool sweater and of course he wore his trail runners. He had left everything else at the apartment in Virginia.

Mary came in from the spa and started taking off her clothes as she said; "I'm getting ready for our vacation in South Florida." They had given her a Brazilian wax and she was now hairless. "They sprayed me with a special tanning solution and I spent a half-hour under the sunlamp. I plan to follow up with another sun treatment in Vegas."

Gus couldn't help himself. He was getting an erection that was poking through the slit in his terry bathrobe as he watched Mary spin around wearing only high heels. He moved over and engulfed her in a hug and kisses as he backed her into the tub area and then turned around. Sitting on the rolled edge of the huge tub, he picked her up and lowered her like she was mounting a saddle. She was more than wet; she was sopping and must have been thinking the same thing on the way upstairs.

That evening after dinner, they made love for the first time in the huge bed. They then went to sleep in each other's arms.

29

Mary woke in the huge bed lying on her stomach. Gus' arm was thrown across her shoulders and at first she thought he must have moved. That was what told her mind to get up. Suddenly she heard it again, a subtle scratching noise from the front door vestibule. She was completely nude on the window side of the bed and someone was trying to get in the room.

Her practical Bulova watch was on the end table, next to her two pistols and the dimly lit Zenith clock radio. One circular dial was still set on a music channel now off the air while the old-fashioned time dial showed that was almost three. The clock dial and a dim light from the opposite bathroom at the other end of the suite were the only light in the almost pitch black room. She shook Gus awake as she swung her legs out of bed to get to her pistols. Both were fully loaded, the S&W with 5-rounds of .38-special and the Armand Swenson Colt Commander with eight-rounds of .45-ACP Super Vel man stoppers. She knew that Gus had a pistol under his pillow and the submachine gun on the chair beside the bed.

Within seconds she was crouched beside the bed with her Colt extending across the sheets, while Gus was still entangled with the covers. Simultaneously a large form rushed into the room as Gus fell out of bed crawling for the Ingram MAC-10.

Mary fired twice at the center of mass before she remembered what Gus had taught her about shooting for the brain stem. A hit there would immediately shut down the nervous system, so she put the next two rounds through his mouth and nose. Her shots were immediately followed by footsteps running down the long hallway. Before Gus could get untangled and she could check the condition of the intruder, she could hear a window at the end of the hall raise as someone stepped onto the fire escape and started down the noisy iron steps.

The next couple of hours were a blur of activity involving the local police followed by the New Orleans office of the FBI. No one could identify the dead man until a copy of his photo was sent to DC and the counterintelligence section identified him as a driver attached to the Soviet Embassy Rezidentura. One of the FBI pros claimed that he was a wet work specialist working for Spetsbureau 13 and they were sending a team to New Orleans. Gus had to call the Pentagon and involve them in the investigation. He discovered that no one had seen Keith Allison since Friday noon. His plane had refueled in New Orleans on Friday evening and left sometime during the middle of last night. Nobody knew where the plane was. From his description, the missing man at the hotel was Keith Allison.

He and the dead man were guest of the Le Pavillion hotel, both with single king beds, one on the third and the other on the ninth floors. Neither had paid and the credit cards they used were bogus. The fix was already under way since nobody in the New Orleans Police Department was interested is solving this case.

On the next morning, they had to rush to leave before six. Mary was still getting dressed when Gus took the guns downstairs to the parking lot next door, positioned them and went through the whole extended routine of starting the car on a cold and damp morning. Driving back to the porte-cochère, he ran in as the doorman watched the idling car and had the restaurant fix two Styrofoam cups of French Quarter coffee, one with hot milk. They also fixed a bag of beignets and mixed pastries.

Mary came out wearing her boots, short skirt and silk blouse, unbuttoned far enough to show some cleavage. The bellman followed with her leather jacket and suitcase. After everything was in place, the bonnet latched and Mary was fixing her seatbelt, Gus tipped both men and got in. It was still dark as they drove out of New Orleans headed northwest parallel to the river. The sun would rise at 6:50, just about Baton Rouge, where they turned west and crossed the Mississippi.

www.ingramcontent.com/pod-product-compliance
Lightning Source LLC
Chambersburg PA
CBHW021224250626
47155CB00008B/2925